MIDNIGHT IN THE GARDEN

Midnight in the Garden

An Anthology of Short Fiction

NOVELITICS WRITERS COLLECTIVE

Edited by
KIM TAYLOR BLAKEMORE & KERRY CATHERS

SYCAMORE
CREEK
press

First Edition 2025

ISBN (ebook): 979-8-9912591-2-5

ISBN (paperback): 979-8-9912591-3-2

MIDNIGHT IN THE GARDEN

AN ANTHOLOGY OF SHORT FICTION

NOVELITICS WRITERS COLLECTIVE

EDITED BY
KIM TAYLOR BLAKEMORE & KERRY CATHERS

SYCAMORE
CREEK
press

First Edition 2025

ISBN (ebook): 979-8-9912591-2-5

ISBN (paperback): 979-8-9912591-3-2

CONTENTS

FOREWORD

PRIDE. GREED. ENVY. LUST. SLOTH. GLUTTONY. WRATH.

I would love to say these emotions—these seven most deadly sins—are of rare occurrence. Yet... how many of us experience some form of them daily? And what are the consequences?

This was the prompt given to the Novelitics Writers Collective. Each writer was assigned a sin at random. Each came through with a story rich in the ways we humans stumble.

None of the sins are labeled. That part is for you, the reader, to discover. After all, one sin can lead to another, and another still...

Do any lead to virtue? Where are faith, hope, charity?

Are we all just a mix of light and shadow, good and evil, stumbling forward through the garden paths of our lives?

We invite you now to walk with us.

Not through a tidy parable, but through the wild and tangled garden of human nature.

May you find something true—and perhaps even a bit redemptive—within.

Kim Taylor Blakemore
Editor

THE CLAIM

SHIRLEY PEREZ WEST

There they were again. Small tracks leading from her garden. The sun had not yet cleared the granite cliff above Estér's claim. The terraces she had hacked into the hillside, long slender rows no wider than a bed or coffin, were still in shadow. She bent close and squinted at the tracks, half the size of her hand, no trace of claws or hooves, nails or toes; not really tracks at all, just smudges in the sandy soil.

Estér had nurtured this garden for three seasons, eventually growing enough to sustain her and the man who had found her hunched at the side of the road, her skirts soaked in her unborn child's blood. He had brought her north in the spring of 1848. There were still patches of snow on the ground then. The icy stream that flowed down the hillside had shocked her when she'd stepped into it, barefoot, skirts tied and tucked into her waistband, which hadn't helped because her legs had buckled with the sting of freezing water and she went down hard on the rocky bottom, flailing, feet slipping, unable to get them under her enough to stand.

The man had laughed, not cruelly; she could not deny she presented quite a spectacle. He did not reach out a hand to help her to stand. Instead, he raised his arms to the Almighty, then built a fire so she might warm herself when she finally found her feet and scrambled past the boulders along the river's edge. She did not step fully into the river again until the July sun burned the back of her neck, and the only relief was to lie in the pool formed by an eddy farther down the hill.

Estér had learned a lot that first year—how to ride a full day in the saddle; to find a straight and true tree to fell with the man's axe; to steer away from a certain kind of man with a hunger in his eyes for more than gold; and how to spot every trace of gold that winked from the wooden batea she used to sift sand and gravel.

Estér scoured her budding garden, looking for signs of intrusion, but the small prints ended just outside the stone borders. She plucked a young radish from the long row, wiped it with her handkerchief, and bit into its crisp, piquant flesh. Whatever was stalking her garden had not molested any of its early bounty which, besides the radishes from the last of the precious seeds she had sewn into her hems before leaving for California, included the tender shoots of peas and beans reaching for the trellis she had yet to build. When the sun shone a full day over the terraces, she would plant the cabbages and squashes and onions that would last into next winter. And she would try again with the corn and chiles from the last of her seeds.

Her shoulders tensed with frustration followed by the familiar cold prickle of fear. Her cache of gold was buried in this garden. Three years of work. Clearly the small indents were not made by an animal, nor had any animal ventured past the stone border of her terraces. Perhaps the marks were etched by something that traveled below the dirt, coming up for air at intervals and leaving a hollow impression. She followed the soft tracks that led from her garden, a low growl in her throat, until, like before, they disappeared into the smooth, granite boulders, some bigger than her cabin, strewn haphazardly down the hillside like God's discarded seeds.

ESTÉR CHISELED a nubbin of tea from the pressed block she had bought on her last trip to the Big Camp and dropped it into the shallow pan of water simmering on the coals of last night's fire. She stretched her back with a deep sigh, surveying the small domain she and the man had cut into the woods. Her eyes roamed to every corner of the cleared land, past boulders and the small turns of the tumbling river to the edge of the woods.

She didn't know what she was looking for. No one had yet bothered her here, though the fear of someone jumping her claim shadowed her. Before he left, the man had given her a folded paper that he said would prove her right to this claim. "Are you crazy?" she'd laughed, because the idea that a woman, a Mexican woman, could claim anything in this land was absurd.

The only visitor they had received in that first year was a tall Chilean on his way to Sacramento. She'd prepared a salve to soothe the blistered rash covering his face and hands and places he would not show. "Not to a woman," he'd said, gesturing to her men's clothing with his chin, letting her know he was not fooled. She looked at him with hard eyes so that he might understand she was done being a woman.

The Chilean and a company of other countrymen had been attacked and routed from their camp, called Spanish Bar. "Do you know it?" Yes, she knew it. She and the man had come through there in the spring of 1848. It was thick with men from Northern Mexico—the first to answer the call to the gold fields of Alta California. She had drawn many stares as they worked their way through Spanish Bar, asking after the scoundrel Alfonso Ruiz who'd given her the ill-fated child and left her behind. There were maybe a dozen other women in a sea of men. Some worked their bateas in the stream alongside men. Others were occupied at their fires cooking food or boiling clothes. The man had insisted they look for

Ruiz, intending to hand her off and be on his way. "I'll not be burdened with a woman and all the temptation of one," he'd said.

They did not find Ruiz, and so she'd followed the man out of Spanish Bar. After a week, they came upon this unclaimed portion of the stream that joined the Yuba River. Together, they'd built a cabin of stacked logs—three walls buttressed against a boulder that reached past the tops of their heads. When the snow and rain filtered through the cracks of the roof that first winter, they huddled under an oil cloth, shivering through the night. She'd disliked being in close quarters with him; had not liked the way he smelled, unwashed for weeks at a time. But he did not bother her in the way many men tried. He'd told her he was a man of God who had spent some years establishing missions in Chile for the Anglican Church. When he'd come down the mountains into Valparaiso seeking passage for England, news of the gold discovery had already erupted. She did not know how he came to be in that desolate valley, or why she listened to him when he commanded that she rise from the pool of her own blood. He'd knelt with her and prayed for her baby's soul, then he'd prayed for her deliverance from grief. She still prayed for it.

Estér strained hot tea into her cup with a bandana then used the warm cloth to clean her face and wipe sleep from her eyes. Later, when the sun bathed the hillside, she stretched strips of cloth behind the stone ledge of each terrace to further block curious creatures from rooting among the seedlings. Her low fence, made from strips of a threadbare shawl no wider than a hand, fluttered with a light wind that swept up from the valley. She smelled chimney smoke and the rotting carcasses of animals. People.

She had last walked to the Big Camp in deep winter to replenish supplies and, in truth, to visit with the woman Josefa. The camp, usually quieter in winter, was full of men, mostly Anglos, with a smattering of others. A cacophony of tongues. New houses and tents dotted the hillsides among fresh tree stumps, pinched between hotels and gambling houses, laundries and stables. There was a new mercantile, but she was unable to go inside. A gang of miners had started a commotion because they could not agree upon the day's date. The commotion had turned into a fight and so Estér retreated, eventually finding a few meager supplies being sold from a wagon.

A banner stretched across the rutted street between two tall buildings with glass windows. She did not read English well, though the man had read to her from his Bible and left it among his discarded possessions. The woman Josefa told her the banner said, "Bienvenidos a Downieville."

Estér had been relieved to find Josefa at home in the small cabin tacked onto the back of a cantina. She'd first encountered Josefa in the street calling to passersby, inviting them to play monte. As Estér passed, she spoke in quiet Spanish, warning her to take care. "The men's wants for comfort are like a fever," she said. Though she had cropped her braids and wore the man's discarded clothes, she knew her stiff brimmed hat didn't hide the soft features of her face. On this last visit, Josefa had offered to help her find a gun. Perhaps it was time.

Rain washed away the snow hidden behind boulders and at the base of trees. Could it have been the rain that caused the imprints? But it was not the first time she had seen them. She watched the river rush down the hill, curling upon itself where it passed over rocks she knew well. Smooth, wide rocks she could sit on while panning in late summer. The morning chill hung in the air, but it was time to get to work.

She pulled off her leather boots near the calm pool and rolled each leg of her pantalones past her knees, then edged into the frigid water. When she found solid footing, she bent and thrust the batea into the gravel and pulled up a panful. The man had said the claim was played out, but every time Estér plunged her greased arms into the water and brought up a batea of wet dirt, she found small bits of gold like baby's teeth.

"Mira," she would say to the man, long-gone. "You of little faith."

She had no good sense of how much her cache of gold was worth. But she knew in the depth of her being it was not yet enough. Once, when she had found what the man called a nugget the size of her big toe, he said it would buy a donkey. She had been pleased to think she could dig up a donkey with one day's effort, but now, two years later, she doubted it.

On her last trip to the Big Camp an ounce of gold was worth $16. But a single egg cost $3 and a sack of flour $15. The man had warned her to carry only dust and offer small amounts. This would keep her gold and her claim safe from those who came too late to this bounty and were desperate.

When she left Sonora, Estér had believed that she and Ruiz, when she found him, would stay only until they'd dug enough gold to buy their own land. She would raise goats and Ruiz would breed horses and their children would thrive. Whenever she remembered this dream, the hollowness inside her filled with sour air, making her bend forward and cough until her ribs ached.

Estér panned until the sun waned and her arms and legs numbed with cold. She revived her fire and sat on a stout log to sift through the last batea of gravel she'd dug. This habit of sifting one last batea at her fire was something she'd learned to do to distract her from the loneliest part of her day. Her eyes darted this way and that as she scratched through the rough leavings until she spied a slight glint.

"Bueno," she said under her breath as she pinched a morsel of gold from the dirt, and then a low hum of satisfaction as a spark coursed through her fingers and warmed her chest. She'd heard of miners who ate bits of their gold.

"Such fools," she said, dropping the last bits into the cloth sack tied at her waist. She weighed it in her open palm. It was time to add it to her cache.

As always, Estér waited until dark to uncover the strongbox, buried in her terraced garden. She'd pieced it together from a discarded crate she'd found at the Big Camp and buried it in the top bed. The box was barely wide enough for her to sit on. If she lay along the terrace, she could reach the bottom where she stowed the largest nuggets. Deerskin bags of smaller pieces were set on top of the nuggets and on top of these she nestled the canvas bags filled with dust and very small bits. The box could hold only two or three more bags. She replaced the wooden lid, covered it with stones and soil, scolding herself for not having spent the dull winter hours making a new box.

The man had said the assayer in the Big Camp would weigh her gold and give her dollars or a note that would be honored by banks in Marysville or Sacramento. Perhaps it was time to start exchanging her gold. A small chill rattled her spine. She dismissed the idea. She needed more gold to fulfill her dream of land and a future without deprivation. The thought brought the familiar vision of her with a family, living on their own ranch, unbeholden to anyone. She reveled in the thought until the image faded as if a cloud had passed over the sun, and her chest swelled with emptiness.

The man had warned her about the desire for earthly things the gold would buy. Every time he ventured among the growing hordes of miners and those that followed in their shadow, he'd spoken of the destruction that would come of gluttonous desires that knew neither bounds nor satisfaction. He himself had woken one day with the conviction that they had retrieved all the gold that God had provided them and, therefore, saved them from destruction. He offered to escort Estér as far as Marysville, three day's walk. She weighed the wisdom of traveling under his protection or continuing to work the claim. As much as the thought of being alone in this place unsettled her, she knew she needed more gold to make her way in this world. Their claim still held more—enough to provide what she needed.

～

THE MORNING DAWNED clear and cold, with no trace of frost. She tended to her ablutions then went to her garden to pluck a radish and enjoy it with her corn mush. She was some distance from the terraces when she noticed a gap in her cloth fence, like a missing tooth. She hastened to the bottom terrace. A handful of radishes lay scattered on the dirt, stripped of their leaves. She scanned for the familiar indentations, but the dirt appeared to have been swept. One half-eaten radish lay among chewed bits. She plucked it up, then dropped it.

"What is this?" she asked, her heart thrumming in her throat. The teeth marks resembled her own.

She spent most of the daylight roaming in widening circles, looking for signs that she was not alone. She found nothing but the occasional droppings of foxes. Her palms buzzed and ached with the need to be in the water before more precious bits of gold washed downstream. The farther she ventured, the more her fears prickled around her neck, and the more certain she became that she had to move her gold. She fried the last of the softened garbanzos and warmed two tortillas before the sun dropped too low. She ate ravenously, clearly depleted from her worry over who or what had invaded her garden. Such brazenness to take one of the cloth strips and discard young, healthy radishes. It was a message: *I am watching you.* She thought again of Josefa's offer to help her buy a gun.

She slept uneasily that night and woke before dawn. She lit a torch and walked to her terraced garden. Nothing looked amiss. She followed her usual routine of panning and early on found a good-sized nugget, like a golden quail egg. She eagerly shoveled and scratched through pan after pan of the river's gravel until the numbness in her arms and hands made it impossible for her to lift anything more. While she had collected the usual number of small bits, there were no more nuggets that day. She checked her garden in deep shadow, but saw no new evidence of the intruder.

As she made another survey of her camp she fingered the nugget in her trouser pocket, letting the smooth side warm in her palm, turning it so that its rough side tickled her skin, then again to smooth warmth. Estér walked wider circles around her camp absently fingering the gold and arguing with herself about moving her cache. It wouldn't be dark for another hour, and she did not have enough dust to make it worthwhile to dig up her strongbox. The nugget was large enough to warrant safekeeping, but she liked the feel of it in her pocket, on her skin.

Her stomach rumbled. She could not remember having eaten anything since her morning bowl of corn mush. She returned to her fire and warmed a tortilla, spreading it with the tiny spoon of lard she wished was butter. She sipped her tea and added sticks to the fire as stars began to show themselves.

Gazing up into the sky filling with twinkling light, Estér wished she had someone here to share this wondrous moment. Her mother had told her stories about the clusters and shapes formed by the brightest apparitions. "See there," she would say, pointing into the night. "There is a mother bear who cannot find her cub so she has taken in a lizard to care for. And there, look. See the hunter with his machete?" Cold filled Estér's chest. She coughed to force it out, catching her breath as hot tears dripped. She groped in her pocket for the nugget, caressed its varied surface until she felt soothed enough to bank her fire and find her bed.

Estér woke with a start. She held still in the black air, listening for the sound that had jarred her from sleep. As her eyes adjusted, she scanned the small space—three walls of stacked logs built around a boulder that radiated coldness in the winter and heat in the summer, a roof of pine boards spread with pitch. Sometime in her second season she had covered the boulder and two other walls with the canvas tent the man had used. She closed her eyes and drifted back to sleep until the whimpering noise she heard in her dream became real.

Estér crawled from her pallet to the cabin's door and pressed her ear against the thin planks. The predawn chill seeped through the cracks. There it was again, a small whimper. She held her breath, her heart beating an alarm. She tried to think through what might make such a sound. A dog or wolf perhaps. A coyote. She had never seen any of these animals roaming the foothills, only deer and fox and other small creatures that scurried about. Once she came upon a beaver working to dam a section of the stream. The man had said there were bears and mountain lions in these wilds, but assured her they would cut a wide swath around human stink.

The whimpering sound came again. No louder or closer. Estér stood and slid the wooden latch, held her breath in her throat as she eased the door open. Her gaze went to the waning coals of her fire some ten feet away. Estér saw the creature at the same moment she heard it whimper. She took an uneasy step outside her cabin and was astonished by the sight of a child, bundled in a thick hide, asleep at her fire. She stepped closer until its eyes flashed open.

She crouched, hoping to help soothe the child's fears, taking in as much detail as she could to assure herself she was not dreaming. She tapped her chest. "I am Estér." Her voice croaked from disuse. The child scampered backward, eyes wide, then jumped to its feet and ran.

"Wait. I won't hurt you," Estér called into the darkness. She trotted after it, repeating her promise that she meant no harm until she found herself in the thick of the forest, shivering, with no good idea of the direction the child had taken.

Estér lay awake until dawn thinking through what she had

seen. A human child, half her size, clothed in rabbit skins, dark cropped hair and plump, smudged cheeks. She was sure this was the creature whose tracks had befuddled her, who had tasted her radishes and spit them out. Had it been watching her all these days? Why had it dared to sleep by her fire? And for how long had it been slumbering within her reach? She felt foolish for not having noticed signs of its nightly visits. She wondered about the discarded radishes and the missing cloth. She imagined the child had been trying to warn her of its presence. Did it know where her cache of gold was buried? But why had it run away? And where was it now?

She turned these questions in her mind, unable to sleep. When she woke the sun had cleared the hills above her claim. She hurriedly dressed and followed small tracks she now understood were made by the deerskin slippers the child wore, up the hillside, between giant boulders until she came to a cave.

She sniffed the air for signs of animals living inside then peered into the low opening. At first, she did not see the child huddled against the wall, staring at her, tear tracks cutting a path through cheeks mottled with mud. Estér dropped to her knees and held out her hand. The child looked at it with bunched brows, clearly battling the desire to trust with the instinct of fear.

Estér glanced about the small cave. There was a mat made of rushes, a carrying basket, and a shallow metal pan for sifting gold.

"Estás solo?" Estér asked. "Alone?"

The child looked away. *Of course it was alone. But how could this be?*

"Come," she said, beckoning with her hand and slowly backing out of the cave.

A morning breeze lifted her hair, reminding Estér it was time to cut it. She wondered if the child thought her a man or a woman. She hummed then sang a song her mother had sung to her—one that made her smile and dance. She glanced back at the empty cave opening. Maybe the best thing to do was to go back to her camp, build up the fire, and cook a pot of corn mush.

"Come, let's eat," she called in Spanish. Her voice echoed off the boulders. She wondered what language the child spoke. She guessed that it was from one of the tribes that lived in this part of California. She was a distant relation to the Yaquis who lived in the hills north of her town. She retreated down the hill, still singing, filled with a new purpose.

The child did not follow at first, though by the time Estér had scooped mush into her tin bowl it appeared at her fire.

"Bueno," she said as she filled another bowl with hot mush. She smiled softly at the child as she handed over the bowl and a spoon the man had whittled from pine. It seemed a familiar implement.

Estér let the silence settle between them, though a river of questions coursed through her head. The child had dark hair cropped to shoulder length. Below a rabbit skin vest was an oversized, canvas miner's shirt that dropped past its knees. Doe skins were wrapped and tied around its legs. Of the native women and girls Estér had seen on her journey north, most wore fitted woven hats and short skirts of reeds or skins and shawls made from skins. A few she encountered wore calico blouses over linsey-woolsey skirts. The child's head was bare. She decided it was female. As to her age, not knowing her people, Estér guessed she was five or six years old. Her breath caught at the thought that one so young would have to survive on its own.

"Soy Estér," she said softly, tapping her chest.

The child's eyes widened. "Tayo," she said, mimicking Estér's gesture.

Tayo licked the last of the mush from the bowl and spoon, then stowed both in the basket Estér had seen in the cave. What did it mean that the girl brought her possessions? Would she retreat now that these newest gifts were packed? Estér could feel herself sink into the comfort of company and the shadow of loneliness that followed close. She shook the thought and set about washing up in the river.

As she scoured the mush pot, Estér could not resist picking through the gravel bits. Here and there a fleck of gold shimmered for her attention. No matter its size, she would drop it into her sack. On her last dip into the river, she found a piece the size of a small bean. She turned to Tayo, holding it between her thumb and forefinger.

"Do you know this? Gold?" she asked in Spanish.

Tayo's gaze dropped. She nodded. Estér sidled back to her and knelt.

"Where is your mother?"

Nothing.

"Your father?"

Tayo looked at Estér, dark eyes glossed with sadness. With broken Spanish, another language Estér did not know, and many hand gestures, Tayo related the story of gold mining with men from a rancheria in the north. Estér felt she understood what was important. Tayo did not have a living mother and had been part of a mining party when white men had attacked them, stealing their gold, and shooting many of the men with guns. Tayo's father hid her in a cave and went back to find others. Tayo waited through a turn of the moon, and then walked to lower elevations as the snow melted. She found the river and took fish from the river and found a good cave.

Estér guessed that Tayo had been in her vicinity for several weeks, perhaps a month. But she had no good idea of when Tayo's father had left, or if he was dead or still roaming the hills searching for his lost child. Perhaps she would ask the woman Josefa if she knew of a rancheria to the north.

Tayo pulled something from beneath her rabbit skin vest: the missing cloth from Estér's garden. With a wide-eyed look at Estér, she tied the swath around her waist.

"So, it was you." Estér stood and started down the hill to her garden. "Come," she said to Tayo. She walked the girl along the borders of the three terraced beds, naming every plant and seedling that was showing itself, naming their uses.

"This one," she said, pointing to a pale, heart-shaped leaf, "is a chayote. Delicious roasted and mashed with tinned milk. We'll have to make a trellis soon for it to climb. The fruit is very heavy." She cupped her hands and let them sink from the weight of a phantom chayote. She glanced at the sky, achingly blue, the sun at its peak. "Another week or two like this and we will plant beans and squashes." She swept her hand to take in the bounty that would feed them.

"This is like gold," she said, though it did not have the solid feel of truth. "It was very wasteful of you to pull the radishes." As she thought of it, Estér believed it was the girl's way to get her attention. No matter. She pointed her finger at Tayo. "Wasteful," she repeated.

For the most part, Tayo hung back acting as if Estér's Spanish was gibberish. When Estér insisted the girl replace the piece of woven fabric, Tayo scampered out of sight.

"I did not give this to you, I gave it to the garden. This was not a gift," Estér called into the boulders. But Tayo did not return. When Estér walked past the fire pit, the girl's basket was gone. A hollow bubble caught in her throat. For a moment she wondered if she had imagined Tayo out of her need for human company—a need she usually denied.

Estér forced herself through her day's work, digging gravel and sifting through it. Her thoughts turned to the need for provisions and her dread of the Big Camp. It was calling itself a town now, with a name. So, what? Going there would still be like stepping into a river hiding nests of cottonmouths. With so many desperate, insatiable men, she risked being discovered as a woman and assaulted, or worse, followed back to her camp.

By the time the shadows grew too long to see much in the

water, she gathered her implements and walked back to her cabin. Her heart leapt when she saw Tayo feeding twigs to the fire.

ESTÉR PUT off going to Downieville day after day, wanting the girl to get used to her and to feel safe. At first, Tayo continued to sleep curled by the banked coals of Estér's fire and did not care to enter the cabin. Estér did not force the matter, though she thought her vulnerable to prowling animals. The season was warming and mild enough to leave the cabin door aloft, the sound of Tayo's faint snores lulled Estér to sleep.

The girl followed Estér around most days, absently digging through pans of gold and occasionally finding bits. When she tired of this, she gathered and wove grasses into mats, or dug tubers. When Estér began limiting their meager rations, still talking herself out of going to Downieville, Tayo showed her where to find wild lettuce and small, tart berries and how to catch trout from the river. The man had occasionally done this, but more often preferred the beans and bacon that were a staple of the supplies he bought at the Big Camp.

It wasn't until Tayo had removed the leggings and canvas shirt to enter the stream to fish, that Estér confirmed she was a girl. In the next few days, she stitched a blouse and pantalones from an old skirt of dark blue broadcloth with red stripes. Tayo liked the cloth very much, though at first, she did not like the way the pantalones covered her bottom when she squatted to relieve herself. So, she went about with her blouse and rabbit skin vest tied with a piece of fabric Estér had given her. Tayo completed her covering with a reed hat she had woven and decorated with three flicker feathers.

One evening as the two of them sat by the waning fire, a lone coyote took up a desperate high-pitched howl somewhere in the trees above their claim. Tayo sat up, eyes wide, listening hard, and then answered the call with a bright trill, like an owl. It wasn't unusual to hear coyotes calling to each other, but Estér couldn't recall ever having heard just one. She gathered Tayo under her arm and sang a lullaby. "Los pollitos dicen, pio pio pio, cuando tienen hambre, cuando tienen frio..." She felt the child relax against her, but she could not shed the shadow of loss that followed her since Tayo appeared, and the guilt sometimes throbbing deep in her chest when she thought of the child's father, perhaps still alive, searching for his lost daughter.

Tayo said she had come from a rancheria in the north, an area Estér had not yet ventured. In truth, she knew she had to make an effort to find Tayo's people; at least ask the woman Josefa what she knew of the rancheria. Anything less would be dishonorable.

Estér let the idea simmer the next morning while she panned, watching the girl come in and out of her sphere. The girl was in her charge, and it was Estér's duty to keep her safe. By midday she decided she would go to Downieville tomorrow. Alone. By the end of the day, she decided it was time to buy a donkey to transport her cache and leave the claim and its dangers behind.

THE SUN SUNK toward the horizon as Estér hoisted two new saddlebags over her shoulder and turned east toward her claim. The bags, filled with flour and beans, fatback and salt, were meant to be carried by a donkey, but for now, Estér would bear the burden. The gold nugget she had brought with her to Downieville that morning, the one the man had told her would buy a donkey, was not enough, even with the small sack of dust she'd brought. Ten more ounces would be needed, she was told by the woman Josefa whose help she sought in making the transaction. She left the nugget with Josefa and spent the rest on a few provisions and the new saddlebags. She would return the next day with more gold.

As she tried to keep a steady pace under the weight of the new bags, she felt a lightness in her step. She would finally leave this place. She would buy a donkey, take her gold to Marysville, and buy land somewhere north near where Tayo's people lived.

The mountain's shadow reached for her as she walked east toward her claim. She did not follow the river closely, but kept south of it to avoid leaving tracks. As darkness settled around her she listened for the echo of rushing water.

The night before, the girl had watched intently as Estér dug up the strongbox and removed the sacks then took a large nugget from her cache. Tayo had dipped her arm deep into the box and brought up fistfuls of small nuggets. When Estér asked her to put the gold back into the box, Tayo shook her head and trotted away. She'd worried then about the girl's fascination with the gold. She wondered if Tayo understood its value. As they lay in the dark of the cabin, Estér told Tayo of her plans to buy a donkey to carry her cache away from this place.

ESTÉR COULD ALMOST FEEL the relief of dropping her saddlebags at the fire, almost smell the salty bacon she would sizzle in the pan. She would add leeks the child had gathered and green radish tops and lettuce to the fry and two precious eggs she had bought. Her stomach rumbled with anticipation. This emptiness could be filled.

The man had warned her that she would never come to feel she had enough gold. He'd read a passage from his Bible about gluttony, deadlier than greed because it could not be fulfilled. A part of her had believed him, felt it as one year passed and then another, her cache growing far larger than what he had taken with him on his horse. It had never seemed enough because she had no life she could envision. With the child, she could see her purpose. Whatever she had, with Tayo at her side, was enough.

She walked toward the sound of the river, letting it guide her to her claim. As she drew closer, she sniffed the air for the scent of smoke. Tayo knew how to rekindle the coals of a banked fire. Past the small pool at the bend, she caught the first whiff of horseshit. She slowed her pace, her jaw tight, but she did not raise her head to look about.

It was full dark when she reached her cabin, the door open and all her belongings strewn about. The fire's coals were covered in white ash with barely a glow from one or two. She set her saddlebags down and stirred the coals, adding sticks from a pile Tayo must have gathered. She let her gaze dart here and there as the light grew. Where was the child? Dare she call for her? She gathered some of her things lying in the dirt: A shawl. Tayo's feathered hat. The man's Bible.

The shovel lay outside the cabin. Inside, the packed earth floor had been gouged and hacked. She shuddered at the violence of it. Josefa had told her to buy a gun, but the price was well beyond what she had with her, more than the price of the donkey. Another chill shook her body as she backed out of the cabin. She added sticks to the fire, unable to summon a clear thought. She should have stayed in the cabin, the shovel in hand. Someone had been here. They might be here still.

A man stepped into the firelight.

Estér gasped. She looked past him for others, for Tayo, but saw only darkness beyond the fire's corona.

"Evening," he said in a high voice that quavered like a goat's. He lifted pinched fingers to his forehead as if to grasp a hat brim and lift it in greeting, but his head was bare. His clothes resembled those the man, the reverend, had worn—a vest and dark coat—and for a moment Estér lost her anchor of time and place. A horse called out nervously. Tayo. Estér imagined the child moving about unseen, undetected by this intruder. Her gaze dropped from his eyes, small and close set, to the pistola handle peeking from his waistband.

"All right then," he said. "Maybe your ingles ain't so good." He rested a hand on the pistola.

Estér's feet were frozen as if caught between two boulders in the icy stream. She could not think of any words or deed that would lead her from this. An owl trilled weakly from the direction of her garden, the sound vibrating down Estér's throat. The child. She wanted nothing more than to run to her and see her safe. The man's quavering voice came to life.

"Okay now. Don't look like you're armed." He nodded toward her saddlebags. "Push those on over." He made a gesture with his foot to show her she should kick the saddlebags toward him. She carried a small knife in her trouser pocket. She had thought it so clever when she found it at the mercantile, the way it folded into itself. It was useless. Better to have a blade sheathed at her belt. She dug a toe under the saddlebag and lobbed it toward the fire.

"Easy now." The intruder pointed his pistola at Estér as he squatted to drag it closer.

She watched him impatiently pull her provisions from the saddlebags, slowly sliding her feet back, claiming distance from him and his pistola, trying to fade into the dark. The owl trilled again, closer.

She couldn't think through any way to be rid of this intruder without giving him what he came for. But what had he come for? Her gold or her claim? Josefa had told her los Mexicanos were being driven from the diggings. Also, Chileans and French, Chinese and Africans, all forced to flee their claims or work for the Americans who claimed all of California. The injustice burned in her. But fear drowned her anger. She could smell it seeping from her skin, feel it hammering at her temples, tightening around her throat.

He stood, pistola wavering in front of him. "Don't go running off. Not yet."

Estér swallowed, dry-mouthed.

"Word is you been workin' this claim some time now. Word is

you're looking to buy a pack animal. I suspect you got a good load of gold buried hereabouts." His eyebrows shifted with the quaver in his voice.

Her gold. She stared back at him, momentarily provoked despite her fear. Tu madre, she wanted to hiss. Days and weeks, months and years of digging and sifting.

"Let's see what you got for your trouble," he said, waving the pistola for emphasis. "Go on and step lightly now. Lead the way."

She turned toward her cabin, picked up the shovel laying in the dirt. Would he shoot her once she uncovered her cache? She glanced at him, his face in shadow, his gun aimed squarely at her gut. He nodded, and she proceeded toward her terraced garden. She trudged forward, eyes darting here and there for a glimpse of Tayo or a hole to drop into.

What if she had left when the man did? Or when the Big Camp filled with more and more Anglo miners. Each time she had ventured there she felt the need to become smaller, invisible with so many ungoverned men filling every space. The chaos kept her away, but how did it escape her that, eventually, someone would come here?

What if she had gathered all her gleanings and left this place before Tayo had found her? She pictured her body hunched against an icy loneliness, the cold, hard gold piled at her feet. She pictured herself standing in a river valley, the child at her side, a field of tall corn fluttering in a warm breeze.

She took big steps, digging the shovel in for balance. She felt strength, not fear, vibrating through her. She would let the intruder have the gold. She would find Tayo and together they would disappear. She had enough. The gold Josefa held for her would be enough.

She stepped onto the top terrace of her garden. The space was indented from her earlier digging, the moon's shadow creating a bowl as big as the shovel's head. She pushed it into the dirt with a hard thrust of her foot, expecting to hit the stones that covered her strongbox. She teetered off balance, confused. The man had followed her onto the terrace and stood out of the shovel's reach. What if she had already been robbed? She tried again, this time scooping and throwing off shovelfuls of dirt. The man started whistling in his quavering way. Underneath the shush of her shovel and the whistling, she heard the owl's trill, quiet but close.

Tayo. At last, Estér's shovel met the nest of bags piled like plump balls of masa. She knelt and pulled a few bags from the hole, quickly counting ten. Far fewer than she had stashed. No nuggets. No strongbox. She stood and backed away, her fist tight on the shovel. "There," she said nodding toward the cache with her chin. How would he know much of her cache was missing.

He peered into the shallow hole. She could swing the shovel with enough force to knock the man off the terrace. Her body trembled as she imagined him tumbling backward, the pistola arcing from his grasp.

"Moo-oo-oove on now," he said, cocking his pistola with a soft rattle. With his free hand he pulled up one of the laden canvas sacks and grunted like a gluttonous boar.

Estér stepped back, nearly tripping on the piled dirt, sweat stinging her eyes, her feet dancing to regain her balance. Again, she danced back, her legs lifting with their own momentum, her body pivoting toward the giant boulders. She dropped the shovel and dashed into the shadows, expecting the report of the pistola, the searing pain of a lead ball piercing her flesh. She slid and climbed and ran past the boulders into the tall pines, unwilling to look back or stop until she could no longer hear the river.

She woke in a hollow with the sound of an owl trilling.

The sun had not reached Estér's garden, but even in shadow she could see the chaos of churned earth. Even the stones that once bordered each bed were strewn like dice. The deep hole that hid her strong box was nothing more than a dip along the slope. She stood with an arm holding Tayo close for the relief it gave her. The part of Estér that had lived through scarcity did not want to abandon whatever food might be salvageable, but Tayo pulled at her, insisting she come away. The girl was right. It was not safe to stay.

Tayo had had the good sense to retreat to the cave when she first spied the intruder and his horse following the river toward their camp. Estér followed the girl up out of the camp to the cave. A weariness hummed through her bones, or perhaps it was a release from the obsession with her cache of gold and the fear that someone would take it. It was gone. But she felt no great loss inside her.

The girl took Estér's hand and pulled her into a dark recess. The deerskin Tayo had used as bedding lay in a heap beside her basket.

"Look, look." Tayo pulled the deerskin away, revealing the strongbox.

IT'S ONLY NATURAL

NICOLE BURRON

Maria maneuvers through the narrow bus aisle, clutching her backpack to her chest. Her shoulders hunched, she scans the crowd of her classmates, looking for recognizable faces. She hasn't seen anyone since school let out for the summer. Her personal social circle was small, consisting of one best friend, Calista, who spent the second half of the summer in Europe studying with an International Honors program. Maria had been stuck with a summer job that kept her locked up most days helping her mom with filing to save up for college.

As she passes each row of classmates, her eyes grow wider. Everyone looks so different. Only the glimmers of their former selves let her connect the dots of who is who. It's as if the entire student body had collectively shed its awkwardness, a group effort transforming them from caterpillars into butterflies. She stands stuck, trying to match a cute boy's face to a name, when a kid nudges her back with an elbow.

"Hey, move it!"

Startled, she scurries down the aisle, stealing glances at everyone. It will be a relief for her to see the familiar face of her best friend.

She reaches the safety of the back of the bus and wiggles her way into the corner seat, nestling into her nook. The bus reaches its next stop and its door opens. She looks up to see a shadowy shape step into the aisle. It blocks the bright glow of the morning light streaming through the windshield. Maria raises a hand to shield her eyes from the glare, and as they adjust, the silhouette takes form.

Hair cascades like a waterfall of liquid gold making a halo around the stranger's head. Sun-kissed skin catches the light, peek-a-boo thigh flashes with each step they take. An hourglass figure framed in a snug Henley crop-top and short denim skirt, she sways down the aisle as if strutting down a runway rather than squeezing through a crowded school bus.

Then, the goddess speaks.

"Maria!"

Maria stiffens. The radiant being makes a beeline straight for her. Before Maria can react, the girl settles into the seat beside her with effortless grace.

"Damn, Maria, why did you have to pick the very back?"

Maria gawks as reality creeps in and smacks her with bitter realization.

It's Calista.

Calista, whose acne had magically vanished in eight weeks and was replaced with a luminous glow and perfectly applied makeup. Calista, whose hair and skin had been adoringly kissed every day by summer sunshine in Europe. Calista, who had shot up at least two inches, all in her legs. Calista, whose previously modest frame had somehow acquired curves that defied Maria's understanding of biology.

Meanwhile, Maria had spent her summer days under the unforgiving glow of office fluorescent lights and eating expired vending-machine food. Her acne had staged a full-blown rebellion, her eyebrows were conspiring to merge into one, and her body remained stubbornly flat and awkwardly lanky. To top it off, her clothes drowned her small frame like she was a child playing dress-up.

Maria hugs her backpack closer to conceal her flat chest.

"Maria! Hellooo?? What is your damage?"

Calista rolls her eyes and fishes a glittery lip gloss from her backpack, swiping it across her mouth with the ease of someone who belongs in *Teen Vogue*. The scent of artificial cupcakes wafts through the air making Maria sneeze. She wipes her nose with the sleeve of her hoodie and shakes her head, attempting to stave off the paralyzing feeling of shock. Calista may look different, but Maria knows this is still her best friend... right? Sure, she changed on the outside, but she was still the same person inside, right? People don't change *that* much.

"Sorry, you surprised me. You look so—" Maria loses her words and scans her best friend up and down.

"Ya, I know. Crazy right? My mom has been so embarrassing about it since I got back."

"You didn't mention anything in the postcards... is this why you didn't want to hang out before school started?"

Calista laughs. "You're totally bugging! I was majorly jet lagged is all." She playfully pushes Maria's shoulder with hers. "Anyways, I met some girls from Italy, and they showed me all these cool makeup tricks. I can show you later. Teenagers in Europe are just *so* much more mature."

The bus comes to a screeching halt at the school and Calista flashes a big smile at Maria.

"This year is going to be so bomb!"

Maria trails behind Calista into their school like a lost puppy. People in the main hallway part like the Red Sea as Calista casually glides through it. Maria notices all the eyes following her best friend, especially the boys. The boys look at Calista like she's a Cherry Slurpee during an August heatwave.

Her ribcage tightens around her lungs. She pulls tightly on her backpack straps, hoping it will weigh her down so she doesn't float away from the humiliation. Meanwhile, Calista, radiating confidence, walks to her locker and opens it, placing a small mirror inside along with a makeup bag, a hairbrush, a few notebooks, and a body spray that surely smells like more baked goods. She secures the locker with a metallic purple lock. Maria didn't even know they made locks in purple. Of course, Calista has a cool new lock to go with her cool new look.

Maria fumbles with her backpack, desperately searching for her mere mortal belongings to put in her locker with the basic standard black lock. She senses a presence come up behind her. First, the cologne—too much of it—fills her nose and burns her eyes. Then, the warmth, radiating off him, causes both Maria and Calista to turn around.

"Hey, Calista. How was your summer?" His voice is deep and calm.

It's Josh, but not the same nerd-alert Josh from last year's math class. This is *Josh 2.0*. The braces? Gone. Baby fat? Melted away, leaving behind a jawline sharp enough to cut glass, and a lean soccer physique beneath his V-neck shirt. His frizzy bowl cut replaced with fresh frosted tips coated in gel that sits like a crown atop his head. Maria's head spins at how handsome he is and her stomach flutters.

Calista blushes beneath her summer tan. "Oh, hey, Josh." She straightens her posture, a move so subtle yet so powerful. "My summer was cool. Spent it in Europe, ya know, nothing major." She rolls her eyes and shrugs, as if her life isn't like an episode of Dawson's Creek.

Maria stands frozen, watching this situation unfold. The air thickens with something indescribable. It's heavier than Josh's cologne and stickier than Calista's cupcake lip gloss. It's animalistic. It's primal. *Oh God,* Maria thinks, *is this what pheromones are?* She vaguely recalls something from last year's science class about chemical signals and attraction. Puberty, as it turns out, is a major stink.

Josh bites his bottom lip, nodding. "That's cool."

The bell rings, signaling the end of the courting ritual. Calista grabs Maria's hand, pulling her away. "See you around, Josh," she says, waving coyly over her shoulder.

Maria looks back as Josh stands, utterly bewitched, like a man who's just been hit by a love spell.

The rest of the first school day is a blur. All Maria can focus on is the undercurrent of *something* in every classroom. The looks. The subtle shifts. *The smells.* The silent choreography of teenage longing. Lust is everywhere, but Maria remains on the outside of it, and by the end of the day, that exclusion aches within her.

Weeks pass and Maria's jealousy of her classmates and Calista grows stronger. With each school day, she becomes more obsessed with the roaring desire pulsating between everyone. The glances they steal of each other's bodies, some lingering, penetrating each other with ravished gazes. Sometimes, the students touch each other in secretive ways, like speaking a hidden language. A brush of someone's thigh as they walk past their desk. Hands touching too long together when they pass a worksheet. A highly questionable consumption of Blowpops while making intense eye contact during lunch time between the cheerleading squad and football team. It's created a friction so sharp and decadent, it makes Maria salivate as she watches everyone. Her hunger to be a part of it eats away at her. Calista eats up the attention from everyone like it's her own personal endless buffet. Especially from Josh, who has a keen interest in being around Calista every chance he can get. Stupid hot Josh with his perfect jawline and teeth and hair and abs. Abs Maria snuck a glance of when he stretched one afternoon in class and his shirt crept up revealing them in all their Greek god-like glory. She thinks about them before she goes to sleep. It drives Maria mad.

Josh hasn't once touched her in a secret way.

She's never seen him, or anyone, pierce her body with their eyes. Who would go out of their way to brush up against her?

Who was thinking about her at night, before they fell asleep? Nobody.

One afternoon, Maria skips lunch to make her way into the school library, searching for books that can provide knowledge on the biology of puberty. She had rationalized that this is the key; that puberty unlocks something within that had made all her classmates beautiful and desirable overnight. There must be something Maria can do to jumpstart her own transformation. Maybe she isn't eating the right foods or a gene had gotten lost when she was in the womb and she needs to consult her pediatrician about it. The craving for answers gnaws away at her, leaving her grasping at what little self-confidence she has left. What could have happened for the puberty fairy to skip her house over the summer?

But the school library's selection is grim. She fans out the books of what she can find onto one of the large study tables. Flipping through them, she scans medical images and dry textbook answers on the process of puberty, but they provide nothing, other than the broad stroke of time called "teenage years." The idea of needing to wait years to experience "the change," as one textbook called it, leaves tears welling up in her eyes. It all is so unfair.

Maria sighs, folding her head into her arms in defeat, and mumbles to herself. "Why can't I just be hot?"

"Oh, are you cold dear?"

Maria looks up, her eyes meet the librarian's, Ms. Cromwell. The *crazy* librarian to be exact. There are different rumors about Ms. Cromwell that have made their way through the school gossip line. Some kids say she is a witch and if you're late with your library books she'll curse you. Others say she only works at the library to protect a secret society that meets in a dungeon built beneath the school. Ms. Cromwell's eyes glint back at Maria beneath her glasses, wrinkles of time magnified behind the lenses as she smiles.

"Oh, no, that's not what I meant," Maria says.

Ms. Cromwell scans the pages of the open books on the table and nods knowingly. "Aw yes. This age can be an unkind time with lots of changes. Change is only natural." She looks at Maria and Maria swears she sees Ms. Cromwell eye her chest, or lack thereof. "Sometimes, the change takes longer. It's called being a 'late bloomer.'" Ms. Cromwell sits next to Maria.

"That isn't exactly comforting." Maria rolls her eyes.

Ms. Cromwell's expression softens, holding a tender gaze with Maria, she mumbles something to herself then nods as though she's agreeing with someone Maria can't see.

Crazy librarian.

"I can see you want answers, solutions, but sometimes to get what you want, you need to leave the restraints of the human mind and turn to the powers of the natural world." Ms. Cromwell motions toward a notebook and pen on the table. "May I?"

Maria shrugs.

Ms. Cromwell scribbles in the notebook. She finishes, rips it out, and folds it in half, handing it to Maria. "The answer to your problem." She smiles at Maria. "Don't forget to put the books in the return bin before you go." A small menacing chuckle slips from Ms. Cromwell as she walks away.

Maria hurries to her locker. She digs through her backpack searching for her next class's homework assignment, trying to balance the bag's weight on one knee, the cloth bottom tilts moving to one side, and it slips. The contents spill onto the shiny, scuffed linoleum floor, including the note from Ms. Cromwell. Maria picks up the folded piece of paper, double checking it's not her homework assignment, and opens it.

You can change—Go to the south end of the school at midnight. There, you'll find a narrow path nestled between the blackberry bushes. Follow the path. It will lead you to a secret garden where a willow tree stands in the center. The willow tree is a magical tree that can grant you your deepest desire.

Be warned. The tree does not give freely. You must bring an offering; something tied to your wish and you must bury it at the base of the tree. Once the offering is placed, speak your desire to the tree three times.

P.S. 16-32-16

Maria could see why there were rumors about Ms. Cromwell. She probably told kids all sorts of crazy things over the years.

A twinge stirs in Maria though, the kind she gets when she knows the answer to a trick question on a test. She rereads the note, and the same feeling tickles inside her.

"Missed you at lunch," a flirty voice says. Maria turns and comes face to face with Calista. "Where were you?" She cocks her head to one side.

Maria crumples the note, fumbling on her words, "Uh, library, had to catch up on some homework."

Calista nods and begins her grooming ritual. She brushes her silky golden hair, reapplies her cupcake lip gloss in long thick coats over her full lips, and drenches her flawless body with sugary-sweet body spray.

Maria stares with envy as she catches her own reflection behind Calista's. Her hair is frizzy and dull brown, her skin dotted with dark spots from summer's acne blow out, eyebrows thick and wild, her lips thin, the dull aluminum smell of her deodorant tickles her nostrils.

This is why no one wants me. Her own voice echoes in her mind. Tears fill her eyes and a sharp pain burrows deep into her stomach.

Josh slides up next to Calista. Maria quickly wipes away the tears hanging onto the corners of her eyes.

"Hey, Calista, can I walk you to class?" His voice smooth and cool.

Calista steals a glance at Maria as she closes her locker, slightly rolling her eyes at her as though she's annoyed by his question. As though attention from hot Josh 2.0 is a burden rather than a privilege Calista takes for granted because she hasn't just changed physically over the summer; something inside her has changed, too. Maria sees it so clearly. Calista has become full of herself and spoiled. Unaware of how good she has it. Unaware of how much Maria is hurting. Calista can only see herself. Maria needs to do the same.

Maria waits for them to leave and for the halls to empty, tightening her grip around the note, her nails digging into her palm as her heart races. She opens the note and rereads it. The same feeling floods in.

Maria faces Calista's locker and holds the lock in her hand, the heavy weight of it giving her the reassurance she needs. If this works, then maybe Ms. Cromwell isn't so crazy. If the combination works, then she'll go to the garden at midnight.

Maria steadies her hands and slowly turns the dial of Calista's lock. 16-32-16. The hinge releases from the lock with a satisfying pop. She cautiously opens it, her eyes scan Calista's things, searching for the treasure she needs. The makeup bag decorated with a daisy print calls to her. She opens it, carefully digging through the products with delicate precision. She can't find the lipgloss she was hoping for. Probably with Calista as she sits in class re-applying it while all the boys watch her, trapping them in a hypnotic spell. Maria huffs and zips up the bag. Her eyes fall on the hairbrush. It's thick with strands that have accumulated over the weeks. A tapestry of spun gold. She grazes her fingertips over the bristles. They poke her skin like small swords, warning her to stay away.

"Young lady, shouldn't you be in class?" a low, sturdy voice asks. The principal's voice, to be exact.

Maria's heart jumps into her throat. "Oh, yes! Sorry. Just forgot something I need for class."

She quickly grabs one of Calista's notebooks and rips a lock of hair from the brush. Shoving it into her pocket with one hand, she holds up the notebook to the principal in the other, waving it dramatically like a white flag.

"Got what I needed." She smiles at him and scurries away.

THE SCHOOL'S grass is wet from the night sprinklers. Maria's sneakers squish through the field as she heads south, her path illuminated by the stale yellow light from the parking lot. The edge of the field is riddled with prickly blackberry bushes, nearly naked from bored teenagers feasting on the berries between classes. Maria crouches as close to the ground as she can, scanning where the grass and bushes meet, looking for any sign of a path. She notices a small opening where the grass has been worn into the dirt, leaving a raw trail like a hollowed-out bone. It's narrow; so small she would never think to enter if she hadn't been told to. She turns her body sideways and forces her way through as blackberry stems and leaves grope at her legs and arms. The path turns downward, and she picks up speed, ungracefully side stepping until she comes to a clearing.

It's a garden, small but lush. Rows of rose bushes spill out hundreds of blossoms, like tongues unraveled. They surround the garden in crimson, hungry for whomever steps inside. The grass is a vibrant green, untamed and free. In the center of the space stands a willow tree, its long limbs gracefully hang like a shroud of ancient mystery, claiming itself as the heart of the garden. It's surrounded by a circle of large, flat, smooth stones engraved with strange symbols.

Maria crouches and touches one of the stones, tracing the etching with her fingertip. It looks old and dirt has settled into it, but the bold black lines stand firm with their meaning. The symbols remind her of ones she learned about when they studied ancient Egypt.

She takes a deep breath and stands before the tree; her heart quickens and body shakes as she moves closer to it. She parts its hanging limbs carefully and steps inside their canopy. Behind the curtain of weeping limbs, the air is sticky and warm. A small chill blows against her neck. Her exposed legs flush with goose pimples. A small bench of twisted wood rests against the trunk. Maria takes a seat on the edge of the bench. She jerks her head and rubs her thighs, trying to combat everything she can't see.

"This is dumb," she says out loud. The willow tree's limbs move in response, swaying back and forth as though in disagreement with her. Her heart leaps into her throat. One limb reaches out toward her, like a yearning hand, and gently rests on her thigh. Its touch is electric; the same way she imagines Josh's touch would be. Instinctively, she touches the top of the branch, and it twirls seductively around one of her fingers. Maria flushes bright red and pulls her hand away, tucking her hair behind her ear. She breathes in a deep breath, trying to calm the buzzing in her body. It's taking over her, in waves. A sensation rushes through, pulsating with an intoxicating current.

"You can really hear me, huh?" Maria asks coyly, tucking one leg under her thigh. The tree's branches creak in unison, the wood making a hissing *yesss* sound.

Maria laughs nervously and her stomach flutters. She reaches into her pocket and pulls out the lock of Calista's hair, the golden strands glow in the dark night. Maria glances at her watch, the digits glare the midnight numbers back at her.

The limbs of the tree whisk together like arms and take Maria from the edge of the bench and press her firmly against the trunk. Clutching the strands to her chest, she exhales a deep and primal breath, relishing in the forcefulness of the tree's touch. She turns her body to face the trunk; her hands and chest press against it and her face burrows into the hard wood. Her lips wet and breath hot, she whispers her wish to the tree three times, each word charged with electric desire. A cool breeze blows through the branches when she completes the third affirmation, and the smell of roses dances in the air. She kneels and madly digs through the earth at the base of the tree, tucking Calista's hair into a small hole and covering it with the moist soil. As she leaves, she blows the tree a kiss goodbye.

EVERYONE'S HEADS turn as Maria struts down the aisle of the school bus, some boys' mouths drop open as she cooly makes eye contact with them. She confidently slides into a seat in the middle, forgoing her usual spot in the back.

Calista gets on the bus at the next stop and flops down next to her. Small pimples dot her face, her hair looks lackluster, her lips ashy, and her clothes look loose on her. Her usual glow seems to have dulled overnight.

"Ugh, I look like shit today." She pinches the bridge of her nose with her fingers. "Does my nose look swollen to you?" She turns to face Maria, her eyes widening. "Holy shit! Did you get a makeover at the mall or something?"

Maria's cheeks flush. "I, uh, tried some makeup tricks from my mom's *Cosmo* and got some new shampoo..."

"*Cosmo* really knows their stuff. I once did this pushup routine I read in one, because they said you can grow your boobs by building your pectoral muscles. It's science." Calista forces a smile; the edges of her mouth curdle and her green eyes study Maria the rest of the ride to school.

Maria and Calista walk through the hallway, side by side as everyone's eyes linger on Maria, like sticky invisible fingers caressing every inch of her. Her skin prickles and the hairs rise on the back of her neck, her body shivers in ecstasy. She can feel parts of her body pulsate and throb, it's almost painful, but delectably glorious at the same time. Her mind dizzies as she locks eyes with some of the senior boys. One licks his lips as she passes, his hot pink tongue glides slick over his rosebud shaped mouth. For a moment, she envisions their mouths colliding and consuming each other. The head cheerleader gives Maria a once over that lasts too long, studying her from the top of her head to her feet, the same way her mom looks for perfect, juicy apples at the grocery store. "I love your outfit," the cheerleader says with approval.

At her locker, a familiar presence comes up behind Maria. The cologne, the heat, she recognizes in a second. It's Josh. She turns and comes face to face with him. His dreamy eyes sparkle under the school florescent lights. His mouth turns upward in a cocky smirk. His face is too close, she can feel his breath hot against her skin.

"Hi." His eyes make direct contact with hers, catching her off guard. Maria steals a glance of Calista and sees Calista's arms crossed and eyebrows scrunched in confusion.

"What's up, Maria?" His direct acknowledgement hits her like an invisible forcefield, leaving her weak in her knees. She buckles and instinctively grabs onto his perfectly toned shoulder for support.

"Whoa, there." He takes both his hands and steadies them on her waist; his touch firm yet gentle. "You okay?"

Maria blushes as her eyes lock onto his; she can't look away from them. "Ya, I, um, didn't eat breakfast. Must be low blood sugar."

"I have a Pop-Tart in my bag." His eyebrows arch innocently over his warm brown eyes. "Maybe we can share it in class?"

Maria nods. It's all she can do. Her brain and body are too stunned by what is happening.

"Cool," he says with a smile. "You want to walk to class together?" His hands slide across her hips as he turns his body next to hers. She nods, and they walk next to each other, a little too closely, leaving Calista behind.

Before lunch, Maria walks to her locker. Calista is applying concealer to the purple rings under her eyes. Maria smiles to herself, still coming down from the high of sharing a Pop-Tart with Josh.

"I didn't know you liked Josh," Calista says while she continues applying makeup and stares at herself in the mirror.

Maria fumbles with her locker, spinning the dial back and forth. "Oh, um, I mean he's—"

"I mean you can have him if you want. I'm not even into him. Senior boys are so much hotter." Maria stiffens, Calista's words hang between them, heavy with offense.

"Anyways, I'm going to skip lunch and go home early. See ya." Calista turns triumphantly and slams her locker shut. She brushes past Maria like an icy breeze.

Maria grits her teeth and opens her locker door. Inside a folded note sits on top of her schoolbooks. Opening it, she recognizes Ms. Cromwell's fancy adult handwriting.

Congratulations, it appears you got what you asked for!

However, there's something crucial you need to understand about the changes. Meet me in the garden at midnight tonight, otherwise you will have to deal with an ugly mess.

❧

MARIA PUSHES her new curves through the blackberry bushes, thorns clawing at her. Tonight seems darker than any other night. She struggles to see where she's going, moving through the jet-black night, feeling her way to the garden.

When she arrives, the willow tree's limbs are drawn open, like stage curtains, revealing Ms. Cromwell sitting on the bench. The librarian is speaking in a low tone as though she is having a conversation with the tree itself. An unsettling feeling crawls up Maria's spine.

Ms. Cromwell laughs and settles her eyes on Maria. "There she is."

Maria squares her shoulders. "What is this about?" Her tone unsteady.

Ms. Cromwell smiles at Maria. "You look beautiful; so grown up." She pats the empty space next to her on the bench. "You'll want to sit for this."

Maria cautiously takes a seat next to Ms. Cromwell, scooting to the end of the bench to put as much space between them as possible

"It's been a long time since I've seen such powerful results. Your desire is very strong." A condescending sigh escapes Ms. Cromwell's lips. "But things like this require care. The natural world is built on reciprocity. Nature gave to you what you could not naturally conjure for yourself, and you gave nature what it needed in order for it to do that for you."

Maria furrows her brow, a puzzled look falling over her face.

"How is your friend Calista by the way?" A wicked smile spreads across Ms. Cromwell's lips.

Maria springs to her feet. "What do you mean?"

Ms. Cromwell sneers and crosses her arms. "You must have noticed that your ripe-as-a-peach friend was a little less appetizing today."

Maria scans her brain, trying to put Ms. Cromwell's word salad together. When the pieces click into place, her eyes dart down near her feet, where the tree trunk and the earth meet, where she buried Calista's hair. Ms. Cromwell takes her boney finger and points at the same spot, putting a spotlight on it.

"*That* offering will last a handful more days, but you'll need to come back with more and always from the original source." She adjusts her glasses. "Thankfully, your friend seems incredibly dedicated to her grooming habits. It shouldn't be much of a problem to acquire more for the tree." Ms. Cromwell chuckles.

Maria's heart flutters in her chest, its beating fills her throat with acidic panic. "What is it taking exactly?"

"Only what it needs. *Nature* only takes what it needs. Your friend may never be as desirable again, but she'll survive." She gives Maria a sympathetic glare. "You know what that feels like."

Maria's nostrils flare and her fists knot. "What happens if I don't bring any more offerings?"

"Then you return to your former self. Which would be such a shame. But if you agree to give nature what it needs, you have nothing to worry about." Ms. Cromwell studies Maria, calculating exactly what Maria needs to hear and feel to accept the deal. "You know, I heard whispers in the library today that Josh is thinking of asking you to Homecoming."

Maria's body floods with excitement. She fumbles with her hair, running her fingers over the silky strands. Her hand grazes her chest that is barely contained in her too-tight top, she gazes at her body, the curves of it, the way her skin glows in the moonlight. She closes her eyes and imagines it in a velvet slip dress for Homecoming. A dress that would hug every curve of her. One with thin straps that would fall off her shoulders too many times through the night, and Josh would carefully use his big strong hands to put them gently back into place. A dress that would get the head cheerleader to nod in approval. A body that each boy would yearn for as she did the

Macarena on the dance floor, but only Josh would be allowed to touch.

She chews on her lower lip, its tender plumpness soft between her firm teeth. Two of the tree's limbs wrap themselves around her shoulders, embracing her the way she imagines Josh would hug her from behind. Her skin tingles all over. She inhales the garden's night air in long gulps. It's fragrant with the roses' sultry sweetness. Savoring this feeling, she knows she doesn't want to lose it. She doesn't want to walk into school and be invisible ever again. She will do whatever she needs to do to keep it this way.

She flutters open her eyes as though waking from a dream. Tracing her fingertips along the tree's limbs, she looks at Ms. Cromwell almost seductively. "How often do I need to leave an offering?"

Ms. Cromwell grins. "Once a week. Always here in the garden, always at midnight. That is the promise you must make and keep to the garden. That is the only thing that cannot change."

But people change.

Relationships change.

And now, Maria understands and accepts those changes.

She nods at Ms. Cromwell. "Okay, I'll do it. I promise."

Maria is mature now. She has blossomed.

Nature is a world of give and take.

What she's doing is only natural.

THE GREAT GREED

TRISH MACENULTY

The Patrol Boys are out tonight. Elena isn't too worried. Their house is tiny, innocuous. The only thing in the driveway is a rusted van with a missing tire and broken windows. She and Dial have nothing the Patrol Boys—or anyone for that matter—want. Except for perhaps the garden, but few people know about that.

"Dandelion," she calls out as she stands at the edge of the garden in the dark. Dandelion is the once-feral calico who hunts voles in the garden. She started coming inside a year ago to avoid the storms and is now, for all intents and purposes—or as they say in the Community for 'all intensive purposes,'—a tame little feline.

It's the time of year for the Geminid showers, but Elena can't see them for the satellites. The Patrol Boys are only a block away in the parking lot of an abandoned shopping center, hollering and setting off fireworks—or is that gunshots? She heard they sometimes put "hostiles" in the middle of a circle of vehicles and then shoot at them like a game of dodge ball. They're nothing more than hooligans with a love for something they call "venging."

"Pss, pss," she hisses for the cat. According to WeatherGenie, no storms are coming tonight, but Elena doesn't like to leave the cat outside with the Patrol Boys roaming around. Something brushes against her calf. She reaches down to swat it away and realizes it's Dandelion's whiskers. "There you are."

Elena snatches up the cat before she can dart under the sunflowers and disappear.

"Just for a little while." She carries Dandelion inside.

Dial is watching an animated version of "Father Knows Best." All shows are developed by VidGenie, now, most of them retreads of shows that were popular decades ago. She and Dial used to like to watch the news, but the news channels were replaced by porn channels during the Wreckoning.

"Is it bad?" she asks, nodding at the TV.

"Stupendously," he answers.

Dial was a history professor before the Wreckoning, but now professors are obsolete. Elena is a graphic artist—another redundant profession. Dial is nearly seventy and she's sixty-five. Not worth re-training. Before the Wreckoning they would have gotten social security, but they are in Group Six, which makes them ineligible.

A sudden POW! startles her. Dandelion makes a low growling sound. It's nothing, she tells herself. Nothing. It wasn't that close.

"Has it really been three years?" she asks.

Dial places his hand on her thigh.

"I'm sorry," he says.

"Don't be silly. What could you have done?"

Elena immediately regrets her choice of words. No one likes to be reminded of their utter helplessness. During the early days of the Wreckoning, the Disloyals were executed on a live Community Feed. Those who weren't cowed by the performance, who continued to speak out, were rounded up by the Patrol Boys, never to be heard from again.

All efforts at resistance these days are easily quashed. Aladdin controls food distribution, monetary accounts, the electrical grid.

One good scarcity and people learn to bend. It turns out you can't do much damage without the means for survival. Try getting anything with your old cash, Elena thinks. She has a drawer full of worthless dollar bills.

Elena's device emits a trilling notification. She inhales deeply before pushing "Accept."

"Millie!" she smiles at the screen. "How nice to hear from you."

Their daughter's face appears on the screen. She wears white lipstick, and her eyebrows have been enhanced so much they look like caterpillars—not to mention the weird light glowing under her skin, a fashion trend Elena finds disturbing.

Dial tenses beside her.

"I'm good," Millie says. "I've been promoted to part-time Inventory Lord."

"That's wonderful."

Millie launches into a description of her new duties at the Aladdin warehouse, and Elena nods her head, pretending to approve. Millie, their older girl, was the good daughter; the younger one, Olivia, always got into trouble. While Millie clawed her way up the ladder at Aladdin, Olivia joined the Leahs, organizing protests, boycotts, and even engaging in sabotage. Then the Patrol Boys came to town. Suspected Leahs were shot on sight. Dial and Elena sold their house and moved into the tiny rental they had purchased for the girls when they were in college. The money from their house bought Olivia's freedom, and Millie has resented them ever since.

"I'll let you go," Millie says. "By the way, Terrence sends his love."

Elena forces herself to say, "Tell him that we love him back." Dial coughs.

Millie gets a sly look on her face. "He knows Moms and Pops love him." The screen goes blank.

"Who the hell are Moms and Pops?" Dial growls.

"They're her virtual parents, Dear. Just like Terrence is her virtual boyfriend."

Dial winces but doesn't say anything. He unmutes the television. *Betty is complaining because Kathy has put her dress in the new washing machine and Father wants to go to the country club while Bud builds a raft.* Elena pets Dandelion who, for once, doesn't seem to mind. Perhaps the noise outside has scared her into docility.

For the first year after the Wreckoning, Dial taught a class in Roman history in the restaurant area at a closed Costco. Some people still wanted to learn in a room filled with other people who wanted to discuss and debate. But the conversation inevitably turned to more recent histories. No devices were allowed in the room, but nothing can be kept secret from Aladdin for long. The cease and desist notice, when it arrived, could not be ignored. So now they stay home, working in the garden in the day and staring at the screen at night.

The screen suddenly flickers, three loud beeps break through their stupor, and a message pops up: "You have been targeted. You have twelve minutes."

The message disappears. Elena's heart thuds against her breast bone. They look at each other. She has never seen fear in Dial's face before, but there it is—color drained, eyes wide, nostrils flared as if smelling smoke.

Dandelion leaps off Elena's lap.

"We have to go," he says. His lips press into a thin line. "It's a message from what's left of the Leahs."

They get up, moving quickly to the kitchen. No time to lose. Elena reaches under the sink for the backpacks that have been sitting there, packed and ready to go, since the early days of the Wreckoning.

"What about Dandelion?" she asks, thrusting Dial's pack toward him.

"She has to stay."

"No!"

"We don't even know where we're going."

He's right, of course. Elena pours the remaining cat food into large mixing bowls and opens the back door.

"There's no time." The harshness in his voice stings.

"She'll be hungry."

"She'll eat voles like she did before," he says.

Elena knows she's being unreasonable, but still she uses up a precious moment to set the bowls of food outside on the patio and take one last look at the garden—carrots, squash, kale, and sunflowers. The food that had sustained them, the food they sometimes traded with their neighbors, their old-age hobby now a source of sustenance. Dandelion has already dashed past her into the dark. The noise from the Patrol Boys in the shopping center has died down. The silence is terrifying.

While Dial collects the contraband bag for bartering from the attic, Elena grabs her device and opens the Community Message Board.

"Please feed Dandy if you see her," she writes. Then she closes her device.

"You can't bring that," Dial says.

"I know."

She takes the device into the bathroom, places it in the tub and turns on the water. It's an old device, not waterproof. She leaves it to drown.

They step out of the house, packs on their backs. Dial carries the satchel filled with contraband. They leave the door unlocked. If the Patrol Boys are coming, there's no point in locking up. An old Grateful Dead song pops into her head: "If they got a warrant, you know they're gonna come in."

She dashes to the side of the house and pulls a tire from behind a hydrangea bush. While she wheels the tire to the van, Dial wedges the jack under the rear of the van and furiously pumps the jack.

They've practiced this a dozen times. Within minutes the tire is on the wheel, and Dial is tightening the lug nuts while she loads their packs and the contraband into the back of the van. She climbs into the driver's seat. Dial hurries around to get in the passenger side.

She turns the key in the ignition. Nothing. Just a click. She tries again. Nothing. She looks at Dial. He shakes his head.

Without a word, they plunge out of the van and grab their bags from the back. Twelve minutes, the warning said. If they were younger, they would have been long gone by now, but when you're old everything takes longer. They probably only have two minutes now.

They trot close to the other houses on the street, avoiding the light of the street lamps. She thanks a God she no longer believes in that there are no drones. If she and Dial were more important, there would be drones.

Don't look back, she thinks. But just before they get to the corner, she can't help herself. She turns like Lot's wife and sees a vehicle with pulsing multi-colored lights in front of their little house. A salty tear runs down her cheek.

Then they run.

They zigzag through the neighborhood and cut through the park, slowing down so they won't stumble over roots from the oak trees. Her knee aches. Both Dial's knees were replaced before the Wreckoning, but the arthritis in her right knee stabs like a box cutter.

"I don't think I can keep running," she gasps.

He slows down. They continue to move along a path through the trees. She pushes the pain down. They lean against the rail of a wooden bridge over a rushing creek to catch their breath.

"I hope the cat will be okay." She rubs her knee.

Dial puts his arm around her shoulder. She can tell he feels bad for sounding harsh earlier. He's a gentle soul. It would be better not to be so gentle these days, but she wouldn't want him to be different. To maintain gentleness in the face of barbarism is a heroic act. She thinks of the vehicle with the lights in front of their house and rests her head on his shoulder.

"The tavern is not that far," he says. "Someone there will know how to find help."

The tavern is a small, rundown bar downtown with no corporate ties. Not the sort of place that attracts the Patrol Boys or the upper echelons. Every once in a while, Elena and Dial go there to trade vegetables for a couple of beers. Sometimes a fugitive Leah shares news from the Movement.

Dial pulls the contraband bag close. Elena hasn't looked inside. She trusts Dial to know what will be worth trading.

"Why aren't there any drones? Wouldn't they be looking for us?" Elena asks.

"I don't know. I don't understand any of this. Why would we be targets? I stopped the history classes two years ago."

"I don't think this is about the history classes," she says.

They leave the park and walk through a tunnel to another street. They try to act nonchalant. Just two people out for a walk. That's still allowed as far as they know.

"We should probably split up," she says when they get to the underpass. "If they're looking for us, they're looking for two people."

"Agreed." He kisses her. "Stay safe."

"You, too." A sob idles in her lungs.

He turns to the left. She continues forward.

She hears a drone and dives behind some bushes as it buzzes past.

A half hour later she reaches the back door of the tavern. She pushes the door open and slides into the hall where she slips off the backpack and stashes it under a table loaded with crates of beer. She passes the door to the kitchen, enters the bar and sits down, hands clenched into fists under the bar. A young couple sits at the other end of the bar. Otherwise, there are no customers. The bartender, a woman about fifty who also owns the joint, glances over at her and then away, wiping a glass.

As the bartender moseys toward her, Elena hears the back door open. She holds her breath but doesn't turn around to see who it is. The chair next to her squeaks against the floor.

"Hey, baby," Dial says. His hand clasps hers, and relief pours through her. She looks up at him, smiles, and curses herself for wanting to cry.

The bartender leans on her elbows.

"Well, aren't you two a sight?" she says. "Come with me."

THEY STAND in the kitchen of the tavern while a young cook stirs carrot soup. She and Dial aren't the only ones to trade vegetables for beer.

"We don't know where to go," Elena tells her. "We don't know why we were targeted."

The bartender takes a sheet of paper from a machine on the counter and studies it.

"I got a fax here and it says you have a daughter in Canada."

"Canada?" Elena asks. "That's so far away..."

"Does Canada still exist? I thought..." Dial asks, eyebrows crunching together in the middle of his forehead.

The bartender shakes her head.

"The old Canada is gone. These days 'Canada' refers to any free zone."

"Are there many? Free zones, I mean," Elena asks.

"More than they want you to believe."

"Wait. You received a fax?" Dial interrupts.

"Sure," the bartender smiles. "It's so low tech it's actually safe."

"You know where Olivia is? Is she okay?" Elena asks. The thought of seeing her daughter again seems too good to be true.

"Your daughter is fine. We'll let her know to expect you."

Dial reaches his arms around Elena, and they clasp each other in relief.

"How do we get there?" Dial asks.

"We have a route," the bartender says. "But you have to pay for passage."

Dial holds up the satchel of contraband. The bartender looks interested.

"What you got?"

Dial opens the satchel and hands her a book.

"Holy shit. *The Odyssey*." The bartender whistles. "What else?"

Dial doesn't answer.

"That's okay. This is good enough. This will get you to the coast. And..." she grins. She walks to the stove, opens the oven door, and pulls out something that looks like a bar code scanner.

"We don't have bar codes," Elena says. "We're Group Six. Redundant and useless."

"This isn't a reader," the bartender says. "This makes the codes."

Elena looks at Dial. She doesn't want a code imprinted on her arm even a fake one.

"It's either this or the Patrol Boys," the bartender says.

Elena thrusts out her arm. The bartender holds the device over her skin, slowly moving it back and forth. The feeling is tingly but not painful. Next she does Dial.

"There ya go. Now you are both in Group Three."

"I can't see anything," Elena says, looking down at her arm.

"No worries. If they check you, it'll register. It'll fool them for a while."

"Do you know why they targeted us?" Elena asks her.

"That's above my paygrade," the bartender says. "Mekos might know."

"Who's Mekos?"

"Your driver. It will take several hours to get to the departure point. You're going on a cruise."

"I used to love cruises," Elena says and turns to Dial. "Remember when we went to Cancun?"

Dial nods. Members of the middle class for most of their lives, they thought that with retirement they would travel, have grandchildren, live off their savings. But during the Wreckoning, their savings had been "re-allocated," and they discovered that everything they'd believed about their future had been an illusion. They wouldn't travel and neither of their daughters chose to be a mother so they wouldn't ever be grandparents either. Elena can't blame them. Who would bring a child into this?

"Mekos will pick you up out back," the bartender says.

Elena and Dial sit at an old picnic table in the alley behind the tavern.

"I should have done more," Dial says.

"Those who did more are dead."

"That might be better."

"Don't say that. We have each other." She squeezes his hand.

A car silently rolls up. They get in the back seat.

Mekos, her hair in dreadlocks, doesn't say anything. Doesn't tell them where they are going or why they were targeted.

The drive is long. Elena falls asleep, leaning against the back door.

She wakes up as the car slows down for a checkpoint.

"Where are we?" she asks.

"At the coast," Mekos says. "You are Group Three tourists. Got that? Name of Wilkins."

Dial reaches over and clasps her fingers.

"Got it," he answers.

Mekos pulls up to the checkpoint. She waves her badge over a scanner. A screen activates and a bored man asks, "Passengers?"

"Two tourists," Mekos says. "Name Wilkins. Husband and wife."

"Occupation?"

"Retirees," Dial says. That much is true.

"Submit your citizen codes please."

The back windows lower; they stick out their arms. Scanners on either side register the codes.

"Proceed," the man on the screen says.

Mekos drives forward.

"We can provide you with more credits, depending on the value of your contraband."

"How's this?" Dial asks and thrusts Ralph Ellison's *Invisible Man* over the seat.

Mekos takes the book and glances at the cover as she speeds down the road.

"Oh my. Worth a lot, this one is. I'll get more credits into your account tonight."

During the Wreckoning, there were bonfires at every corner of their neighborhood on Freedom Day. The populace was directed to free themselves of tyranny and bring out their books to be burned. Elena and Dial dutifully brought armfuls of books and watched them burn while music blared from loudspeakers in the back of the Patrol Boys' trucks. One of the books that Dial tossed on the flames was *Fahrenheit 451*. She had never liked that book, and liked it less after she had lived through its premise. Who would have thought that the books they had withheld and hidden in their attic would now buy their freedom?

Mekos drives through the quiet tourist town, streets with shops and handsome Victorian houses that have been turned into B&Bs. To think there are people who can afford to be tourists. Maybe they have important skills? She isn't even sure what skills are valued anymore. Maybe it's just random.

"Mekos, do you know why they targeted us?" she asks.

"Someone wanted your house."

"But it's such a small house. Two small bedrooms, one bath, linoleum floors. No dishwasher." They'd never been wealthy, but they'd had a lovely two-story home once upon a time, the home where they had raised their two girls.

"Does it have a garden?"

"Yes."

"There you go. According to our information some Aladdin techlord wants new housing. With a garden, your house would be a prime pick."

Mekos looks over her shoulder at them before turning her eyes back to the road.

"You don't really think all this happened for the betterment of society, do you?" she asks. That was the claim during the Wreckoning. Aladdin had to be in control because their leaders made such a mess of things.

"I figured the world had just gone mad," Elena says.

"Historically, it's because 'they' want something," Dial says. "The Romans wanted gold and slaves. In Germany during the Third Reich, they wanted the Jews' apartments, fine furniture and paintings, even dinnerware. America wanted oil during the Mideast wars. Not to mention all the colonists everywhere wanting land."

She's heard this reasoning before, and to her all that wanting seems a sort of madness itself. Elena had believed she and Dial had nothing that anyone would want. They had intentionally let their front yard go wild and didn't bother to repair torn screens or repaint. As long as they were ignored by the drones and the Patrol Boys, they believed themselves safe.

"You're right. It's greed," Mekos says. "We couldn't survive without at least a little greed. Wasn't it greed that made you keep some of your books? Once Aladdin took control, the Great Greed began. Houses, businesses, savings. *They* want it all. And it's never going to be enough."

"But who are *they*?"

"*They* are the ones who are not us."

Mekos pulls into a parking lot. Holding out a pair of pamphlets, she stares at them grimly.

"You must be able to pass as Group Three. I've got two suitcases in the trunk. We'll place your backpacks in them so you don't look like refugees. Get some breakfast and then buy new clothes from the shops."

"Shops?"

"Yes, people shop in stores here in these enclaves."

Elena looks at Dial. She hasn't shopped in a store since before the Wreckoning. They receive a monthly allotment for goods on Aladdin's servers and that's how they get everything—medicine, non-perishable food items, toilet paper.

"How do we pay for the clothes?" Dial asks.

"With your bar code."

"How long do we stay here?" Elena asks.

"Later today you'll board a ship for a five-day cruise. When you get on it, look happy. Laugh at the things the Group Threes laugh at. Be sociable. Whatever they believe, you believe the same thing. Don't worry. No one talks about anything that matters. It's not permitted.

"On day two, you'll get off in Grand Cayman to go shopping. Once you get there, go to the Starbucks and order two cappuccinos with soy milk and two chocolate-covered cookies with almonds. Don't forget the almonds."

"Then what?" Elena asks.

"The barista will check your code. Then someone will fetch you and take you to a boat, not a cruise ship, and you're off to Canada."

Elena has a hard time imagining Canada as a place somewhere

off the coast of the "Free State of Florida"—a place that is anything but free.

Mekos drops them off in front of a diner in a shopping district near the cruise line, each with a roller bag with their backpacks inside. Dial hooks the strap of the contraband satchel over his shoulder.

"Be. Careful." Then she drives away.

Inside the diner they order breakfast, but they are too nervous to be hungry. Elena looks at Dial over a plate of eggs and hash browns. "Honey," she says in a soft voice.

He looks into her eyes.

"It was..." she whispers and mouths Millie's name.

He nods in agreement. They both know. Millie requisitioned their house. There is nothing else to say.

"I'm so excited to go shopping," Elena says in a cheery voice for the sake of Aladdin's ubiquitous ears.

After breakfast, they go into town to shop.

In spite of their situation, Elena enjoys being in actual stores, running her hands over the fabrics, perusing shoes and handbags, trying on necklaces and sunglasses.

"How do I look?" she asks, a silk scarf around her neck, straw hat with a cerulean blue ribbon on her head.

"Like a girl," he answers. "A pretty girl."

She glances in the mirror. She's definitely no girl. The last three years haven't been kind to her face. Every freedom taken left her with another wrinkle and another patch of gray hair. A parenthesis has formed around her mouth. But she's beginning to think that their situation maybe isn't so bad. Their lives have become so narrow—the cat, the garden, the little house, the occasional walk through the neighborhood if the Patrol Boys aren't around, never talking too long to their neighbors, never "congregating." Like the proverbial frog in boiling water, she hadn't realized how the constant wariness and fear had begun to petrify her emotions.

So when they board the cruise ship, smiling at their fellow passengers, it isn't an act. For the first time since the Wreckoning, they have hope. They join in the shipboard activities, playing foosball and shuffle board, lounging in the sun, attending a magic show in the evening.

But that night as they lie in bed in their Group Three state room, Dial's jaw clenches and he says, "I should have done more. I should have fought."

She remembers when the auditor came to their house after the Wreckoning.

"Would you call yourselves *loyal* citizens?" the auditor had asked.

"Of course. We love our country," Dial had said.

Then the auditor went over every one of their Community feeds. Most were innocuous, but sometimes she had "liked" a post later found suspect or hostile or disloyal. Those posts eventually stopped appearing. It was the text feeds with Olivia and the phone calls to her own parents that were damning—especially the phone calls she'd had with her Papi, who had escaped from Cuba when he was a young man in the 1950s.

"Papi, life under Aladdin is no better than any dictatorship," she'd argued after the Wreckoning.

He'd gotten furious with her.

"You know nothing. I know what it's like not to have freedom!"

"But freedom to do what? To express an opinion? To disagree with others? We can't do that anymore, Papi. Our jobs are all gone. No one's allowed to read anything not written by WordGenie or watch anything that isn't from VidGenie. There's no press anymore. Anyone who resists is systematically deprived until they have no choice but to acquiesce."

The auditor had played her words to them.

"You should have listened to your father," he'd said. "He was loyal."

"Too bad he died during the Second Pandemic," Elena had retorted.

"There was no Second Pandemic," the auditor had assured her. "There's also the matter of your younger daughter. She seems to be gone. Do you know where she is?"

They'd shaken their heads.

"Your classification is Group Six," he'd said abruptly.

"Sounds like we're waiting to board a plane," Dial had said.

"It could be worse. You'll at least have a monthly allotment of goods from Aladdin. Group Eight doesn't even get that."

WHEN THE SHIP reaches the port at Grand Cayman, Elena piles on four pairs of underwear and stuffs her purse with silk scarves. They can't take their suitcases or even the backpacks with them or it will raise suspicion. The only thing they'll take is the leather satchel with their remaining contraband.

"Ready?" she asks Dial as she puts on her new sunglasses and the straw hat.

"Ready as I'll ever be."

Then he takes her in his arms and kisses her deeply. Endorphins rush through her body. They have not kissed this like in a long time.

"I love you," he says.

"Of course you do," she responds, their own little in-joke. She hugs him hard, inhaling his scent.

They disembark the ship with the other tourists and place their feet on the solid ground of Paradise.

"All those going to Stingray City, come this way!" a cheery guide calls out to the crowd.

"We should find the Starbucks," Dial says.

They walk along a sun-drenched street filled with tourists and upscale shops and restaurants. The heat is cloying. They pass a shiny new CoffeeGenie, and at the end of the block they find the rundown Starbucks. Inside, a whining window air conditioner tilts at windmills.

A young man with a flashing smile and a Caribbean accent takes their order. His smile disappears when he brushes the scanner over their arms.

"You're running out," he says so softly they don't hear him at first.

"Did you say running out?"

The young man glances around, sees no one listening and whispers, "Leave a payment in the bathroom in the vent above the paper towels. I'll refill your credit."

Dials nods and exchanges a look with Elena.

"How much will the collected works of Shakespeare bring?"

The barista grins.

"Enough to get you to Canada. Then you won't need it."

He hands Dial the key to the men's room.

THEY SIT AT A SMALL TABLE, drink their cappuccinos, and nibble the chocolate almond cookies. Elena can't wait to be with Olivia. They always had a good relationship even during Olivia's rebellious teen years. Elena realizes now how important those small acts of rebellion were. Millie, on the other hand, had been so complacent, never questioning of authority. She fits in perfectly with the Aladdin apparatus. Elena can't imagine Millie actually doing the work to keep the garden alive, but taking care of a cat shouldn't be too hard. Unless she already has virtual pets.

The door opens and a bell tinkles.

Elena looks up to see a sun-burned, blond woman in her thirties with two children—a boy and a girl about nine or ten. The woman's thin, foxlike face looks vaguely familiar.

"Where do I know her from?"

"She was on the ship, I believe."

"I think I remember her from before the Wreckoning. She had a feed where she railed against Aladdin. I thought she was probably in prison."

The woman, tall and bony, leans over the counter, furtively conversing with the barista. Elena can't hear what they are saying, but the barista is shaking his head. Now the woman bites her knuckle. She turns and ushers the two children out of the coffee shop. Elena watches through the window as the woman stands on the sidewalk and surveys the street.

"Uh oh," the barista says.

He rushes to the window and bangs on it. A drone buzzes above the woman. Dial leaps up and runs outside.

"Wait, where are you going?" Elena frantically follows. "Dial, honey, stop! There's nothing you can do."

The woman screams at her children, "Go! Run!" But they stand dumbfounded.

The woman's eyes boil with panic. A shrill alarm sounds and a beam from the drone envelops her. As she sinks to the ground, trying to avoid the beam, her eyes meet Elena's, conveying some sort of plea. Elena reaches for the two kids and pulls them close to her.

"No!" Dial bellows.

He leaps forward, yanks the woman out of the beam, and slings her onto the sidewalk. The beam swivels over to Dial. He looks up at the drone and laughs. The beam grows brighter. As her husband disintegrates into dust, Elena sinks to her knees, screaming.

A loud BANG silences her screams. The drone topples out of the air and bursts into pieces on the road. She looks around, trying to understand what is happening and sees a gray-bearded man behind the wheel of a Chevrolet Suburban, holding a sawed-off shotgun. He pulls the vehicle beside her and rolls down a window.

"Get in!" he shouts.

The blond woman leaps up, grabs her kids and shoves them into the back seat. She turns to Elena, who hasn't moved.

"Come on!"

She pulls Elena onto her feet and shoves her into the back seat of the car with the children. Then she leaps into the front and slams the door.

"Let's go!"

As the car pulls away, Elena sees Dial's satchel on the ground.

"Stop!" she cries out.

The driver hits the brakes. Elena opens the door, leans down, and grabs the satchel. The car speeds away as she shuts the door.

"I was only supposed to pick up an old couple," the driver says and looks at the blond woman. "Who are you?"

"I'm on the run from Aladdin and these are my kids. Our contraband was stolen. We have nothing."

"I don't know how I can help you," he says. "The boat isn't free."

"Then we're fried," the woman says, looking back at the kids. The little girl beside Elena whimpers.

"I have credit," Elena blurts out.

"How much?" the driver asks.

"I don't know."

The driver pulls to the side of the road and takes out a bar code reader. He runs it over her arm.

"Looks like you've got enough to get all of you on the boat," he said. "Is that what you want to do?"

Elena looks at the blond woman, who is holding her breath, and then back at the driver.

"Yes."

The woman weeps in relief.

"What's your name?" Elena asks.

"Penelope, but people call me Penny," the woman says, brushing away her tears. "My kids are Franny and Zooey."

"What? That's…"

"I know. It's weird… I'm a Salinger fan."

Elena looks at Franny and Zooey. They each have fluffy hair, nut-hued skin and sparkling green eyes. Elena wonders what has happened to their father.

"Take us to the boat," Elena tells the driver.

THEY WAIT in a shed at a boatyard. It's hot. The children nap, leaning against their mother who waves away buzzing flies. Elena sits in the doorway and watches the sun melt into the horizon. She feels the breeze that always seems to stir at the end of the day. At least she can feel that. How is she supposed to go on without Dial, she wonders. It feels as if concrete is settling inside her chest.

When the driver returns, he leads them along a dock to a white boat about twenty feet long. Two shiny outboard motors hang on the end. The boat has a name painted on it in Brush Script: Charon. That's fitting, she thinks.

A woman with arms and neck covered in ink, wearing a captain's hat, helps them on board.

"The kids will need to wear life jackets," she says.

"Can we fish?" the boy, Zooey, asks.

"We'll be going a little too fast for that," the captain says. The driver and the captain untie the boat.

"Good luck," the driver calls out as the boat drifts away from the dock.

"How soon will we get there?" Elena asks the captain.

"A few hours. Depends on the weather. There's a bed in the cabin big enough for one person. You can take turns sleeping."

"I'm not tired," Elena says. How can she possibly sleep without Dial next to her?

They sit on cushioned seats in a horse-shoe at the stern of the boat. The captain stands at the helm and starts the engine. They putter out of the harbor. Once they are out on the open water, the captain pushes the throttle forward. The engines roar, and the front end lifts. Soon they fly over the surface of the dark blue water.

Elena gazes up at the satellites beaming in the night sky. Beyond them stars and planets flicker dimly.

She has somehow compartmentalized the grief lurking below her, waiting to pounce. No matter how fast the boat goes, she knows she won't be able to escape it. She thinks about what Mekos had said about the Great Greed. She has her own share of greed. She did not want to give up Dial, did not want to give up her last strand of hope for happiness. She grew up believing that happiness was her due. What an insane idea. Dial was willing to relinquish it all in a single heedless moment.

"I'm sorry about your husband," Penny says. "He saved my life."

Elena merely nods. Dial felt like a failure because he didn't "do something" and this woman's predicament gave him a chance to go out in glory. She knows he did the right thing, the strong thing, but she can't make herself feel good about it.

The kids hang their arms over the side of the boat and laugh the way kids do as the boat slaps against the waves.

"I'm friggin' exhausted. I haven't slept in days. I've been so worried. I can't thank you enough for helping us," Penny continues.

"It's what Dial would have wanted," she says.

She looks at the children. How oblivious they seem of the peril surrounding them. Penny faces the wind, hair streaming behind her. She yawns.

"Why don't you go into the cabin and rest? I'll look after Franny and Zooey," Elena says.

"You don't mind?"

"I don't mind."

Penny gets up, stretches, and then descends the stairs into the belly of the boat.

"I'm bored," Franny says, turning away from the waves.

Elena opens the satchel and extracts the last piece of contraband.

"Would you like me to read you a story?"

Franny and Zooey stare at her, eyes wide, mouths agape.

"Come, sit beside me."

Obediently they sit on either side of her. She opens the book. The boat hits a large wave and sprays them with droplets of salty water. The children giggle. Elena waits for the boat to slip back into its groove before she begins. The children snuggle closer to her. They smell like feral kittens.

"This is called *The Secret Garden* by Frances Hodgson Burnett. It was my favorite book when I was child. And it was my daughters' favorite, too."

Zooey rhythmically kicks the storage box beneath the seat while Franny plays with a strand of hair as she reads, "When Mary Lennox was sent to Misselthwaite Manor..."

By the end of the second chapter, the children are asleep on the cushions. Elena looks at her watch. It's midnight. The captain drinks from a thermos, staring straight ahead.

Without warning, the grief lurking below the surface engulfs her. She sobs and turns to look behind her at the endless expanse of black water. It would be easy to dive off the back. She's a good diver and can easily make it over the sharp propellor blades of the speeding boat. Then she could swim until her arms gave way and sink into the dark oblivion and she would not have to face the future alone. She stands, slips out of her sandals, leans over, and sees the wake churning behind them. She feels an irresistible pull as if the water is commanding her to leap into the abyss.

Something brushes against her calf. She reaches down to swat it away but there's nothing there. With a sudden pang, she thinks of Dandelion, waiting for her in the garden.

A movement in her peripheral vision causes her to look toward the front of the boat. The captain is waving to her from her perch at the wheel. With her other hand, she pulls the throttle down. The engine's roar lowers to a hum and the prow settles. Why is she slowing down, Elena wonders.

"Come here," the captain calls.

Elena crosses the deck to the captain's chair. The captain points to a smattering of lights up ahead.

"What is that?"

"Canada. Or as you probably know it, Cuba."

"Cuba? You're taking us from one dictatorship to another?" Elena asks, horrified.

"They've tricked you into thinking Aladdin controls the whole world. But it's not true. Africa, most of South and Central America, and yes, Cuba—all part of an alliance. You'll be safe there."

Penny emerges from the cabin.

"Did I hear you say Cuba?" she asks.

"Yep. We'll be there soon," the Captain says.

"Thank God."

"Do you think we'll ever get America back?" Elena asks.

Penny pulls her long hair behind her head, twists it into a knot and says, "I guess that depends on us."

The mound of land grows bigger, the lights brighter now. Soon she'll be reunited with her daughter, and she'll have to tell her about her father.

Penny checks on the sleeping children, comes back, and nudges Elena.

"Your book," she says, holding it out to her.

Elena shakes her head. "Keep it for them. Let them have their own secret garden."

To her surprise, Penny hugs her, and the warmth of the woman's embrace loosens something inside her. Above them a clutch of shooting stars streams across the sky. The Geminids are finally visible.

A FINAL KEEPSAKE

CARRIE HAYES

Tragedy was a word the old woman had learned when the actors came and performed their Greek plays. The plays explained a lot, and she recognized the twists and turns of her own story in them. How her mistress cared not for rules, desiring passion above all else.

Then one day, she'd returned to give birth. A beautiful boy and his two sisters, all born on the same day together. As the three babies grew up, they'd watch their mother leave and not return, sometimes for months. When she did appear again, she would be silent and sorrowful, waiting for the next burst of wandering to lead her away from them.

During her last absence, when the children were still little, yet big enough to understand, the old woman attempted to explain why their mother had left. "Something inside her is always empty."

"Does she not have enough to eat?"

"Oh, she has food enough. It is a different kind of hunger. It is not in her belly, and we cannot fill it up for her. It is something else. It is—perhaps your mother's tragedy."

~

MANY YEARS LATER, when the children's mother returned, she stumbled and collapsed upon the ground.

"Quick, quick!" cried the old woman. "Get your brother!" She said to the girls, "She needs our help."

Their mother's hair was matted and gold, reaching to her knees. Her skin had turned brown from the sun and her tunic was torn to rags.

"Was this the last time?" the old woman asked her.

"Yes, yes," their mother whispered. "This was the last time."

AS THE CHILDREN GREW UP, the old woman could not help but notice how the boy became caught in stories of the Crusades, until his own desire was not unlike his mother's obsessive need for passion.

"I will go to the Holy Land!" He'd wave a toy sword in the air, imagining the multitude of infidels he'd kill. To which the old woman would nod, smiling to hide her sorrow that his nature was so similar to his mother's, although his was to make war while hers was to make love.

FOR THE OLD SOLDIER, it was a long journey back from Jerusalem. This last Crusade, the Children's Crusade was to be the last one for him. There had been battle, the decimation of infidels, the re-establishment of the Christians and installation of a ruling governor. Every time he'd been to Jerusalem, it always ended with decrees and edicts, hangings and the confiscation of valuables. Then the soldiers would divide the spoils. But that was a younger man's game. For the old soldier, this last foray, what others called the Children's Crusade, had been a disaster.

Who would have known that a young blonde boy, not even fully grown, would whip the crusaders into such a frenzy? Looking back, the old soldier considered those final months and how the boy's insatiable craving for God's approval, and by extension, the old soldier's approval—had inspired those many thousands to follow Romain into battle. Romain. So many things had gone wrong.

At first, Romain had shouted, "We'll bring the true faith back to the Holy Land!"

But then, the horses became lame, and the food turned rotten, making everyone sick. Then there were the drownings. Romain insisted the sea would part for them, leading those boys into the water over their heads. Only a handful of adults whose constitutions were hale had survived that wretched trek.

Now, after many years and many stops, the old soldier was on his way back to his feudal lands. Sitting down, he readily accepted the assistance from his new page, Karim, a Moorish lad he'd engaged out there who was willing to remain by his side. As the ship pulled away from the docks at Civitavecchia, it occurred to the old soldier how crusades such as these, be it waging war or no, brought men together. They shared everything. Their food, their weapons, their shelter, and whatever women they might ravish along the way.

"Rest, my lord," Karim said. And the old man nodded, closing his eyes, grateful for the respite.

It was a fig that the old soldier often dreamed about. When he was a boy, there had been a fig tree in their garden, and sometimes, if the moment was just so, the housemaid would take a pause from her chores and reach up to pick a fig from that tree. Then, smiling at him, she would tear the fruit apart and offer him some while she ate the other half. It was both tart and sweet and smooth, yet his tongue felt strangely itchy afterwards.

This made him laugh and want her, but smiling, she would decline and go back to her chores. "You're just a boy!" she'd laugh.

During his trips to the Holy Land, this delicious dream stayed with him for many years. It stayed with him even after the crossing with the strange golden woman who'd paid for the voyage with only her loins as currency. That had been years ago and he was one of twelve crusaders on that boat.

She had been trying to get to Jerusalem and the other men had said, "We can only bring you aboard if you pay your way with your legs."

The woman had not been such an innocent. But still she asked, "Pay with my legs how?"

"Open of course, for each of us. Then, by the time we arrive, you'll have paid for your journey."

Ha! The look she gave them! The old man smiled at the memory even in his sleep. He did not recall whether she spoke again before she got to work. She certainly didn't say anything to him.

But during that trip, each of them took as much as they wanted and as much as they could, while she lay prone and silent. And truly, she was a mystery, in that she gave away nothing, save for her person, which, like the housemaid and the fig, was tart and sweet and made his tongue strangely itch afterward.

On that trip, approaching the shore, the silent woman had removed a fig from her inner sleeve. The other crusaders were occupied with how they'd disembark, but the old soldier (he was not so old at the time) had watched her wordlessly tear the fig apart and eat it, the juice dribbling down the side of her mouth.

"I love figs," he had said.

"This came from the garden at my home." Her voice was smooth and very soft. Then she had gathered her robes, and left the boat. She neither looked at the crusaders, nor did she acknowledge them as she walked away. The next time he saw her was on the steps of a church, where a priest was physically ejecting her, pulling her arm, yelling the way they shout at common prostitutes. And, after all, it's how she paid for her crossing, so that's what she was, was she not? Yet the rough treatment by the priest seemed harsh.

On the eve of the raid against the infidels, he had seen her once again. That time, she was begging for food in the market, where people ignored her or the merchants spat at her, and tried to beat her with their brooms. It was most unpleasant. But that had been years ago. Now, he was just an old soldier, performing a final obligation and making his way home.

The dream of the housemaid blended with the memory of that crossing. In the old soldier's mind was the sensation of the fruit and the woman, and the taste of a fig with its luscious flesh and perfect skin. In his dream, the soft silence of the golden woman's yielding made him shudder.

"My lord?" Karim gently tapped him. The soldier did not want to wake up. Clinging to the dream, he imagined the housemaid's perfect backside, not unlike that delicious fig.

"My lord," Karim said again.

With his eyes still closed, the soldier brushed Karim's arm away. To imagine it even now, many decades later, filled him with such a desire that was so distracting he could just —

This Children's Crusade had been an undeniable disaster. How many of them had died? Scores of them. The ones left living had been sold, because, in truth there was no other way for the soldiers to get back, unless they pooled their resources by selling those unfortunate boys.

And whose fault was that? That scallywag, Romain, had been so besotted by his own faith, believing the Lord spoke to him, directly.

He swore up and down this was the case, and he convinced anyone who'd listen that the Children's Crusade would bring about the kingdom of Heaven on Earth. Romain, that incorrigible little—the old soldier pulled his cloak over himself and sighed. His fig dream was ruined now.

Groaning, he stretched and watched the French coastline straight ahead. The water was a bit choppy, and the sky was grey, but they would alight before any serious weather arrived. The soldier shifted, feeling something in his mouth with his tongue. Hmm, that could not be good. Slowly, he slid his finger along his gumline and tenderly tapped a tooth which had given him some trouble during the last fortnight. It was loose. He inserted his thumb and gingerly pulled the offending incisor out. The tooth was nearly black.

"Ah well," he sighed, and spit the bloody phlegm into the sea.

"That tooth won't be bothering you now, my lord," said Karim.

The soldier wiped his hand on his cloak, "No, indeed, Karim. It won't."

Arriving in port, Karim helped the old soldier hoist himself up onto the dock. They had few belongings. The small package the soldier carried in his arms was the last of his obligations before returning home. It was Romain's cloak which he'd pledged to the dying boy he'd return to his family. Somehow, Romain's long and painful death had been the final tragedy of the whole disastrous campaign.

At the soldier's direction, Karim hired a pair of horses from a nearby stable, and they began the journey several hours inland where Romain's family was said to reside.

Gradually, the skies cleared, and they took in the beauty of that part of the world. Fields of lavender and yellow crops of brilliant rapeseed grew on either side of the path, lending their surroundings a sensual aspect. The old soldier wondered if there were any fig trees at Romain's family farm.

It was still light when they arrived on the edge of the old soldier's feudal lands. The village was, in truth, a hamlet with only three buildings. The first was a blacksmith, the second an apothecary, and the third was the hostel connected to the farm where he'd been told that Romain's family took in paying guests. Between the old soldier and his page, they had just enough coins to stay a couple of nights. After that, they would begin the final trek home.

An elderly woman welcomed them and told them to drink from the well in the garden at the back. "The water there is sweeter," she said. "Then if it please you, we will bring you something to eat."

Karim and the soldier followed her instruction and sat themselves down at a table across from the kitchen. Adjacent to the kitchen was a cauldron, where a pair of sisters washed two large bucketfuls of snails and cockles, oysters, and clams.

The old soldier thought the girls looked strangely familiar. But then, all pretty girls seemed to look alike. One was fair-haired and the other had freckles. They barely noticed the men who'd arrived, as there were often travelers at the table, and they weren't much interested in anything an old man or his page might have to say.

The soldier and Karim listened to the old woman gently scolding the girls.

"Well, that certainly took you long enough." She plunged the snails into the cauldron. Then she flicked her cloth to shoo away a goose poking around for scraps.

The old woman stirred the contents of the cauldron. "This had better be enough for tonight."

One of the girls sighed. "There's too many! And they are just... ewww." She wrinkled her nose. "I can't imagine anyone eating them!"

To which the other girl burst out laughing, and the old woman said, "I shall box your ears if you two cannot behave."

"Slugs!" one of the girls hissed.

"They're not slugs; they're snails. We don't eat slugs. There's a difference. Prepared properly they are delicious. People have been eating them for centuries. Now give the men their soup, please."

Silently, the girls obeyed and served the steaming broth. The old soldier took care not to let it dribble down his beard too much. The soup was filled with carrots and parsnips, dandelions and peas, bits of turnips and cabbage. He let each morsel rest inside his mouth until he carefully chewed it into a mush that might be swallowed.

The blonde girl asked, "Will you have some bread, my lord?"

She was really very pretty. "Ah yes." He nodded. "But my teeth, they are not what they were."

"I will break the bread for you," she offered. "Then you can soak it in the soup."

"Thank you, my child." He watched her ample bottom sway as she walked back to the kitchen. He realized that his page, Karim, was watching him watch the girl and he shrugged.

She then re-emerged with a large loaf of bread.

The girl with the freckles asked, "Where have you come from, my lord?"

"We were in the Holy Land."

"Really?" Both girls came closer to the table.

The freckle-faced one said, "Our brother went there."

Careful, he reminded himself. That was when he noticed a figure sitting in the shadows by the edge of the building.

"I have been many times."

"What happens there?" asked the blonde girl. "Before he left, our brother had said that he was sure it would be Heaven on Earth. But if that were true, he would have come back and told us so."

"In a place like Jerusalem, which is the site for so many holy things—" The old man was suddenly nervous, unsure whether this was the moment when he should get Romain's cloak out or not. "We—by whom I mean those of us who go on Crusade—are often confronted by every sin imaginable."

"Really?" the freckle-faced girl sat across the table and leaned on her arms to listen better. "Like what?"

"Well, there are mortal sins, of course, and then there are venial sins."

"Which sin is worse?"

"Yes, my lord," Karim was struggling not to laugh at this. "Tell us which one is worse."

The old soldier smiled. "I think we can all agree that coveting your neighbor's sheep or wife or taking another man's life are as wicked as can be imagined."

The freckle-faced sister said, "I can't imagine any of those things."

The old soldier admired her full lips and her wide set eyes, which were so innocent. She might have been a doe on the edge of the forest, oblivious to his bow and arrow. He studied the curve of her breast and felt a strange uptick in his own bosom. Was that life? Was it the power of God, reminding him that he was still alive? Her bodice strained across her front, and he imagined holding her, or at the very least, touching—

"May I offer you the next dish, my lord?" The old woman stood over them. She placed their now-empty soup bowls at the far end of the table.

"Oh, yes." He nodded, hoping she hadn't noticed his voice trembling just the smallest amount.

One of the girls brought another dish, filled with steaming snails and clams, cockles and crayfish. "My granny steams them, rather than with the usual preparation." It was the blonde. He marveled at how this pair of girls could be so deliciously beautiful.

"Oh, yes?"

"It keeps them moist, and soft, yet makes them warm at the same time." She smiled, and her teeth and lips shone as if she had covered them in oil.

The soldier's hands were curled with age and he struggled with the small tool needed to remove his supper's flesh from its shell.

"I will help you, if you like," the fair-haired girl held out her hand.

"Oh yes, I would like that." In spite of himself, he could not resist the notion of these sisters, no doubt Romain's sisters, serving him, tending his every—

A figure stepped from the shadows and approached the table. It was a woman, more of a crone, really, ravaged by time, or was it disease? Perhaps she was the younger sister of the old woman who had welcomed them?

Hard to say really. The crone's hair was gold but streaked with white. Her skin was brown from the sun. Beside her was a wolfhound. She took the empty soup bowls and placed them on the ground so the dog could lick the remains. There was something familiar about her, too. But her age! He found the crone's demeanor somewhat offensive and turned back to the blonde girl, who was pulling succulent meat from the shells of his food.

"Did you see him?" The crone asked the soldier.

"Did I see whom?"

"The girls' brother. His name was Romain. He was very blonde. Just like this one, here." The crone gestured to the fair-haired sister.

If there was something the old soldier didn't like, it was being put on the spot. "Where is the party responsible for these girls?" He particularly didn't like it when the person doing so was a woman. No doubt, this crone had weathered a bumpy road but that did not mean—

"I am that party." The crone said. Where did he know her from?

"Well, madame, as your feudal lord, your daughters should come with me."

"And do what?"

That look. The old soldier knew that expression. But he knew it from where? He drew his chest up, "I am in need of a wife, and shall marry one of these girls. The other will serve in the household." He pounded his fist on the table. "Not that I see it's any business of yours. As the feudal lord, I am entitled to do whatever I want with whomever I want to do it."

"And re-live the story of Lot?"

"What?"

"Genesis nineteen, my lord. Ask them their age."

"When were you born, my child?" He asked the daughter with the freckles.

"This will be our eighteenth summer, my lord. We're twins. Well, we were three originally, when Romain was still with us."

The old soldier whispered, "And where is your father?"

"We've never met," said the fair-haired girl. "Our mother said he was a crusader."

"I only knew him during a crossing to get to the Holy Land," the crone said. "It was a... I don't think anyone on that boat really took the time to know one another. I was fulfilling a different need."

The old soldier felt that flutter from earlier in the evening fold in sorrow. That meant, Romain, that passionate boy, the boy whose cloak he had yet to give her, who was so fearless and filled with the Lord—

It was dusk. The nightbirds and crickets began to sing.

It was time to give that woman the cloak. "Karim," he said, "fetch the small package from our room. And bring it here, to this lady."

Wordlessly, Karim brought the package out. He then knelt, and offered it to the crone. When she took it from him, she held it to her chest, her fingers spread across the front. Her golden hair fell forward, hiding her face, but the soldier knew that she was weeping. Eventually she lifted her head and looking at him, nodded. "My lord. The crossing was long ago. I seem to remember you're mentioning a love of figs that day. May I offer you one? Those in our garden are very sweet."

REMAINS

GAIL LEHRMAN

D r. Philippa Flynn sat erect in the wide, round room. It wasn't the surrounding columns, inlaid with gold and ornate plaster scrollwork, that rendered her slack-jawed. It was the niches. Scores of niches. Two-foot square, glass-fronted, embedded in the walls around the entire circumference of the room. Each niche was decorated in high style. Each niche was unique.

There was a Victorian niche, an Arte Deco niche, a Cubist niche. One, on the right close to the floor, contained a Star Wars universe, complete with LEGO Millennium Falcon fronted by LEGO Luke Skywalker battling LEGO Darth Vader. The niche above it, paneled in high-gloss black plastic, held a miniature Steinway grand with candelabra and the score of Bach's Brandenburg Concerto Number 4.

As a tenured professor of English literature for twenty years, it was Philippa's job to guide her students to look for universals. *Come now, find the common theme.*

She cocked her head, like she did in her classroom, picturing some over-eager apple-polisher, waving frantically for attention.

"I know. I know. It's Death. Look. Every box showcases an urn with human remains."

"A cinerary urn," Philippa imagined herself correcting. "Death has its own vocabulary."

Add another word: columbarium. She rolled it around on her tongue. Col-um-bar-i-um: a building for storing funeral urns. She would never come back to San Francisco without thinking of the col-um-bar-i-um because the niche directly in front of her held a brass urn with the ashes of her dead lover.

Brandon's box was done in the style of an Edwardian library— flocked red velvet wallpaper, tiered wooden bookshelves with an ornate circular stairway. The tiny books were bound in leather and covered with miniscule gold letters.

Reasonable. Not inappropriate for a poet storied for his return to classical tropes. Cultured, courtly, urbane—certainly that was the Brandon Van Duyne of Instagram and Facebook. Of course, his trendy author wife, Rebecca, would want to institutionalize his image in a literary meme.

Philippa drew a ragged breath. A tsunami of rage overwhelmed her. What a farce. What a slap in the face of authenticity. Her very soul was appalled. How could her passionate, torrid lover spend eternity as a trite cliché?

Cultured, courtly, urbane... that was a charade. Only she, Philippa Flynn, had been granted entrée to the hidden extravagance of the man's true essence. She clutched her bulky leather purse to her chest as if it were Brandon's body, vibrating in memory of his lusty, amorous thirst. Her breast swelled with pride at the unquenchable fire they'd ignited in each other's arms.

She was here in defense of that pride.

Just twenty hours ago she'd been home in Brooklyn watching PBS when she chanced on an interview—Rebecca standing in this very rotunda, promoting her latest piece of literary trash, a memoir of her life with Brandon Van Duyne. Phila almost choked. What villainy—profiteering off of Brandon's death.

Seething at the maudlin, mawkish chatter, Philippa was gripped by an iron resolve. In life, Brandon had anointed *her* keeper of his secret self. Their love demanded a final fidelity. She must be the one to curate that self in death. She'd rescue Brandon from this Disneyland of death and return him to his rightful place—home with her.

It took shape in an instant. Call in sick to work. Fly, as an anonymous East Coast tourist. Car rental. Hotel. Poof.

And here she was, her Holy Grail mere inches away, but locked behind glass. She had come to retrieve it, but how? How? Frustration drove her to her feet, her palm slamming the glass door of his prison. To her utter shock, it wobbled and the latch at its base clicked open.

God in heaven, what just happened? She jerked around, looking for a guard or curator, but the room was empty. She pressed close to the glass, covering her actions, just in case. Gingerly, she tested the door hinge. It slid right up. She was in. Grab the urn and run.

Her fingers reached out but stopped a hair's breadth from the urn. Wait. Think. Brandon was a celebrity. The missing urn would be noticed. There would be a hue and cry. An investigation. Phila tapped a finger to her brow, working the problem till she solved it. Simple, really. She needed the ashes, not the urn. If she emptied out the ashes and put the urn back, no one would be the wiser.

She almost giggled because she even had an appropriate receptacle in her purse. Attending a myriad of academic conferences, she'd developed the habit of hoarding the plastic drawstring laundry bags provided by the hotel in case she encountered travel items she wished to save.

Phila felt like the brilliant nemesis from an Agatha Christie story. As if on a movie screen, she watched her hands close around neck of the urn. The thing was awkward, but manageable. She lowered it to the floor, slipped her fingers through its brass handle. A slight moment of resistance, then the lid gave way, revealing the grey powder within.

Brandon.

Phila wrapped the plastic bag over the mouth and upended the urn. With the faintest whoosh, the contents fell into the bag, a whiff of grey dust escaping into the air. She secured the lid and put the urn back in the exact place it had been. She pulled down the glass, making sure the latch caught completely. Then she dropped the bag into her purse and walked out the door.

As PHILA STRODE the long yards to the parking lot, still thrilled by her audacity, logic kicked into high gear. She was flying back to New York this afternoon. The bag weighed easily five pounds, maybe more. It punched out her purse like a pregnant woman's belly. She pictured the pregnant purse on the TSA conveyor belt. She pictured the TSA agent pausing the belt. Moving it backward, his eyes narrowing, trying to figure out what might be in the purse. She imagined him pulling it aside, calling her to open it, asking her what was this bag of powder she wanted to bring onto the plane?

No. That would never do, but she could figure it out. Certainly she could. Philippa Flynn had a gift for management. It was her proudest super power. So many academicians were flighty nincompoops. Not Philippa Flynn. She was a solid, concrete planner. That's why, as chairwoman of the English Department, she'd gotten funds for the great Brandon Van Duyne to present a lecture at her community college in Brooklyn. It was why he was her *enamorata* by the time he left.

As soon as she popped the trunk of her rental car, the answer stared her in the face. Her roller bag—a purposely easy-to-spot red tartan—was half-empty. She'd put Brandon in the rollie and check the bag. Splayed out so as not to lump, the cremains shouldn't set off any alarms. Normally, she hated checking bags... all that loitering, watching luggage circle the carousel while you twiddled your thumbs. But these were special circumstances.

She hefted the plastic bag from her purse. She zipped the suitcase open and nestled Brandon between layers of her clothing. She zipped it closed, laying her palm on the bag in momentary exaltation. Then she got behind the wheel and put her keys into the ignition. The rental car roiled to life. The dazzling San Francisco sun ricocheted off the hood. She donned her sunglasses and pressed her foot to the gas. A triumph of passion with planning. "Passion with planning." Her lover's description of her.

It had been a bright day like this when Brandon Van Duyne stood at the front of her lecture hall reading from his magnum opus, *Classical Canticles*. Surrounded by grungy nose-ringed undergrads in torn jeans, he was the essence of literary elegance in his blue blazer, yellow paisley ascot and black goatee. It was painfully obvious that the students—required to attend—had no idea of what they were being offered, but his deep, sonorous voice sang out verses that enthralled her with their verbal gymnastics. The language was so erudite, so controlled. Was she alone in catching the subterranean ardor at their heart? She had to find out.

Sipping wine at the post-lecture reception, the poet was philosophical about the muted response. "I don't take it personally." Heaving a dramatic sigh, "Ah, callow youth..."

"Sadly so." Phila grimaced in agreement. "But perhaps I can make it up to you. Can I offer the compensation of a home-cooked meal?"

He hesitated. She understood. He was married to a bestselling novelist and must be cognizant of possible gossip.

"I pride myself on my cooking, as I guess you can tell." She patted her plentiful hip, hinting that no one would consider a slightly dowdy, middle-aged academic to be grist for the rumor mill.

His lips twitched in poised amusement. "What a tantalizing offer. Who could resist that, Dr. Flynn?"

"Please, I'm Phila."

Their eyes met over his mock bow. "Pleased to meet you, Phila. I'm Brandon."

AT THE AIRPORT, she printed a luggage tag at the self-serve kiosk and wrapped it around the handle next to the leather tag with her name and address. The suitcase rode the conveyor belt through the x-ray machine before dropping into the bowels of the airport. No whistles screeched, no sirens blared. With a satisfied sniff, she ambled through security and out to her gate. Two hours later, she was ensconced in a window seat, floating over billows of white clouds in a perfect blue sky. Soon she'd have Brandon home where he belonged.

HOME WAS the ground floor apartment of a Park Slope brownstone.

He'd arrived on the dot of seven, offering up a bouquet of lilacs. "A lovely gift for a lovely lady." He'd gone casual in slacks and a charcoal turtleneck that set off the twinkle in his grey eyes.

"Such good manners, sir," she curtsied. She'd chosen a flowered caftan that obscured her hips and complimented her dark hair. "The place is a bit cramped," she said as she led him past the galley kitchen to the narrow living room.

"But full of books." He moseyed to the floor-to-ceiling shelves that covered one whole wall of the room. "Now I will find out who you really are, Dr. Philippa Flynn." He ran his hand down the spines of her collection. "Chaucer. Shakespeare. Pope. *Paradise Lost.* Another edition of Milton. And yet a third..."

"I did my thesis on Lucifer in *Paradise Lost.* Pride is such a maligned emotion. Why is it sinful to recognize your gifts? For example..." She sashayed to a wall of drapery at the far end of the room and pulled a hanging cord. "Come see mine."

Brandon turned and his brows arched skyward. "My word."

With a wave of her arm, Philippa ushered him into a backyard garden so lush and green it harkened to another reality. In the deepening dusk, a string of fairy lights lit the trail of pavers that wound through pockets of high grasses. Artfully spaced shrubbery created haloes of deep shade while beds of scarlet tulips, azure hydrangeas, and purple irises popped out like surprise birthday presents. Concrete pedestals held classic pottery, a Grecian urn *ala* Keats, a bust of Homer, a sundial. In the far corner, the wrought iron table was set with porcelain plates and crystal wine glasses. Bordered by stone walls and facing the windowless brick building next door, the long, narrow space was utterly secluded.

Brandon drifted around the path, bending to catch the scent of the iris, brushing his fingers over the silk of a tulip, running his palm over a mound of warm moss as if caressing a woman's body.

He turned to her, eyes burning. "This is a sensual feast."

She dipped her head in acquiescence. "A labor of love. I call it my Garden of Earthly Delights." She offered him her hand. "Come. The moon's rising and there's so much more I want to show you."

∽

"Pretty out there, isn't it?"

Phila jolted. "Excuse me?"

The guy squashed into the middle seat was craning his neck to look out her window. He pointed to the sky. "I always appreciate that pure blue. The air is so pristine." He was a crisp-looking fellow in a starched white shirt, his tie loosened for comfort around his collar. "There aren't many pure things left these days."

It was an intriguing comment from a corporate type. She smiled agreement, then turned back to her window. But he'd jostled her memory. *An Ode to Phonic Purity* was one of Brandon's signature poems. She dove into her purse for the worn, cloth-bound book that was always with her.

"Oh, hey... isn't that the writer who died?"

Still twisted her way, the middle guy was reading the large block letters *VAN DUYNE* slanting across the front cover sandwiched between the smaller, italicized *CLASSICAL* above and *CANTICLES* below.

At Phila's startled jerk, he sat back. "I didn't mean to invade. It's just... Well, it's been all over the place... him dropping dead at the podium like that."

Even after six months, the memory stabbed her heart. The twenty-four-hour news stations playing the clip over and over, relishing the grisly spectacle—Brandon, elegant and perfect in a black tuxedo, Rebecca, next to him in a diaphanous designer gown. He steps toward the dais. His hand reaches toward the speech tucked into his breast pocket. Suddenly, instead of the speech, he grabs his chest. His other arm swings back, catching and ripping the fabric of his wife's dress as he doubles over and falls across the podium. Every news channel. Every hour. For days. And she couldn't look away.

"I do a lot a reading myself, though not poetry." The guy chatted away. "I gather he was some big deal."

Phila's pride in Brandon overrode her desire for solitude. "He was the best poet working in America."

"Wow. That's a ringing endorsement." He pointed at the well-worn cover. "Looks like you would know."

"I'm an English teacher, so... yes I do know."

The guy's smile broadened. "Good for you. Kids don't do nearly enough reading these days. As a student of human behavior, I learn more from books than anything else."

Phila's hesitation drained away. "Oh, yes. That is the mantra of my life."

The fellow shifted to face her more, his brown eyes crinkling. "My name is Joe, by the way."

"And I'm Philippa... Phila." Her cautious self yelped, but it was too late.

"I caught an interview with his wife on YouTube." The guy reached for his cell phone but stopped, remembering where they were. "He advertised himself as this traditional proper gentleman, but it turns out he was a regular Casanova who couldn't keep his pants on." The guy didn't notice Phila's spine going rigid. "Just goes to show. You can't tell a book by its cover," he chuckled, "if you'll pardon the expression."

Keep Your Mouth Shut, flashed in red lights across Philippa's brain. But fugitive aircraft hours were a world unto themselves. All her words would be scattered into the molecules of the air.

"That interview was a complete distortion. I knew Brandon Van Duyne intimately. There was not an underhanded, dishonest bone in his body."

The fellow's brows shot up. "You knew him? Really?"

"Those stories are base fabrications, the accusations of a greedy woman out to sell books. Brandon Van Duyne *was* his poetry. Anyone who says different is a foul liar."

"You sure? His wife was really open about it..."

Before Phila could spit out more words for Rebecca, the flight attendant popped in with a perky, "Anything to drink?"

Phila waved the woman away, but Joe smiled. "Sprite in the can, please. And I'll take a second unopened can as well." He put one in the mesh seat bag and snapped the tab on the other. Looking to

Phila, he winked. "They don't make it back for a second round, so I always get two. You gotta travel smart, you know?" He took a long chug of soda.

Phila turned her face back to the window. Rebecca's stories about Brandon's sexual adventuring were vile. Phila categorically rejected them. That night with Brandon was her own doing. He'd been nothing but professional until she worked her magic on him. She knew, *knew* to the core of her being, that the passion Brandon exhibited in her garden was unique—for her and her alone.

Her eyes drooped in uneasy rest. Through half-closed lids, she watched the sky darken to blue dusk and then to velvet night as she flew Brandon east, away from the sun, away from Rebecca's loathsome world, back to her own.

At last they got the trays-up, seatbelts-on announcement. The plane began its circular descent, banking to give a perfect view of the sparkling Manhattan skyline. More circles, a steeper bank, that sharp change in the engine sound as the flaps came down and then, with the appropriate thud, they were back to earth.

People turned on cell phones, gathered their belongings and undid their seatbelts. When the plane came to the gate, those with enough room stood to stretch, waiting for the front door to open. Joe slipped his untouched soda into his pack. "Back to the salt mines."

Focused on getting off the plane, Phila fell into automatic politeness. "What is it that you do?"

The elderly woman in the aisle seat exited and Joe stepped out to pop the overhead bin. "I'm in law enforcement." He pulled down a black suit jacket and put it on, straightening his tie in the process. "Detective Joe Bianco, NYPD, at your service." He flicked her a salute. "Nice talking with you."

Phila watched Joe Bianco squeeze down the narrow aisle. She'd spent the flight opening up to a cop.

Frozen at her seat, Phila replayed the afternoon. She said she knew a famous dead person. Okay. She said she thought the rumors about him were lies. That's allowed. Nothing she'd said connected her to the San Francisco Columbarium where, as far as the world was concerned, Brandon Van Duyne's ashes rested in peace. In truth, nothing had changed. A man she'd never see again was told she knew a poet who had died. Big deal. Fate added a dollop of danger to her venture, but she was still Philippa Flynn. She was still the master of her fate, still the captain of her soul. Satisfied, she gathered her belongings and sauntered out of the plane.

The airport was jammed with weekend travelers. She elbowed the sea of bodies, down to the lower-level baggage claim where peevish passengers circled empty carousels. This was why she hated checking her bag. On a night like this, it could take forever. She staked out a spot facing the conveyor belt, hoping to escape another interaction with Detective Joe Bianco. At last, she heard the loud clunk. With a blast of warm air, an invisible outer door opened and the carousel rattled into motion. God be praised, Phila's red tartan suitcase was the first to drop through the heavy plastic ribbons. She jerked it off the carousel and cantered outside to grab a cab.

The gritty New York air was dense with car exhaust. Irritated drivers honked and cursed in the jolting stop-and-go traffic. Phila barely noticed. She leaned back, keeping a steadying hand on the suitcase next to her on the seat. Her pulse quickened when the cab turned onto her street. She gentled the rollie to the ground, tipping the cabby well. She slipped the key into her lock. Her home was waiting as she'd left it. The walls were clean and white. The books were neatly lined up on their shelves. The place felt still from the lack of activity. She wheeled the suitcase to the center of the room.

"We did it, Brandon. You're home."

There was no need to rush now. She washed the travel dirt off her hands and face, checked the mail that had fallen through the door slot onto her rug. When she was ready, she pulled back the drapes and slid back the door to her garden, breathing in the fecund aroma of the fertile earth. Her Grecian urn sat on a pedestal near the far corner. She put a hand to her heart. This was what she'd pictured in that awful Columbarium. Like Keat's frozen lovers— *"Beneath the trees, thou cast not leave"*—Brandon Van Duyne's remains, preserved forever in her Garden of Earthly Delights.

She lugged her suitcase up onto her coffee table. Resting on her knees, she sang a silent prayer, then undid the flap to retrieve the bag nestled in her clothing. Only... it wasn't her clothing.

Philippa dropped back on her haunches, staring at neatly folded button-down shirts, balled-up men's socks. There was a brown leather shaving kit, a pair of black business shoes and another pair of running shoes. Two ties coiled around an empty toilet paper roll. Pajamas. Fruit-of-the-loom briefs.

"Wait. What? No. No, no, no..."

She tore through the alien garments, searching for her own. Shirts, socks, shoes and briefs went flying. Nothing of hers was here. Impossible. Insane.

She'd grabbed the wrong bag.

In a fit of fury, she flung away the empty suitcase, knocking her table lamp to the floor and sending weird shadows against the white walls.

Brandon. She'd lost Brandon.

Clenching her fists, she fought for clarity.

"Think, Philippa, think. Organize yourself." She jumped to her feet, running her fingers through her hair. "Okay. Okay. Okay..." *Figure this out.* "If I have somebody else's bag, that person probably has mine. My bag, with my name and address buckled to the handle. So, I'm findable, right? Oh, God." Her hand shot to her head. Maybe that person's name is buckled to *this* bag.

She dashed across the room, scrambling for the handle. Yes. See. A leather tag, just like hers. She dragged the suitcase to the overturned lamp, squinting to read the tiny script.

Her knees buckled and she sank to the ground.

You have to travel smart these days. He was smart, like her. He'd picked a bag that was easy to spot. Just like her. *Joseph Bianco, 212-555-8732.*

Prone on her living room rug, Philippa imagined Detective Joe Bianco at the carousel. There's only one tartan roller bag. Like her, he grabs it without checking the tag. He gets home, tired after a long flight. He throws the suitcase onto his bed to unpack, unzips it and, *ta-da.*

Her name and address were on the tag.

After an eternity, Philippa sat up. Her mouth was dry and her head ached. In the shadowy light, the living room felt foreign and claustrophobic. The open door to her garden beckoned. Stumbling across the room, she stepped outside.

The earth was night damp. The fairy lights twinkled off the tree branches. The high walls kept the street sounds at bay. It was a night just like this that they'd lain together in the soft moss under the Japanese maple. When they were finally sated, Brandon got up on one elbow.

"I sure have enjoyed this trip, Dr. Flynn."

She sat up, adjusting her caftan and straightening her hair.

"It's no accident. I've been planning it for quite a while."

"Oh. So it's passion with planning, hunh?"

"Exactly."

HER PASSIONATE PLANNING had finally failed. She was undone by chance and a tartan suitcase.

"Oh, Brandon, what happens now?"

His ghostly image shimmered before her, ascot, goatee, and all. She could almost hear his acerbic *Well, what* does *happen now,*

Philippa Flynn? Submit? Cave? Yield without a fight? Tsk, tsk. What a disappointment.

She went red with shame. Brandon would have been mortified at her childish theatrics—throwing things, giving into despair. Really. She'd have no more of that. Head down, she circled her garden, scanning for a strategy. It took one rotation. Then she snapped her fingers, hooting, "That's it."

Joe Bianco's phone number was on the suitcase. She could call him, right now even, apologetic about the muddle. *Isn't it droll, after we flew together? Could we meet and make the exchange tonight? What? You found a bag of ashes? Oh, yes, I was flying my uncle's cremains back east.* (Hopefully he doesn't ask for details.) *Required special arrangements? I had no idea.*

She went to caress the urn that would soon hold her lover's remains. "This was a nothing, a pittance, a minor glitch on the way to perfection."

In the quiet of that triumphant moment, she heard the thrum of a car engine turning down her block. Flashing red and blue lights breached the pale moonlight on her wall. The thrumming died outside her house. Then came the doorbell.

Phila didn't flinch. It could only be Bianco, of course. Her address in hand, he'd beaten her to the punch. No problem. She was prepared. Regal and serene, she walked to open the door.

"Joe." She radiated warmth. "I was about to call you. Isn't this funny? We've had a little mix up, haven't we?"

She waited for a reciprocal smile, but Joe Bianco's face was studiously blank. There was a uniformed officer behind him.

"Funny? Not really. SFPD put out a bulletin. The security camera at the columbarium caught footage of a woman stealing the ashes of your friend Brandon Van Duyne. I thought *Damn, what a coincidence.* Then I opened my suitcase." He nodded to the uniform, who took hold of her arm. "Jesus, lady, how could a woman with your smarts make such a dumb move?"

Philippa's soul summersaulted. The floor dropped away and the walls collapsed. Her books, her couch, her lamps, slithered in a Daliesque dance. Her hand shot out to the doorframe, clawing for solid ground. Then, in the roiling chaos, she found it. Out in her garden. The Grecian urn, glowing in a halo of golden light, a lifebuoy in a churning sea. Like a freight train screeching to a stop, the spinning world slammed into stillness.

So what if she'd been discovered? Nothing could malign the purity of her motives. She'd meant for Brandon Van Duyne's remains to rest in a place of grace. Let these simpleton cops try and condemn her. Language and rhetoric were her meat and drink. Once she told her story, the world would applaud.

Philippa took a deep, cleansing breath. Her chin came up. Ramrod straight, she faced Joe Bianco.

"Beauty is truth, truth is beauty—that is all ye know on earth, and all ye need to know."

A policeman on either arm, she strode proudly out the door.

ROSES SHOULD BE RED

KERRY CATHERS

Upward. Step after rushed step. A layer of sweat coated Ilsa. Lines of it trickled down her back, soaking her mourning garments and dampening the hair around the edges of her reddened face. Lungs worked like bellows, drawing in the sickly aroma of pitch on the ornamental torches lining the stairway. Too many had been lit for the lateness of the hour and the heat they spat out made the air stifling. She was lightheaded from it, and the wide curve of the stairway made her dizzy as it had never done before.

A third of the way? Halfway? Surely no less than that. Her legs were weakening, slowing her pace, making every movement sluggish and clumsy. The skirt she clutched and held to her knees was quickly becoming too great a weight to bear. She would collapse before reaching the top.

And die there.

A step higher and she faltered. Another and Ilsa tumbled, knees cracking against stone, hands landing with a stinging slap moments afterward.

Her body shuddered with a sob she refused to release. This was neither the time nor the place for tears. For days she had held them back, refusing their release, no matter how much they pooled at the sides of her eyes or how securely grief lodged itself in the back of her throat. Weeping would come later. When the work was done.

How had it come to this? When the messenger had alighted upon the baron's court, carrying news of a royal visit, there'd been such hope, such exultation. How had that joy turned to this?

Near-ceaseless work, was how. A fortnight of orders and tasks and scoldings and chores. Clean this. Clean that. Clean that again. Barely a reprieve and not a single night slept through.

Her body ached as never before. Her whole being cried out for relief. To sit. To rest a moment. Only a moment. That was all that would be needed. Ilsa breathed a tiny laugh. If she lowered her body onto the steps, there'd no be no strength to lift herself from them.

And there was an urgent summons to be answered, for which she was already late. Late before the messenger had brought it to her.

One more task and there'd be rest. After all she had weathered, she could weather this. Weather it or starve.

A deep breath to fortify her resolve. Another to push down all the emotions that threatened to tip her into hysteria. She balled them up. Set them inside an imaginary fortress that sat low in her belly. And welcomed the numbness that followed.

Ilsa straightened, hands on her back to ease the ache of her muscles, and went upward.

She heard their voices before she came upon them. Bess and Meg, tittering about the next day's royal procession. Gossiping about the monarch that they knew only from rumor and reputation and the face on the coins.

"Come. Come, child." Squat, round-faced Meg scurried down a few steps to take Ilsa by the elbow and haul her to where Bess waited. "No time to dawdle."

"I was moving—"

"He's in a rage." Bess, lithe, tall, and the senior of the two, spun

Ilsa to face away from her, and tugged at the knots of her apron strings.

"When's he not in a rage?" Meg scrunched up her face.

"You can't deny he's been worse of late. Angry the wine's too sweet. Angry it's not sweet enough. Furious there are too many flowers. Enraged there are too few. No pleasing him." Bess tugged at the laces of Ilsa's gown with the grace of stampeding cattle.

"Is there a reason I'm being disrobed? I prefer—"

"Shush, child. Prancing about like a peacock, he is. As though the king were coming to visit him personally." Meg made a face, rolled her eyes.

"You're soaked with sweat," Bess scolded. "Did you not think to bathe before coming up?"

"The summons—"

"Don't answer back, child. Not to your betters." Meg looked over Ilsa's shoulder to Bess, shook her head in defeat. "There are those you can't teach. Folks from the country. Not manners. Not propriety." Meg pulled at the shoulders of Ilsa's gown, then let Bess pull it down at the waist.

"Come, child. Lift your feet so I can get it off you. Is there no sense to you at all?" Bess pinched Ilsa's calf hard enough to bruise.

"And this nonsense." Meg held up a forest-green gown trimmed with embroidery the color of autumn wheat. "What's he got her wearing full livery for? She'll only be scrubbing something. A sow in silk."

"And in this heat. The bugger has gone daft."

The two women took hold of the livery skirt and raised it above Ilsa's head.

"Arms up."

Ilsa obeyed. Her limbs almost too heavy to lift.

Ilsa maneuvered her arms into sleeves that were too tight. Bess gave it a vicious tug at the waist that almost sent Ilsa toppling. Ilsa grabbed a handful of Meg's sleeve and was rewarded with a scowl.

"I think we brought someone else's." Bess gave another tug.

"There's no time to correct it."

"I don't think it will lace properly." Bess pulled the string through the eyelets with rough jerks.

"It has to or he'll be in a rage the rest of the night and I'm not tolerating his sharp tongue telling me I can't do my job. Put your knee into it." Meg looked at Ilsa as though, somehow, bringing the wrong gown had been her fault.

"I could wear the other." Ilsa pointed to the crumple of black material half a dozen steps down.

A knee pressed against the lower part of Ilsa's back. Then a pull. Hard and unexpected, pressing the air from her lungs.

"It's not closed at the base," Meg commented, circling the gap with her finger.

"I can't breathe."

"It'll have to do. Only way we'll get that closed is if we cut some flesh from her middle," Bess declared.

"It's quite tight." Ilsa curled her fingers over the neckline, pulled at it. Anger flared, threatened to unleash itself, but she tamped it down.

"Be grateful for the assistance." Meg came around to face Ilsa, her expression changing from disdain to horror. "Look at your hands, child." Meg plucked Ilsa's right hand, turned it over and back in her own. "He's made you ruin them with all the scrubbing these past days."

It was the softest Ilsa had ever heard Meg's voice. Her heart eased and she went to offer an apology and gratitude.

"They're almost worse than your face."

Ilsa's heart hardened and a spark of defiance lit deep in her gut. Quickly doused. There were mouths to feed and work was scarce for women from the country.

"Enough of that." Bess swiped at Meg, hitting Ilsa instead.

"We've got to get her dressed and on her way before he comes to fetch her."

"Has he said why he needs you in such haste?" Meg asked.

"No. He—"

"It'll be nothing of significance. Not with her being the one called." Bess gave the gown a vicious twist at the waist adjusting the bodice.

"Likely more scrubbing." Meg took the gown, twisted it back.

Annoyance showed on her face. She knew it from Meg's reaction.

"You could show a prettier face to the world. I know you're not long a widow, but that's no excuse to wear your grief, expecting everyone to share in it. Especially not with His Majesty on his way."

Tears welled up and Ilsa blinked them away, biting down the sickening grief that rose with them.

"You listen to me well, child. You've few reasons for tears. His was a worthy death, and you should be grateful of that."

Ilsa swallowed back a laugh fearing it would unhinge the precarious hold she had on her emotions. The notion was absurd. A death was a death and its method amounted to nothing. A worthy one didn't feed the children left behind any more than a shameful one did. Neither did it ease the pain. Dead was dead.

She gave Meg the best smile she could muster. It was what was expected when a compliment was given.

"Must be a comfort knowing your husband helped bring about this visit. If in a small, unintentional way."

Ilsa opened her mouth, a scathing retort poised on the tip of her tongue. But the woman's glare silenced her.

"You'll want this." Meg wrapped Ilsa's waist with a black belt. The sheathed knife that hung from it slapped Ilsa's thigh like a punch. "Kind of his lordship to honor the dead of Sarak Don with such a gift."

Coin to buy food would have been kinder.

"Off with you now." Bess gave a shove and Ilsa stumbled up the first few steps before righting herself.

"You'll have to show more grace than that," Meg called up after her. Her words ringing with amusement. "Or they'll never keep you on at the palace."

The words echoed in Ilsa's mind longer than in the air. One rolling over the other like the red light that dances over hot coals.

At the top, Ilsa stepped into an octagonal chamber whose walls, ceiling, and floor were whitewashed; a dullness to cleanse the visual palette before stepping into the magnificence of the garden.

Not a real garden. Not in the living way. But still a thing of beauty.

Ilsa trudged to the elaborate gate at the chamber's far side. It stood taller than her by half and stretched wider than the reach of her arms. Plain black iron rods twisted and wove around each other so tightly that what lay beyond could only be glimpsed through tiny gaps. In places iron had been wrought into petals, fruit, leaves, or flowers.

She pulled the velvet cord that hung to the gate's left side; heard the distant ring of a bell. And waited.

Her breaths were slow and even, to gather her fortitude against what was to come. Exhaustion had changed, progressed into something else. Something almost ethereal. Her body didn't feel like hers. Her mind was somehow distant. She was here, but not here. The world at arm's length.

In the stillness, her thoughts drifted to him. His face. She closed her eyes to fix the image better. Ilsa thought of his laugh and drew in a deep breath, imagining the aroma of horses and hot metal that lingered on his clothes. A sob rippled through her. She could not cry. The Master of the House was not the sort of man who understood grief. Ilsa twisted the emotion, changed it to resentment; a safer sentiment. Misery had its own life, coming upon its victims unexpectedly, without beckoning. But resentment was cold and could be controlled, contained.

"Are you *sleeping*?"

The words cracked like a whip, jolting Ilsa back to awareness. She gaped, forgetting, for a moment, where she was.

"You are late. The moment I set eyes upon you, I knew you were no good." The Master of the House looked over her. Thin and jagged of face and frame, he used his height to bully. His visage an appropriate vessel for the man he was. He'd come to the position young, arrogant, with an inflated perception of his competence and importance. He oversaw the baron's household servants and accounts and did so with the compassion of a harsh winter; stealing the accomplishments of others while laying blame for failure on the shoulders of people he was jealous of. Those who could not defend themselves.

"Beggin' pardon." Eyes lowered, shoulders rolled forward, Ilsa offered a shallow curtsy. "I came when called."

He huffed and turned away. "I've no time for lies. Since there is no one else about, I have no choice but to tolerate you." He moved beyond the gate and Ilsa followed behind into the baron's garden.

Generations ago, before a king had come to rule and the land was spotted with petty nobles, a fashion had swept through the courts. No one knew from where, or whom, or why, but its rumor became unquestioned truth. The mark of nobility and civility became inextricably entwined with gardens. No building could bear the name palace without one. And without a palace, there could be no seat of power. No nobility.

A trifle for most lineages, but for this territory the task had seemed impossible. To guard against its enemies, the palace had been built on an island that rose like a tiny mountain from the sea. Rock buildings and roads constructed upon a rock foundation, leaving neither room nor soil for a garden. The baron's long-dead ancestor had built a citadel at the top of his island, and there he had carved his garden from hard stone.

"Time runs short." His voice burrowed through the haze of numbness thickening around her.

"Beggin' pardon," she replied from reflex, scurrying to match his pace.

"I doubt you can comprehend the importance of the king's visit. The *first* visit by a monarch in living memory. *Longer* than living memory."

Ilsa's eyes drifted to the walls and pillars that lined their twisting route. At the intricacy of stem and leaf and blossom of every flower known. At the clusters of grapes that hung from weaving and drooping vines. At the acorns that dangled from leaves and branches and the rough bark of its trees. The skill, the hours, the talent that had created the breathtaking beauty. Every vein, crevice, turn of leaf or petal rendered so well, they seemed real.

"The Wars of Succession have stripped the king's court of many of its greater nobles. Leaving titles ripe for the picking."

Above, the cloistered ceiling was turned into a wild pattern of canopied branches and leaves so tightly layered they left no space for an imagined sun.

"We must show the king that our lord—the baron—exceeds his title. A baron by name only, capable of managing, and deserving of greater honors. An earldom. Or duchy. It is *our* sacred duty to convince the king our lord is of nobler stock than his ancestors."

Lamps sat in sconces, their flickering flames casting the illusion of movement throughout the garden. Her fingers danced over the rough surface of the walls. When first carved, the garden had been painted. Vibrant colors that must have made for a magnificent illusion. But fashion changed, and sometime long ago, the colors had been left to fade and the paint to peel, leaving only a few spots amid the stretch of brown stone. Her only disappointment with the practice lay with the bunch of roses that sat near the Lady's Chapel.

Her favorite flower. Her husband hated them, insisting their aroma made him think of funerals.

Roses should be red, no matter the fashion at court.

"Are you daft?" The force of the Master's voice pulled her from her reverie. Like waking from a pleasant dream into something awful.

"Beggin' pardon." Ilsa dropped her gaze and lifted her skirts no higher than the top of her shoes, rushing to catch up to him.

"Your sort will not be aware of this, but a few short months ago the baron exceeded himself at the Battle of Sarak Don. Held off the encroaching army and kept the crown from falling into the hands of the Pretender."

"My husband died in that battle."

He regarded her with disbelief, then his gaze dropped to the blade that sat at her hip. He huffed and looked her with contempt. "Inexplicable why the baron honored fodder such as your husband. They were sent to Sarak Don to die so their betters could live. They served their purpose. Why waste good metal and leather on gifts for their families?"

His words and their conviction drove deep into her heart. Her husband had been a good man. A decent one. Far more deserving of life than most of those who had come back. Or those who had not gone to war.

With a sneer, he was off at a pace she struggled to match. "Keep up."

Ilsa's stomach soured. Surely, he was not returning her to the chapel.

"Stay abreast."

But Ilsa faltered. He turned, spied her, sent her in retreat when he barreled back down the hall, taking her arm in a painful grip.

"Look." He barked, pointing a spindly finger toward the arching window at the end of the short hall and the landscape beyond it.

"*Look* where the moon sits. Near its midpoint." He leaned closer, hissing his words in her ear, his anger palpable.

Ilsa folded in upon herself.

"His Majesty arrives tomorrow. *Tomorrow*. We have from midnight to midday to prepare the baron's palace. I will tolerate nothing less than perfection."

"Beggin' pardon." She managed another curtsey.

"Your work has been sorely lacking."

Her head snapped upward toward his.

"I'll not have you spoil this for me—for the baron. If we fail on this day, we fail forever."

Her work had been exceptional. She'd made certain of it.

"The enclave around the Lady's Chapel being the worst of all."

Ilsa paled. No. No no no. She'd scrubbed her fingers raw cleaning it.

The Master of the House released his grip, turned on his heels and strode away, leaving Ilsa gaping and fixed in place. The garden around her swirled. Dread rippled up from the floor, through the top of her head. He could not have spoiled her work.

She hurried after him.

The enclave came into view. Ilsa halted, hands shaking. Hours had been spent scrubbing, wiping, washing dirt from the intricate curves and angles of the walls and floor. All the while her body had begged for sleep.

She closed her eyes, wishing herself away. Somewhere kinder. She slowed her breath. All her defenses shuddered inside of her, threatening to crumble.

"Avoiding this will change nothing." Each of his words dripped in arrogance. He took her elbow and pulled her deeper into the enclave.

She stood in its center, the space a perfect hexagon, the Lady's Chapel to her right. Ilsa sank to her knees at the destruction. The pots of flowers she'd arranged around the enclave to add color and aroma were broken, the soil spilled out, ground into the stone by boots. The delicate leaves, petals, and stems torn and scattered across the stone.

"Unnecessary as it is to say, the Chapel's enclave cannot remain in a state such as this. The king and his wife are to be brought here, to show off the magnificence of the baron's garden."

Ilsa ran her fingers through the debris. What had they done? "It was pristine when I left it."

"Perhaps, but such is irrelevant. It is a disgrace now."

"What happened?"

"There was work to be done to fix the gate and sconces." He spoke it as though it was obvious.

Evidence of their carelessness dotted the space. Scuffs on the pillars, windowsills, along the base of the wall and onto the floor. Scuffs that would take hours to scrub clean.

"I had cleaned it." She crushed foliage in her fists.

"And there was work to be done afterward," he reprimanded. "A wiser woman would have waited for the other work to be done before beginning."

"You commanded it be done immediately."

He huffed. "I recall no such instruction."

"Clean the space to perfection or I'll have you flogged." She gathered fragments of the spoiled gardens about her. "Your words."

"I would never utter such a vulgar threat."

"My head had barely nestled on the pillow when you had me pulled from it."

"I would—"

"Urgent, you said."

"Circumstances change."

She rose in a single motion, turned so she looked him in the face. "You could have come to tell me. To say that I could stop."

"You are wrong in your presumption. I could not have done such a thing."

"Nothing happens in the baron's household that you do not know of." Her fists balled. Body tensed.

"I can hardly be expected to oversee what happens while I am asleep."

It was like running headlong into a wall she did not know was there. "You slept? This afternoon? After denying me that luxury. Set me to a task you knew would be ruined. *While you slept.*" A kernel of something awful formed low in her abdomen.

He brought himself to her, standing tall, his face inches from hers. It should have intimidated her, but he seemed small, petty. "Know your place," he seethed. "If not for how your sodding husband met his end you'd not have been brought into service at the palace. Keep. Your tongue. Behind your teeth."

She croaked a laugh of surprise. The furnace set low in her abdomen glowed hotter, danced around the metal casing of her resolve into which she had sealed her emotions. Her hatred. Her exhaustion. Her fear. Her grief for his death. It heated to molten that filled her veins. It must have reflected in her face, for his expression soured and his venom turned biting.

"On the morrow, I'll speak with her Ladyship. Have no doubt, I'll have you sent from this house in disgrace. You and your children."

"My husband served her husband. Died for her husband. That should gain some sympathy."

"Sarak Don was a culling." He lifted his voice, his contempt unfettered. "Eliminating the ignorant and worthless—"

Ilsa flinched, her fingers curling, uncurling. The knife a weight against her thigh.

"The only injustice was that it awarded them with a death nobler than they deser—"

His expression altered. Rage shifting to disbelief. To confusion. His gaze dropped to the space between them taking her eyes with it. She saw it. Her knife in his chest.

Her heart thudded with the horror of what she had done.

The kernel of emotion expanded and everything she had tamped down, ignored, locked away, came free, like the awakening that blossomed with the first kiss of sunlight.

Anger beyond anger engulfed her.

She withdrew the blade. Plunged it in again.

The Master of the House slumped to the floor. She struck him even after he'd gone still. Wrath moving the act beyond murder to something grotesque.

Exhaustion overtook her, slowing, then ceasing her motions. The haze of emotion breaking and laying bare what she had done. His robes soaked red, hers spattered and spotted with blood. On her hands. His blood.

Uncurling her fingers, Ilsa settled back against the wall, eyes fixed on the weapon that had carried out such violence. A gash of deeper red ran along the pad of her thumb, down to her wrist. She'd cut herself on the blade that had cut him.

How curious. And careless. What a mess it would create.

Crimson rivulets chased down her forearm, warm and sticky, mingling with the blood that was his and dripped from her elbow, onto the floor she'd scrubbed clean not that long before. Someone else would wash the mess away.

Setting the hand on her knee, her body freed from years of tension, her eyes lifted to the carved flowers on the wall across from her, letting them dance over the beauty of the false flowers and leaves until they settled on the majesty of the bouquet of roses. She smiled.

Some good had come of this. The roses were red again.

BY ANY OTHER NAME

SUE ANN HIGGENS

Ella Johnson squeezed into the orange plastic chair across from yet another job counselor's desk. "Call me Dominic," he'd said, showing her into the cubicle. She dutifully reported to this stuffy Unemployment Office once a week. Faded posters extolling SUCCESS and PERSISTENCE hung from yellowed tape in the windowless waiting area. She'd spent five and a half months through the Detroit winter hunting for jobs, dropping off her resume and calling recruiters. The end of her six months of unemployment loomed. Her rent was due. What would happen to her and Felixia, her cross-eyed Siamese?

At least this job counselor was well-dressed. Maybe he could really help her. His cubicle felt nicer than the others'. Instead of a messy cupful of pens or a tape dispenser asking 'Is it Friday Yet?' a brass nameplate announced Dominic Washington. A classy framed photo showed him laughing alongside several other Black men. The bottom of the frame had Greek letters. His bookshelves were heavy. She was impressed that even with no natural light, his two plants were thriving.

"Looks like you have the touch with philodendrons," Ella said.

"Oh, uh, yes. My grandmother made sure I knew how to grow a thing or two. What brings you in today, uh, Ella?" Dominic asked.

"Well..." Ella opened her purse for a Kleenex. She could never be sure if telling her story would bring her to tears. "I had a successful career in the mail-order wreath business. I don't mean we just did wreaths. We specialized in them. And our cedar garland was always very popular. Return orders year after year. I helmed a sophisticated shipping department and had only the rarest complaint. I practically ran the company for twenty-three years." She opened her bag again and took out the worn manilla folder that held copies of her resume, passing one to him.

"Then, last year, Leonard, that's my boss." She hesitated, then realized it was obvious he was no longer her boss. "Leonard says, 'As we face the end of the twentieth century, we're expanding our product line to meet the needs of the market. No one wants dry pine needles dropping on the floor in the new millennium,' or some such crap."

Ella clapped her hand over her mouth. "Sorry, I don't have a potty mouth. I'm just disappointed. Suddenly, our main products were from a catalogue of Christmas junk. Ceramic birds on skis. Santa Hat string lights. Or, uh, cheapo ornaments of armadillos. And there I was, overseeing Quality Services. How was that heap of complaints and returns *my* fault?"

Ella picked lint off her too-tight chinos. Damned email had made everything feel urgent. All the time. Why did they think she'd gained thirty pounds? It wasn't from going out for spinach salad lunches. The vending machine might have been her best friend in the whole office. "Anyway, they replaced me with *two* people. That's all I have to say." She paused. "Well, that and I've taken my resume to over thirty places and gotten no bites. So, here I am. My unemployment runs out this month. What do I do now?"

The counselor sat very still.

"Okay, one more thing. I was named Employee of the Month so

many times, they deeded me a parking spot next to Leonard's. That's how good I was. I mean, imagine you've got a good thing going, and then suddenly, it's gone."

WELL, he thought, looking up at her, that was something Dominic could imagine. These so-called 'clients' at the employment office never imagined he'd been the respected leader of a sizable counseling department at an esteemed Chicago university. Instead of a smelly cubicle like this one in downtown Detroit, he'd had a title, an office, and a secretary. He'd earned them, after all. He'd been important. His fall from glory had been so unfair.

"'Employee of the Month so many times I got my own parking space.'" Dominic minced her words in his head. This lady's ego likely awarded her: Colleague Whose Car I'd Most Like to Key. Nearly all his meetings at Bloomfield County Employment Access started with this litany of excuses and abuses. He took her resume, noticing her nails were bitten to the quick. His face remained therapist-neutral. He needed just one more solid re-employment placement to qualify for a promotion.

His boss, Luisa, did weekly verification visits to work sites of recently placed clients. She then reported to the county how many people their office had re-employed. He was so close to meeting the quota and getting what he deserved: a raise and an office with a door.

This white lady, Ella, had all her teeth. And she smelled better than a lot of the people who sat across from him in that chair. He knew that lily of the valley scent. It wafted off older ladies at his grandmother's church. Dusty, but making an effort. If her resume was true, she could probably run an office or at least work phones. This had to be the one.

"Your resume looks good. But you've just got the one reference listed here. Are you confident this, uh, Leonard is speaking highly of your work?"

"Why wouldn't he? I kept that place afloat. Should have been promoted, not canned."

He remembered speaking to an employer who was looking for help at a new botanical program. Something to do with plants. The owner had come in two weeks earlier looking for office support. Where was that plant lady's business card?

How had he ended up here? Gone were the days of a secretary outside his office door screening the nonsense so Dominic could focus on his passion: counseling college students. God, he'd been good at tackling their problems: broken hearts, parents' expectations, unfair grades. Part motivational speaker, part student schedule ninja, he'd worked his tail off. He knew he made a difference.

Maybe he drank a bit. But he burned all that stuff out of his system at the gym. He was there at five-thirty every morning to sweat, steam, and suit up for the day. And wasn't he proof forty-two wasn't old? At his old job he played pick-up hoops on Friday afternoons. And made time every Tuesday to join the grad students on their pub trivia team, Blood, Sweat and Beers. Occasionally, he'd hit the juice before leaving the office for the day. So what? On a college campus where he knew for a fact plenty of profs were up to no good, he'd been singled out and pressured to leave. It still pissed him off. One of his colleagues had ratted him out, saying he was regularly drunk at work. *Which* he wasn't. He shook his head to clear the cloud of disrespect again. He found the business card and studied it while Ella droned on.

"I could usually get people who complained about their orders talked off the ledge, then send them a twenty percent off coupon for their next order. I honestly think I could be a hostage negotiator."

"Ella, not to cut you off." Dominic stared at her until she

quieted. "Since you're clearly so good with plants and the whole mail-order industry…"

"Not plants so much, though that was the origin of our company. I mean *their* company. Obviously, they had no loyalty to me…"

"Right. So, there's this exciting new enterprise just getting started." Dominic leaned back in his chair and looked at the business card. Topium Enterprises: Plants from Out of This World. Duma Rind, President.

He remembered meeting Duma. She was looking for office staff. She smelled like roses—a scent that made him sneeze. Too cloying. Like vanilla. It always made him wonder what the person was trying to cover up.

"I think it would be right up your alley. They're looking for skilled individuals to help at a new agricultural company. Topium Enterprises. Catchy name. You'd be an incredible asset, don't you think?" It was coming back to him. "She mentioned the salary and benefits were *very favorable*. Why don't I get the president on the phone right now and we'll see when you can interview?"

He dialed the number on the card. Dominic rolled his shoulders feeling the ten extra lat presses he'd added to the morning's workout.

"Topium Enterprises," the call was answered. Ella scooched forward on her chair.

"Hello, this is Dominic Washington from Bloomington County Employment Access. May I speak with Duma Rind?"

"That's Rind. Rhymes with sinned. Not Rind, as in kind."

Her voice had a reedy quality. He could picture her. Tall. Dressed in a navy pantsuit, sporting gold loop earrings, and an aquamarine ring. Around his age? A slight accent he couldn't place. She was the most put-together business owner he'd met during his year in this humiliating job.

Dominic nodded to Ella and put the desk phone on speaker,

carefully annunciating, "Ms. Rind, we met a couple of weeks ago when you came by seeking an office employee to help with your new enterprise."

"Yes, I recall our meeting, Mr. Washington. When I said I'd been a professor of botany, you mentioned you were previously in academia. You also lamented the lack of a good gym near the office, though you looked like you were faring just fine in the fitness department."

Her laugh. He remembered that edge of flirtation, a constant annoyance in higher education. Everyone dangling some intimate possibility. His neck tightened. He could use a drink.

"Yes, I do miss that campus life, ma'am," he laughed. Ella scrunched forward in her too-low chair, mashing the handbag on her lap.

He'd just switched to a new gym near the Un-E office. He didn't like changing routines, but the gym was the best way to fulfill what his grandmother had drummed into him: *Avoid doctors. They'll take more from you than they give.* He humored her old-fashioned ideas. Sure, Black folks had been used for research without knowing it. Or denied a doctor at all. Awful stuff. But at his college jobs, he'd always had an annual check-up with the campus doc. *Which* he passed with flying colors. Rum and Coke was his apple-a-day. Or two, or three.

"Well, Ms. Rind, I have a very strong candidate for your position. I am here with Ella." He flipped the page back on his clipboard.

"Johnson," Ella croaked.

"Yes, Ella Johnson." Dominic nodded to her. "Ms. Johnson has been in the horticultural products industry for years, overseeing customer satisfaction."

"And quality control," Ella blurted.

"And she's ready for her next venture. I think she's just who you've been looking for. Is the position still open?"

"Why else would the company president have answered this call?" That throaty laugh again.

"You won't find another resume like mine. I can oversee phones, inventory, shipping, returns—I've done it all." Ella gabbled. "When can I interview?"

Dominic held up his hand to slow her. "Yes, Ms. Rind, Ella is enthusiastic and has deep company loyalty on top of her honed workplace skills." Ella gnawed her nails like a rodent. Dominic looked away.

"One thirty today. Come to the farm. Mr. Washington has the address. It's a very long driveway, but you'll know you're in the right place when you see greenhouses at the end of a long fence. Just press the buzzer when you get to the security kiosk. Our guard is off on Wednesdays."

"This is very exciting, Ms. Rind. You'll see Ella this afternoon at one thirty."

He had a good feeling about this match. He printed MapQuest directions for her, and Ella Johnson was off.

ELLA ARRIVED AT A GATE. Long rows of greenhouses were surrounded by a high fence. At a security shack she pushed a button and slowly the gate dragged itself open. She drove through and parked near a tall woman in dark slacks. "I'm here to meet Ms. Rind?"

"You must be Ella. I'm Dr. Duma Rind, double PhD., Immunology and Molecular Botany. But please, just call me Duma." They shook hands and she turned toward the gate. "The gate's been on the fritz. Now that I have some help around here, I'll have time to get it fixed. Step into the greenhouse and see where you'll work." Ella clutched her handbag, scrambling to keep up with the woman's long strides.

Rows of worktables stood on a gravel floor. Long rails overhead held baskets spilling flowers. "Let's see... petunias, fuchsia, and blue lobelia," Ella announced with confidence. This lady's credentials were important—she'd never heard of a double PhD. She had some expertise of her own. It was a point of pride for her, knowing not just the difference between a Norway pine and a blue spruce—any fool knew that. She knew which amaryllis could share a pot with tulips and narcissus for sequential blooms.

Ella sniffed the long strands of orange nasturtium trailing from overhead. Instead of their usual peppery kick, she smelled roses. Strange. She rummaged in her bag to retrieve her resume.

"You travel light. Is that your overnight bag?" Duma asked.

Ella chewed the side of her pinkie finger. Overnight bag? She couldn't lose this job.

"Your counselor did explain this job is residential, yes?"

"No, but, uh, I can do whatever is needed." She reached up to smell a stem of geranium from another row of baskets—it, too, smelled of rose.

"How do you like our cultivars, Ella?" Duma asked.

"I must have a cold coming on. It's almost as if they all smell of rose."

"Yes, indeed. You have a nose for the job. You will start at the computer desk in the corner here, cataloging our current stock of hanging baskets. And, if all goes well, soon I'll show you the real focus of Topium, a product we call Midnight Oil. Now, if you'll follow me, I'll show you to your room in the dorm."

There was a dorm? Ella had never lived in a dorm. She'd gone to the local community college for a few classes. This would be fun.

"Um, Doctor, er, Duma. There's a problem." Ella gnawed on her left thumb. "I thought I was only coming today for an interview. If the position is, uh, residential, I'll need to get my things. And, I have a cat I'll need to bring. Felixia."

"Oh, a cat?" Duma nodded slowly. "I suppose we need a cat—

it's a farm. Yes, let me finish the tour and you can go and get your things."

"The other thing is," Ella didn't want to sound whiny, "I don't sleep so well—at home or away from it. I mean, not even in hotels. I find it hard to—"

"You'll sleep just fine here, Ella. I'm a doctor. I guarantee it." Duma walked to the next doorway.

THREE O'CLOCK ON A FRIDAY AFTERNOON. The week had hollowed him out. How many sad people and bad luck stories was a man built to take? Babies on laps wanting another sip of mom's soda. Old folks and young people searching for the illusive dream of a decent job for decent pay.

Technically, he worked until five, but he needed to see a man about a Bacardi. A couple rum and Cokes would help put this week to bed. Grandma said you could trust rum better than a doctor. *It staves off colds and keeps down the sugars.* If that were true, there'd be no diabetes for this grandson.

Dominic reviewed his past week's appointments. On Wednesday, he'd found a job right away for that nail-biting white lady. Since then, it'd been nothing but duds. How the hell had he ended up dispensing pitiful jobs to the destitute when he'd been so good? His coworkers were jealous, that's how. It wasn't like he was getting Adderall from students and snorting it off the metal toilet paper holder in the men's room. He knew a couple guys who did that. One more call and he could leave for the weekend. Dominic called Topium and, as he'd hoped, Ella Johnson answered.

"Uh, hi, Ms. Johnson. It's Dominic Washington from the Bloomington Employment Access office," he spoke fast. "I hope all is going well for you at Topium. It seemed you'd be a natural there."

"This is a really special place," Ella oozed. "The week has flown by. I mean you can't believe how nice it is to work around plants and flowers!"

"I imagine it is." Dominic remembered his former office. He'd brought in fresh flowers every Monday. He made sure birthdays and work anniversaries were celebrated—always cupcakes—and he wrote thank-you notes like his grandmother taught him. Here he was in this cubicle maze at the Last Chance Suckers Club. This lady loved her new job. He was so close to the promotion he deserved.

"Since your monthly benefit runs out on the thirtieth, Ella, I want to make sure it's going well. My supervisor and I will be making a site visit to you next Wednesday afternoon." It would be the bright spot of his week, showing his boss a successful placement. One more and he'd get the supervisor role he'd told his grandmother he already had. There'd been no point in telling her he'd been canned by the university.

Ella yammered on about how she was killing this new job. "Uh huh." He rolled his eyes and reached for his jacket. He kept a couple of those airplane-sized rums in his car's glove box and they were calling his name. Finally, she caught her breath and told him the place was hard to find. "Yes, I have the directions," he clutched the chance to sign off. "I'll look forward to seeing you Wednesday."

ELLA LIKED the work and realized she was no longer fighting the constant urge to snack. At her old job, she'd spent the day see-sawing from sweet snacks to salty ones and back to sweet. She liked the healthy food Duma's cook prepared. She didn't really miss television. Maybe *The Sopranos*. At home, she never slept through the night. Her first night at Topium, Duma handed Ella a tube that looked like clear lip gloss. "Here's some enhanced rose oil we've developed. Dab some on your wrists at bedtime; you'll sleep like a baby." And she had.

All manner of books lined the shelves in the so-called dormitory. It was more like a guest house, really. Sometime, she would have to ask Duma where everyone else slept. Easy chairs tucked in a corner of a common room made for comfortable evenings for her and Felixia. She was already three books deep into a zany detective series.

"Tomorrow, Ella, I'll start training you on the medicinal qualities of roses," Duma said as they finished dinner. Ella nodded. She had no experience with roses. "Rose extract has analgesic, anticonvulsive, and hypnotic properties, you see. All of those are essential to our top-secret product."

"But tomorrow is Saturday." Ella knew she shouldn't talk with her mouth full. "I mean, I'm here. I can work. I just didn't know."

"Distilling our hybrid rose oil is but one of our plans at Topium. Most people love the smell of roses and have no idea that certain varieties relax them and make them healthier."

Had Duma heard her? "I don't know what it is, but I've sure been sleeping well here," Ella interjected. "Probably why I got through the inventory so fast."

"I appreciate your enthusiasm, Ella. Yes, I believe we have a winning formula—we are so close to sharing it with the world. My research has been published many times, but only in obscure technical journals." Duma dabbed her lips over the pistachio lime cake they'd just finished. "Our competitors are breathing down our backs—but they won't succeed."

"What kind of competition is there for hanging baskets?" Ella asked, licking the citrusy icing from her fingers.

"I'll be famous in medical circles if I can get this product right. We are so close. I'm still trying to dial back the sedating elements. The target is for a patient to feel calm and pain-free, but not necessarily drowsy. If only the pharmaceutical companies would have listened to me. Instead, pain medication has caused more harm than good—anyone can see that."

"I'd be honored to work up a catalogue for you." Ella's pulse and voice both rose. "Other people need to get some of this rose oil stuff. It will catch on like wildfire!"

Duma didn't seem to hear her. "I'm working to extract and dilute comforting oils from other flower species, too. Poppies in particular. We plan to start the new millennium with a line of medicinal oils. By prescription only, at first. We've distilled a hypoallergenic, non-sedating formula—groundbreaking in pain management. But this..." Duma laughed, looking toward the greenhouse. "This will make me famous. Finally." When her gaze returned to Ella, she looked surprised she was there. "I'll see you at breakfast," Duma said flatly as she stood to go.

"Oh, and I meant to tell you," Ella wished Duma would stay and talk longer. "Wednesday afternoon my job counselor, Dominic, and his boss, are coming here for a site visit." Duma's eyes narrowed. "Just checking up on me, I guess. The county wants to be sure people are really doing the jobs they say they are."

Duma's face was unreadable. "Did that security gate and our high fences suggest to you just anyone can visit Topium?" Duma barked. Ella didn't know what to say. Eventually, Duma said, "Fine. They're only county workers. We've got nothing to hide from them."

"It ain't much, but it gets the job done," Dominic joked about his car as his boss, Luisa Velasquez, got into the passenger seat of the '93 Tercel. His friends ribbed him for his utilitarian car. He'd had the latest BMW before his job was ripped from him.

Before she got in, he'd stuffed his rum under the maps in his glove compartment and stuck two pieces of cinnamon Trident in his mouth in case last night's bender was lingering on his breath.

"So, what do we know about the client and the job they've

taken?" Luisa asked as they drove from downtown through the suburbs out toward farmland.

"We are visiting Ella Johnson. She had a career in mail order Christmas wreaths or something. She was probably very competent. When the work got more complex, she was laid off. She'd done a diligent search, but I was able to connect her to the perfect employment opportunity." Luisa nodded. Dominic liked the always-calming cocoa butter scent of her hair cream. Most of the Puerto Rican women he knew used something similar. "I placed Ella with a new agricultural company. I believe inventory and initial marketing are the job tasks. She confirmed today's appointment."

"Since this is so far afield, we'll probably be stuck in rush hour on the way back." Luisa rubbed her temples.

"Headache?"

"Just my usual stress-induced migraines. But what can you do?" She shrugged and looked at the scenery. "In the future, let's try to keep site visits to the Detroit metroplex, okay?"

"Certainly." Did she think he wanted to drive to the end of the world to visit a client? He'd be gasping for a drink by the time they got back to the city.

They drove in silence for several miles. Dominic finally turned down a very long fence-lined driveway that ended at a security gate. It stood open so he drove through to a group of fenced greenhouses. He set the handbrake and they walked toward the nearest building.

"Do they grow roses?" Luisa asked as he knocked at the greenhouse door.

"My nose tells me they do," Dominic said sniffling.

"We meet again," Duma stepped through the door and put out her hand. Dominic shook it and gestured to his colleague.

"Ms. Rind," rhymes with sinned, he remembered, "this is Luisa Valezquez, my manager. We do site visits to see how our workers are settling in to their new jobs. Thank you for allowing us to visit. May we see Ms. Johnson?"

"Yes. She's doing almost as well as she thinks she is." Duma gave him a knowing smile. "She seems very comfortable here— wasn't even troubled that it's a residential position."

"Excuse me?" Dominic's neck prickled. How had he not known a critical detail like that?

"Oh, yes. Upon reflection, it seemed the best thing for workers here. Our products are developed specifically for their, uh, *calming* properties. Not advisable for someone to spend the whole day around these elements and then drive home. She and her cat have moved into our dorm and seem to like it here."

Luisa's scowl telegraphed concern. Dominic followed Ms. Rind, ignoring his many questions. He was desperate to climb out of his godforsaken cubicle and into an office.

"Oh, it's you, Mr. Washington!" Ella scuttled toward him. She shook Dominic's hand vigorously, as well as that of his boss.

"Mr. Washington should be your Employee of the Week after finding me this great job," Ella trumpeted. "Have a look around." She swept her arm showcasing the hundreds of hanging baskets. "I'm nearly done with the inventory, aren't I, Doc...Duma?"

"Indeed. Ella has gotten a good start." Duma spoke over her. "And she'll start more complex tasks related to our product development next week."

"What sort of products do you develop?" Luisa asked.

"Over here you can see Ella's progress on recording our inventory." Duma strode down an aisle of hanging baskets to a fancy desk in the corner supporting a large computer.

Dominic coughed. His palms were sweating. This place was making him itch. Was it the sappy rose fragrance? Why was Ella expected to live here? Why was it all fenced? And what was up with the security gate?

"I must ask again, ma'am. What sort of products are you

developing?" Luisa gave the woman a stern look he'd never seen before.

"That information is classified." Duma spoke in a low register.

"Pardon?" Luisa shot back. "It is essential we understand the role our client is placed in and the conditions of their work environment." Luisa held her clipboard tight to her chest. "Lest they be taken advantage of. That's why we do site visits." She cocked her head a few degrees, expectant.

"You're right to wonder what we do. And even why this is a residential position," Duma said softly, taking a half-step toward Luisa. She indicated with her head they should follow her toward the back of the greenhouse. Dominic followed, Luisa trailing him.

A large silvery cat walked past, its pale blue eyes large under black-tipped ears. "What a gorgeous cat," Dominic said. It curled between his ankles.

"Oh, thanks. This is Felixia; she loves it here at the farm." The cat sauntered out the greenhouse door.

"Ella will be helping us as we develop the next phase of our product line. She's already confirmed that our Easing Oil brings calm and solid sleep. Hence the need to reside on site."

Luisa stopped short. "She's what? Please tell me you're not experimenting on her?"

"Of course not," Duma snapped.

"Ms. Rind, we have a duty to fully understand what is going on here." Luisa's short stature belied her power. Dominic coughed, nodding in agreement with his boss.

"I've had tea and a light afternoon snack prepared for us. Let's sit on the patio and discuss it. You will see Ella is in the ideal place to use her skills." Dominic's agitation was growing. Could Luisa see how he was sweating?

~

DUMA TOOK them outside to a flagstone patio under a pergola of white wisteria. Shrubby pink and white rose bushes lined the path. A round table for four was set with tea, cheeses, and delicate pastries. Ella knew they were in for a treat.

"Please," Duma said and motioned for them to sit. Ella sat first, between Duma and Dominic. Luisa was the last to sit and looked wary. Ella couldn't understand why. The food and setting were lovely. Ella loaded food onto her plate as Duma poured them tea.

"You can see why I don't mind staying here," Ella said through a bite. "It's just one lovely meal after another."

Dominic took a slow bite of cheese. Then another. "I actually skipped lunch today. This is very nice of you, Ms. Rind" He felt the tickle of a sneeze coming on, or was it a cold?

"Just a small thanks for you sending me the ideal employee."

Luisa looked at the tea cup with caution. She took a small bite of pastry and chewed it, pleasure growing on her face. "I can't tell you when I've had a meal outdoors that wasn't from a box, standing outside a deli, between meetings." She broke into a near-smile.

"So, your questions are a little tricky to answer, Ms. Velasquez," Duma said. "I am developing a hybrid oil here. One with the calming attributes of, say, opium and the analgesic elements of rose essence."

"Opium?" Luisa choked. Ella was surprised by this news and saw Dominic stiffen in his chair.

"I know how it sounds. Your reaction is the dilemma I encounter when explaining the work. I'm hybridizing opium-producing poppies to lower their toxicity and addictive elements. I have a research grant from the FDA and that funding ends soon. At the millennium, if you will.

Duma took a bite of pastry and smiled at the taste.

"The research is heavily monitored," Duma continued, "as we need to avoid commercial appropriation of the products by pharmaceutical companies. We are, in fact, trying to undo the damage they've wrought in the world of pain mitigation."

Ella could not believe her luck. This woman was a hero! And she, too, was part of this exciting work. She turned to see Dominic was scratching splotches on his neck.

"Physical pain is one of the great plagues of human existence. And most forms of pain medication lead, in their extreme, to attachment. We see growing evidence of an addiction crisis. Less habit-forming pain medication is needed. I'm using rose-infused oil as the neutral base to deliver the product, code named: Midnight Oil. You can obviously smell our rose distillation."

Ella stared at Duma. What a great idea. Nothing that Leonard had ever done could compare with this!

"Ella's role here is residential not only because we don't want staff to drive after work." Duma smiled. "But, frankly, to limit possible shared intel about the research with others. We strictly limit who comes and goes essentially by having no visitors, and staff who reside on the premises. Comfortably, I believe."

"I for one love it here," Ella said to Dominic. "Very homey. And, as you can see, the food is amazing." She held the pastry platter out to Luisa.

"Our poppies are controlled varieties—utterly illegal to the general public because heroin can be made from them." Duma looked off toward the fence behind them. "Poppies have been cultivated as far back as Neolithic times—ancient Minoans used them for comfort and pain relief. Think of it." Ella felt a streak of pride in the work she shared with Duma. "And our research is limited by seasonal availability of poppies. Beyond that hedge, we have our top-secret cultivars. About two acres of *Papaver somniferum* poppy, and ten acres of *Rosa damascena*, which translates to about five thousand bushes from which we distill rose oil. We're about to commence our final test harvest, balancing the calming effects of rose extract and the pain mitigating effects of opium. Another lab is working on reducing the addictive elements."

Ella was stunned by it all. No wonder she was sleeping so well at night.

"Your hanging baskets are a front?" Luisa accused. Ella hadn't considered that.

"Not a front, so much as a sideline." Duma sipped her tea slowly.

"This work is going to make Duma famous in medical circles, I can tell you that much," Ella parroted. She saw her boss go rigid. But she'd said so last night.

"This important work is focused on relieving the plague of pain while removing the risks of addiction. After alcohol, opioids are the most abused drug family."

Dominic looked at Duma, shook his head, and reached down to pet the cat. Ella hoped he saw how great this project was.

"What is our client's involvement in the experimental work?" Luisa sounded tough, acting like someone was pulling the wool over her eyes. Ella could almost laugh because she knew she was safe here. Dominic sneezed several times. His eyes were red and his face blotchy.

"Is it the cat?" Ella asked. "Siamese cats are considered less allergy-causing than most."

"Uh, no." Dominic sneezed hard three times in a row. "Ironically, I think I'm sensitive to roses. Never could abide the scent. But I've certainly never reacted like this." Dominic's eyes were red and bulging. He produced a handkerchief from his back pocket and stepped away to blow his nose.

"Allergic to roses?" Duma's head jutted back. She looked down at her tea. Shaking her head, she started to chuckle. Ella wasn't sure what was funny. Mr. Washington stood several feet from them coughing and sneezing even though Felixia had run across the lawn. "Allergic to roses." Duma laughed at some unknown joke. The cook approached with a fresh pot of tea.

"Cook." Duma tried to calm her giggles. "We seem to have triggered an IgE immune reaction in one of our guests. Could you please bring me the First Aid Kit? The blue one. Not the red." The cook set down the tea pot and turned back to the house.

"Bless you, Unemployment Office!" Duma barked, laughing like a seal.

"We're from County Employment Access," Luisa tried to match her volume.

Duma nodded and cackled. "Right! Employment *Access*!" She bellowed the last word and her head dropped back in gasps. Ella found Duma's laughter rude. Was she mocking them? What was so darned funny? She took another pastry.

Duma's laughter subsided and she shook her head. "Allergic to roses," she said. "Unheard of."

"Care to tell us what's so funny?" Luisa crossed her arms.

"You cannot imagine the isolation and strain of a project like this." She shook her head. "I have prepared multiple formulae, documented hundreds of possible scenarios. And while not everyone likes rose fragrance, it is tolerated exceptionally well by the general population." She dabbed her eyes with her napkin.

Duma looked serious again. "We predict a growing, vicious attachment to opioids. So widespread it might even tackle whole communities, breaking them down with crime and overdoses."

Luisa was nodding, as if she had already seen exactly what Ella's boss was describing. Duma's hair was messy, her precise lipstick gone, replaced by blanched lips and a scowl. Luisa eyed her with caution. Dominic reached for a napkin on the table and turned his back to them to blot his streaming eyes.

"Mr. Washington, I see we've made an error. And caught it just in time. We have, thus far, believed that rose oil, with its own complementary characteristics, was the ideal carrier for our product. She paused and clenched her hands. Dominic was coughing, almost doubled over.

"Rose oil is considered hypoallergenic and does not become rancid. Rose pollen is not airborne. It is exceptionally rare for people to react to it."

Dominic unbuttoned his collar and scratched his neck. Welts were rising.

"Allergen testing is the most difficult part of product testing. Ethically speaking, I mean. And we have, unwittingly, seen our first such reaction."

Poor Mr. Washington. He looked miserable, pacing and itching his back, his neck. Coughing. Why wasn't Duma doing something? Wasn't she a doctor?

"One finds rare mentions of rose allergy in the literature. But only in Turkish villagers where rose distillation is a lifelong constant." Duma spoke directly to Mr. Washington. "My research suggests that, like the rise in opioid over-use, exposures to general pollutants are on the rise. And they may cause people living in the twenty-first century to have more and more allergies. Even, possibly, children. I'm determined to fight that with my new products. I can tolerate no allergic reactions."

DOMINIC'S TORSO and face were on fire. He felt buzzed. Sped up. Not like the long, low buzz he got from a drink. He'd steered clear of drugs. His grandma made sure of that. No one in her family was going to fall prey to the junk that brought down other neighborhoods near theirs.

The cook brought a blue plastic case to Ms. Rind. "Mr. Washington, I have an antihistamine I think will help. But it will make you drowsy. While you've not shown signs of anaphylaxis, I suspect your throat feels strange."

"Yek," was all that came out when Dominic tried to speak. His heart punched away like he'd just run a sprint. "Tight." He rubbed his throat.

"As I feared." Ms. Rind removed a blister pouch from the blue case. "Diphenhydramine. Common name: Benadryl. Take two. It will help." She handed him the tablets. He wondered if his grandmother would trust her. But he was so fuzzy. Ella moved his water glass closer to him.

"Are you sure you want to take that?" Luisa said. Worry wobbled her voice. He gulped down the pills.

"As Ella can attest, we have a very comfortable dorm here." Duma said. "Why don't you rest in one of the unoccupied rooms? I'll show you in."

Dominic worried he'd blown it, bringing his boss to this unexpected scene. But he wasn't in the mood to argue. He looked at Luisa and raised his eyebrows. He slumped onto Duma who carried the blue first aid box.

~

"I CANNOT BELIEVE THIS. I never should have agreed to this site visit," Luisa muttered. She rubbed her temples, scowling. She paced around Ella, impatient to get on the road toward town. "I know I can't just leave him here. It's his car," she grumbled. "God, I hope he's okay. He really is one of our best. Ready for a promotion, too. I'd hate to lose him."

"You won't be sorry if you stay for dinner," Ella said. And once dinner was served—halibut in a butter sauce and roasted potatoes —Luisa seemed to relax a little.

"I am so glad I could bring my expertise to this job," Ella said between bites. "Thank goodness I didn't get hired at any of those other places I took my resume to. They wouldn't have known how to use me. I will really be able to steer this ship." Luisa looked at her, still rubbing her head. "And obviously, this work is really important. Think how it will help people with pain problems."

After dinner, Ella sank into her cozy chair in the dorm, Felixia beside her. She gestured to the other chair and handed Luisa the rose oil Duma had given her. "Just put a touch on your wrist. It's really good for relaxing."

Luisa hesitated, then took it, and dabbed it on. She sat across from Ella in the other chair, shoes kicked off, feet on a stool. From down the hall, they could hear Dominic's soft snore. He'd been out for five hours. Luisa had taken Ella's suggestions to start reading the mystery series that she'd been racing through since she'd arrived last week.

Luisa yawned and looked at her watch. "Goodness, eleven-thirty!" she laughed. "At least my headache is gone."

Dominic walked in.

～

"GOOD LORD." He stretched, buttoning his untucked shirt. "Where am I and when's dinner?"

"Well, look who's alive," Luisa said. "You'll be a lucky man if you can get a plate of the halibut we had for dinner. And herbed potatoes—a real treat."

"As far as I know, I'm not allergic to fish." Dominic shook his head. "Can't be too careful." He rubbed his hand over his face. "Pretty sure I'm not going to be buying roses anytime soon."

Ella laughed. "You look like yourself again. You can't leave without having dinner."

"Dinner does sound good. But, Luisa, I've held you up long enough. What time is it?

"Going on twelve o'clock." Luisa adjusted her watch. "As in midnight." For all her pacing and fuming earlier, Luisa looked relaxed. "And I'm loving this book. Any chance I can borrow it, Ella? I don't know when I've enjoyed reading a book."

"I'm pretty much second in command here—of course, you can. And I'll go tell the cook you're awake," Ella said to Dominic.

He excused himself to the restroom and splashed water on his face. His eyes were puffy. And his hands were sweating. There was something he didn't like about this place. He recalled several times he'd taken roses to a date only to start sneezing and coughing. Each time, things quickly became less than romantic, but he'd never put two and two together. He'd been struggling to breathe. Why hadn't Duma called an ambulance?

Never mind dinner, he was awake and needed a drink. Dominic looked down and noticed his right sleeve was rolled up. There was a bandage over his inner elbow. The panicky feeling in his throat tightened.

They had to leave.

He felt his pocket for his car keys as Duma approached.

"Thank you for the chance to sleep in your lovely dorm, Ms. Rind." He wanted his voice to sound calm. "But I don't think I need a standing reservation." He laughed.

"Are you sure, Mr. Washington." Duma stepped closer to him, the clang of her rose fragrance choking him. She put her hands on his shoulders. "I've been in touch with my research associates. We'd like to offer you a position here at Topium. Not only for the opportunity to study your particular blood enzymes, but to..."

Adrenaline shot through him. She'd taken his blood. He stepped back. His grandma had warned him about experiments done on unsuspecting people. *'Now you hear my words,'* Grandma's voice echoed in his head. *'They think it's okay to research on us. You can't trust them.'* He'd always thought she was paranoid. But he was no lab rat.

"Uh, no. No, thank you." His heart raced. "Uh, but thank you anyway," he croaked. "It's gotten late. Let's go, boss."

"What's the big rush?" Ella asked, her head lolling.

"You need to think of all the people you'll help, Mr. Washington." Duma looked desperate. He pushed past her, took Luisa's elbow, and trotted toward the car.

"Don't you think it's a bit rude to rush off like this, Dominic?" Luisa resisted his grip on her arm. "They've been so nice to us."

He shot her a look and saw her face was soft, released from her usual anxious scowl. He propelled them both toward the car.

"I could show you the ropes, Mr. Washington," Ella chimed. "I've really got a feel for this place now. I'd like to add you to my team."

"Ella, come with us! Get in the car," Dominic urged, desperation cracking in his tight throat.

"No, I'm happy here," she said. "We are making history. You should join us, Mr. Washington."

He shivered as he stuffed Luisa into her seat and leapt into the car. Good God, what he'd give for a drink. He gunned it toward the stuttering barricade. The gate inched shut, threatening to trap them.

"What is your problem, man?" Luisa growled. "We were having a perfectly nice time. You really should have had the halibut."

The gate nicked his back bumper, but he made it. He shot down the long, fenced drive. "What did they give you, Luisa? What did you take?"

"I just put a drop of that oil on my wrist after dinner. My headache disappeared."

"I knew it!" He shuddered. "Study my blood enzymes...? She knocked me out and took my blood, Luisa." He held out his arm for Luisa to see. "She wanted me as her specimen! My grandma always warned me... I mean *that lady's* the one who brought up the ethics of testing... Damn." Dominic coughed. "What kind of Tuskegee-style hell is that place?"

Her hand flew to her mouth. "No! Oh, Jesus. I'm so sorry,

Dominic. We'll report them tomorrow. It's, that's... it's not right." She scrubbed her wrist on her slacks over and over, trying to remove the oil.

They shot through the countryside toward the interstate. He was breathing more calmly. His eyes had stopped itching. He'd only sneezed once in the car.

"I don't know what it was." She shook her head. "I just felt so calm there, I didn't want to leave. My headache went away. I guess it was the oil."

On the highway on-ramp, he shifted into fifth gear and stepped on it. They crossed miles in silence. Approaching the city, Dominic spoke into the dark car. "Do you think it's safe for Ella to stay there?"

Luisa's silhouette shone in the strobe of the highway lights. "I was wondering that, too." She rubbed her temples and sagged back into her seat, dropping the book she'd borrowed on the floor. "She seemed okay. She was happy."

"Yeah." Dominic leaned toward the windshield, shooting down the freeway, willing the miles to pass. "And maybe like she says, she's the best in the business."

GARDEN ART

MICAH THORP

From: Modern Art Today, The Critic's Corner
By Mitchell J. Critterdon

As a professional art critic, I am occasionally asked to comment on a private collection. Most inquiries are made by wealthy collectors who believe spending massive sums acquiring mediocrity is an extraordinary feat. Typically, I nod politely, try not to say anything too offensive, and walk away. I never write reviews about these collections because they are both irrelevant and uninteresting.

Never.

But, it seems, every absolute has an exception.

A few weeks ago, I was asked to view a group of sculptures purchased by an enthusiastic, if unenlightened, individual of great means. Based on an independent description of the works in his possession, it seemed he had amassed one of the most significant collections in the Western Hemisphere. The list of pieces was impressive enough I was intrigued, and scheduled a visit.

Like many solicitations, there were a few wrinkles that were not mentioned during the initial entreaty. Most notable was that this substantive array of art was exhibited in a sculpture garden. To be clear, no piece of sculpture should ever be displayed in such a manner. Three-

dimensional works are best viewed against a two-dimensional backdrop. Layering a Hellenistic marble against a midcentury Kinetic doesn't engender appreciation nearly as much as it induces nausea.

While the venue was bad, the sheer number of pieces was overwhelming. It was as though this collector (who shall remain nameless) suffered from the same psychological malady as a common hoarder, but instead of piling up newspaper and Tupperware, he had stuffed Donatello and Rodin into his backyard plaza. The unbridled quantity of pieces was so great, and they had been so closely spaced, it was nearly impossible to assess.

Shortly after my arrival, I informed the host I did not feel well and excused myself.

~

ON MOST DAYS, the Monvoy Gallery was like every other art gallery on Manhattan's Upper East Side. Except for a few lost tourists, or the occasional collector, it was usually empty, a sign of either exclusivity or irrelevance. In either case, it's non-descript façade, perfectly white walls, unblemished floors, and industrial ceiling hosted an ever-changing mixture of the art world's most commercially viable work, either sculpted or painted. It was as staid and unchanging as anything in the modern art market.

Founded in the late 1980s by brokers seeking a tax shelter for their newfound wealth, the Monvoy's board consisted of ageing financiers less interested in running a gallery (or for that matter displaying art) than in attaining social mobility. Thus, the gallery's staff consisted of little more than a curator and his apprentice, whose primary responsibility was ensuring a never-ending series of showings, exhibitions, and auctions, designed less to generate income than attract the avant-garde of the art world and their associated followings. Whether the Monvoy turned a profit was never clear.

With a lack of fiscal pressure, the curator at the Monvoy, Nigel Ostermond, had enjoyed a stable, if predictable, career. He understood his role was simply to ensure that fine art made its way in, and, at some point, made its way out, with some level of fanfare. The how and why were not as significant as the mere presence. A celebrated artist or work was as valued as a centerpiece for a soiree as it was a margin-generating product. Nigel's role at the Monvoy was clear, and his acquiescence to it made him a longstanding fixture within its walls.

For years, Nigel had avoided hiring any help, but when a board member's millennial daughter, Maxine Trout, applied for a job, he assumed her hiring was a mandate. He soon learned she had been sent to the Monvoy in the hope she would develop some modicum of societal sophistication, which she seemed to avoid.

As it turned out, Max was enthusiastic about art, if somewhat unschooled in its history, form, or market. A rather successful junior bond trader, her professional interactions had developed on the trading floors of several large firms where profanity-laden screaming was considered a polite form of communication. Filled with a never-ending well of interesting, if somewhat hair-brained, ideas to help promote the Monvoy, she'd managed to increase both its profile and margins. Over the months that she had worked as an assistant curator, Nigel had come to appreciate his young charge... until a gentleman in black visited the Monvoy Gallery.

∼

WHEN MAXINE ENTERED Nigel's office, she looked excited and a bit flustered.

"There's a representative here from the Burton Ross estate," she said, her fists clenched like a small child standing in line to see Santa Claus.

Nigel looked up from his computer. "The Burton Ross estate? What does he want?"

A big grin came across Max's face. "I don't know, but it must be good."

Nigel stood and followed Max from his small office onto the gallery floor. Standing in the midst of several Degas-inspired statues was a short, stout man staring at a small painting. He was wearing a long black overcoat, dark glasses, and a crimson tie. His thinned grey hair was neatly combed and his pale face clean-shaven. He smiled as Nigel approached.

"You must be the curator," the man said.

Nigel nodded. "What can we do for you?"

"I represent the Burton Ross estate. Mr. Ross has recently acquired..." The man paused, searching for the right word. "Modern art. Yes. Modern art."

Nigel folded his arms. "And he wants to sell it?"

The man shook his head. "No, no, no... Mr. Ross is a collector. He never sells anything. He needs a valuation. For insurance purposes."

Nigel raised an eyebrow. "And why have you come to us? I'm sure the insurance company is capable of finding an appraiser."

The man's smile faded. "He requires someone who understands the market." He paused and lowered his voice before continuing. "And is capable of a certain level of discretion."

Max rubbed her hands together. "And what exactly is the piece?"

"A sculpture. Something Mr. Ross has acquired for his garden."

Nigel cleared his throat. "I assume the provenance is available."

The man paused before answering. "It isn't. Thus, the need for outside expertise."

Nigel frowned. "We aren't really in the business of providing appraisals. And I'd hate to disappoint your client. Particularly if he's looking to help offset the cost of loaning it to a museum or selling it."

The man took off his darkened glasses to reveal deep-set bloodshot eyes. "Not to worry. This piece will never be loaned or sold." He reached into his coat and pulled out a card. "Mr. Ross will pay generously for the service." He handed the card to Nigel. "Please consider it."

~

"WE AREN'T DOING IT." Nigel said flatly, as he rocked back in his office chair.

Max frowned. "What do you mean? Why wouldn't we? He's going to pay us a lot of money."

Nigel shook his head. "Because whatever it is, it's been stolen and sold on the black market."

"What do you mean, 'stolen?'"

Nigel motioned for Max to sit in the seat across from him. He pressed his fingers together. "A man with that much wealth, who doesn't want to pay for a formal insurance appraisal, isn't going to loan the piece to a museum, and is uncertain about its provenance? What else could it mean? He probably purchased it from a black-market broker."

Max pulled her hair into a ponytail. "I think it would be fun."

Nigel frowned. "You're at the beginning of your career. Something like this could end it before it starts."

Max cracked her knuckles. "Gee, I'd have to go back to Wall Street and get rich selling securities. Sounds terrible."

Nigel put on his best I'm-trying-to-mentor-you face. "Max, these things never end well. We'll have to sign some kind of NDA, sign off on something about how we won't say anything about it, and eventually be found out. After that, we'll be ostracized. It isn't worth it."

Max paused for a moment. "We don't know if he actually has something that's been purchased on the black market, right?"

Nigel nodded.

"And if we see it and think it's stolen, we aren't obligated to write an appraisal?"

Nigel nodded again.

Max leaned forward. "Think about it. No one will know. There's no risk. No paper trail." She waited before continuing. "And if it turns out we're wrong, we still get paid. Well paid."

When Nigel failed to respond, Max intoned. "And, you need the money."

Nigel looked up, flustered. "What do you mean?"

"You left your portfolio on the counter in the break room."

"That was private!"

"Well not that private if you left it in the break room," Max retorted. "You know, I could help you increase your returns."

Nigel's shoulder slumped. He sighed. "I made some investing mistakes. Don't see retirement coming anytime soon."

Max cleared her throat. "So again, you need the money." She leaned on the desk. "And it might be fun? Maybe this is a new line of business for this place. We start doing valuations on questionable pieces."

Nigel closed his eyes. "I know better than to do this. But I know I'm going to do it anyway." Nigel opened his eyes. "I suppose it doesn't hurt to look. As long as we decline if anything appears nefarious."

Max rubbed her hands together. "What fun!"

THE BURTON ROSS estate was larger than either Nigel or Max expected. It took ten minutes of driving to make it from the front gate to the large manor atop a small hill in the middle of Westchester County. Max stopped her Subaru in front of the marble steps. As Nigel and Max made their way to the front door, they noticed a series of large obelisks astride the silver-encrusted front doors. Before they reached them, the doors opened and the man who had visited them at the gallery stepped out.

Adorned in a black waistcoat, shirt, and tie, he wore his familiar dark glasses and shiny black shoes. It wasn't apparent at first glance whether he was a butler, a curator, or an estate manager.

"Thank you for coming," he said and motioned for them to enter.

As they walked down a long hallway, Max noticed several paintings lining the walls on each side of the hall. She whispered to Nigel, "Is that a Pollack?"

Nigel nodded. "It was purchased at Christie's seven years ago by an anonymous collector. I guess he isn't so anonymous anymore."

At the rear of the house, the man in black opened a pair of double doors and stepped onto a patio. He extended his hand out toward a large courtyard. "Welcome to Mr. Ross's private sculpture garden."

The man in black scurried ahead of Max and Nigel who paused when they stepped out onto the patio. Nigel looked up and noticed two figures standing on a small veranda looking out at the garden.

"I think that's the critic from *Modern Art Today* up there, standing next to..." Nigel trailed off.

"That's Burton Ross," Max said. "I looked him up."

"Is that one person?" Nigel replied.

"He's morbidly obese." Max nodded. "Like Jabba the Hutt morbidly obese."

"A man of significant appetites," Nigel said. "Literally."

Nigel and Max stepped into the garden. The ground was covered by a well-manicured lawn broken up by knee-high hedges surrounding a variety of different sculptures. So numerous were the pieces of art that if one looked across the lawn they could not see the building on the other side. Mannerist, Neoclassical, Hellenistic,

Relief, Equestrian, and other styles had been placed on small pedestals spaced only a few feet apart.

As the man in black marched toward the center of the garden with Max in tow, Nigel lingered at each sculpture they passed, a look of surprise and awe on his face.

In one corner of the garden, the man stopped in front of a small round pedestal. He pointed at the object sitting on it. "This is Mr. Ross's newest piece. He would like a written appraisal."

Nigel caught up and stood stone-faced, staring at the object. Max slowly circled it, scratching her head with an incredulous look on her face. Finally, she stopped and laughed out loud. She pointed toward the pedestal. "Is that what I think it is?"

The man in black didn't respond.

Max shook her head. "It's a toilet."

MAX PULLED her Subaru off the freeway and into a rest stop before she spoke to Nigel. "What was that?" she asked. "Burton Ross has clearly lost his marbles. No wonder he didn't want an insurance company appraiser to come look at his sculpture, which is just a toilet. He's crazy."

Nigel smirked and didn't respond. Max turned her head, realizing he knew something she didn't.

Nigel closed his eyes and pressed his fingers together. "Mr. Ross is not crazy."

Max shook her head. "Then what? What happened back there?"

Nigel continued to smirk. "In 1917, a Parisian sculptor named Marcel Duchamp entered an art contest sponsored by the Society of Independent Artists, of which he was a member. The contest was held in New York, and the sculpture he entered was shipped from Paris. The sculpture he submitted was little more than an upside-down urinal with the name R. Mutt written on its side. He titled it

The Fountain. It was rejected by the jurors as they deemed it not to be "art." Duchamp quit the society in protest, and the society's refusal to display it ignited a controversy that has persisted ever since. Namely, can day-to-day objects be considered art?"

Max stared at Nigel for a moment, absorbing the information, before speaking. "That urinal was *The Fountain.*"

Nigel nodded.

Max looked straight ahead for a moment. "And it's been obtained without permission?"

Nigel nodded again. "It's worth millions. There is a replica in the Philadelphia Museum of Art, but the original was lost, though many believe it's been traded back and forth on the black market for years. I have little doubt Mr. Ross obtained it in some back-alley deal."

Max sat silently as she drove the rest of the way back to the Monvoy.

Nigel was finishing a purchase order when Max burst into his office.

"We have to steal it back," she said.

"Steal what back?" Nigel said without looking up.

"*The Fountain,*" Max replied.

"Why would we do that?

Max shrugged. "Because it's the right thing to do. He obtained it illegally. It should be displayed somewhere the public has access to it. And why not? What's he going to do, report it to the police?"

Nigel leaned back in his chair. "If he caught us stealing it, then yes, he could call the police."

Max crossed her arms. "And say what? That we were stealing a stolen piece of art? Which is a urinal? Not sure I'd worry too much about that."

"How about getting caught breaking and entering?"

Max's eyebrow rose. "I've got that one covered. We aren't going to need to burgle anything. We are simply going to help Mr. Ross with a problem at his estate."

"Assuming we wouldn't get caught, why do we want to steal this valuable piece of art and what will we do with it when we steal it?"

"I haven't figured that out yet. As far as anyone knows, it's lost. It's really about the principle of the thing."

Nigel raised an eyebrow. "Principle? What principle is that?"

"Duchamps wanted to make a point that art belongs to everyone. It's all around us. The idea that his representation of everyday art is being hoarded by a rich collector in his private garden is anathema to everything he was trying to prove. Obtaining his work by nefarious means and hiding it from the public isn't acceptable."

"And so, we steal it?"

"Like Robin Hood."

Nigel rubbed his temples. "We aren't taking from the rich and giving to the poor."

Max put her hands on the desk. "Yes, we are. Sort of. And either we need to steal it or report it."

"This isn't the sort of thing one reports."

"Of course, you do. And then the world knows Mr. Burton Ross is a corrupt underhanded bad guy." Max leaned forward even further on the desk, putting her forearms on it and staring at Nigel. "And..." She paused for effect. "If we get caught, we'll be seen as heroes for trying to bring art back to the little guy."

Nigel opened a drawer and pulled out a bottle of sherry and a glass. He poured generously and drank the entire glass before responding. "Fine. Let's go steal a precious piece of art from a megalomaniacal rich guy."

~

WHEN MAX PULLED a van with a large "Plumbing Repair" logo on the side up to the Monvoy entrance, Nigel scratched his head, initially wondering why someone had called for a plumber and why Max had changed careers.

Max stepped out of the van and into the gallery's lobby. She handed Nigel a coverall. "Put this on."

"Why?"

"So, we can steal a urinal from a rich guy," Max said matter-of-factly.

Nigel held up the coveralls. "I don't think these go with my Faloni."

Max marched past Nigel. "You're right. A shirt with that high a thread count would never be covered by denim. Unless it was during fashion week, where that sort of thing is considered edgy. You should go find something else."

Nigel shuffled by her into his office. "I think I've got something a bit more pedestrian in here." A few moments later he returned wearing a slightly less ostentatious shirt beneath the coveralls.

Nigel touched one of the buttons on his shirt. "I don't feel like a plumber."

"You don't need to feel like one. Just look like one. Now get in the van!"

IT WAS midnight when Max pulled the truck up to the small speaker at the front gate.

A buzzing sound was followed by a raspy voice. "Can I help you?"

"Mario's plumbing. We're here to fix the toilet," Max replied. She leaned across the console toward Nigel and whispered, "If they ask, you're Mario. I'm Luigi."

Nigel, white and trembling with anxiety, whispered back, "From the video game?"

Max smiled. "Exactly."

The voice emanated from the speaker. "I wasn't expecting any plumbers."

Max sighed loudly, "You called us in the middle of the night for a plumbing emergency. You told me Mr. Ross would be very very upset when he finds the bathroom sink didn't work." She paused. When the voice didn't respond she continued, "We drive all the way out here in the middle of the night because you guys called us, and now you're saying you didn't expect us? What kind of operation are you all running?"

"Um, I can check with the house manager, but…"

Max tapped the speaker box. "Hello. It's the middle of the night. I'm not waiting for you to contact anyone. That's it, we're out of here. You can tell Mr. Ross the water destroying his house was preventable." Max paused and turned the ignition on in the car. "And good luck finding another plumber in the middle of the night."

"Wait! Wait!" the voice pleaded. "Fine. Just come around the back of the house. Someone will let you in."

As the black gate opened, Max turned and smiled at Nigel. "I love bureaucracy."

Nigel sighed and followed as Max led him to a door near the loading dock. As they approached, a small woman wearing a black dress opened the door. She had tortoiseshell-framed glasses, and her hair was disheveled. "Thank you for coming at such a late hour. Follow me."

The woman led Nigel and Max down a long hallway. Around another corridor she stopped and pointed to one corner. "The guest lavatory is in there."

Max cleared her throat. "Very well. We've got it from here."

The woman stopped and looked at Max. "Don't you need some tools?"

A flash of nervousness crossed Max's face before she responded. "Oh, of course. We just wanted to see what was wrong before we decide what we need."

The woman frowned. "Fine. Just get it fixed before morning." She turned and walked away.

Nigel whispered to Max. "What now?"

Max shrugged. "We go figure out what's wrong with the bathroom."

"What if there isn't anything wrong?"

"There won't be."

Nigel began to shake nervously. "We're going to jail."

Max put her finger to her lips. "Quiet. Just go into the bathroom, run the sink, flush the toilet, and pretend you're examining things." She pointed toward the hallway. "I'm going to get the tools." She made air quotes around *tools*.

Nigel wasn't sure what to do when he entered the bathroom. There were three sinks, a stall, and two urinals. He stood silently for a moment wondering why the mansion had such a large restroom. He turned on one of the sinks. Then another. He flushed one of the urinals. He tapped on the side of the stall. He stood in front of the mirror and made a face. Not sure what else to do, he stood in front of a different urinal and unzipped the fly in his overalls. As he stood urinating, Max burst into the room breathing heavily.

"It's done," she said as Nigel awkwardly flushed the toilet and zipped up.

"What do you mean it's done?"

"The sculpture is in the van," Max whispered.

"Why are you whispering? We're the only ones here," Nigel said loudly.

As he spoke, the woman opened the door. "How's it going?" she asked.

Max turned and held up her hands. "We're done!"

"Splendid." The woman looked at Max and then Nigel. "And you did it without any tools."

Max coughed. "I just put them away." She pointed toward the door. "In the van. They're in the van."

Nigel took Max's arm. "Yes, we've fixed the locking gasket. Took but a moment." He pulled Max toward the door. "And now we have to go. Another emergency."

The woman looked at her watch. "At one in the morning?"

Max pushed past her and through the door. "Yep. A plumber's work is never done."

Before the woman could say anything, Nigel and Max were in the hall, nearly running back to the van. Once they had left the estate, Max pulled off the road. Nigel immediately opened the door, stepped out and vomited. After a few minutes, Max stepped out of the van and walked around to where Nigel was leaning against the door.

"Do you want to see it?"

"I suppose I should."

Max slid the van door open. On a large tarp sat *The Fountain*. Nigel touched the porcelain just above the base. "Any idea how soon the cops are going to come looking for it?" he asked.

Max smirked. "No one will even know it's gone."

"How?"

"I simply replaced it with a different urinal," Max replied. "I even wrote R. Mutt on it." She put her hands on her hips. "Mr. Ross will probably get someone else to do the appraisal, they'll declare that it isn't real, and he'll simply assume he bought a fake."

Nigel scratched his head. "I see."

Max sighed. "I just don't know what to do with it now that we've stolen it."

Nigel took a deep breath. "I know exactly who to call. It will reside in a proper museum. The public will have access to it. Even Duchamps would approve."

THE MUSEUM OF MODERN Art in The Bronx was like the MoMAs in Manhattan and Queens save for its tawdry reputation and general lack of esteem. Considered the trashier and more transactional branch of the MoMA institution, it did what it could to attract avant-garde and upscale artists, high-society patrons, and donors interested in funding something more attractive than the colonial, washboard surfaced façade facing Third Avenue, not far from the St. Barnabas Hospital Emergency Room. But despite these efforts, it remained a wanton stepchild to the more venerable purveyors of the modern art world.

Originally given to the MoMA foundation by a wealthy slumlord, the Bronx Museum was still often mistaken for the methadone clinic that had once occupied its premises. The museum's ticket booth had once been the clinic's dispensary, leading to confusion among formerly-treated addicts, who upon relapse would find themselves in the same line as school children, wondering whether they were experiencing hallucinatory withdrawals.

Inside the museum, a variety of unimportant, uninteresting sculptures and paintings adorned the series of different rooms and anterooms extending across a large hallway. A wall of small plaques listed various donors, which included Mel's Auto Shop, the Bronx Teamsters, and a bodega a block away from the museum. A small gift shop was filled with sodas, artistic tchotchkes, and posters of various famous paintings, none of which had ever been displayed in the Bronx MoMA.

Across from the gift shop were lavatories, for both men and

women. In accordance with New York City ordinance, three individual, family restrooms stood next to the men's and women's. And while two of the individual restrooms were clearly functional, the third didn't have a door. A waist-height barrier had been erected with a small sign that said, "under repair." Those who peered over the sign saw a bathroom that appeared empty, save for a urinal, upside down in the middle of the floor with the name R. Mutt written on its side.

SCULPTURE GARDENS ARE OFTEN FILLED *with untended artistic foliage that in the best of circumstances is overgrown. In the worst, they are uninteresting and dead. It was only after a short period I found the need to extract myself from it. I am certain there were a great many classical pieces I never saw and would be quite interested to see in any other environment.*

Within the art world, gluttony is often a topic, but seldom an act. Bruegel's The Land of Cockaigne *or Steen's* The Dissolute Household *are emblematic of many artists' efforts to render the deadly sin on canvas. But none of them, not a single one, would have contemplated that the overconsumption of art could be considered a form of gluttony. Yet here we are.*

Art is, in its purest form, an expression of humanness. When best acquitted, it reaches out and builds common cause with others. It nourishes the part of us that necessitates empathy, purpose, and even love. But in a world where "supersized" fast food lends itself to cardiovascular and hepatic congestion, eventually killing the consumer, one is left to wonder what the overconsumption of art does to the soul. I have to suspect an analogous set of maladies befalls anyone so ravenous as to create the morass of statues and carvings I recently witnessed.

I have no doubt that the creators of most sculpture gardens have the best motives in mind, namely creation of a place where great works can be exhibited and displayed. But this is impossible in such a milieu. My advice to others considering the construction of a sculpture garden: Save your money. Buy a gnome.

THROUGH THE GARDEN OF EARTHLY DELIGHTS

ANNIE TUPEK

Amelia Fessden pushed through the door to Dr. Malachi's Virtual Pathworking Therapy office. She crossed the waiting room with its invitingly empty chairs and brochures advertising the various services the good doctor offered strewn across the coffee table.

"I'm so sorry I'm late."

The receptionist buzzed Amelia through to the back. "A meeting went long." Now that she was on her temporary job assignment, all she had these days were meetings. Until she finished these paths.

"You're right on time, Ms. Fessden." The receptionist joined her. In her mid-twenties, pretty with blonde hair and surfer tan skin, the receptionist wore a plum-colored suit and carried a tablet.

Amelia had missed the receptionist's nameplate on her way in and wasn't sure if she'd met the woman before. All of Dr. Malachi's receptionists looked and sounded the same. Bright and airy and overly helpful.

"I've checked you in."

"I know I should relax. Pathworking works best when one is relaxed," she blurted. Amelia forced herself to match the receptionist's steady pace down the corridor.

"Don't worry about that. The simulation entry will help relax and orient you in the world. You've walked over a dozen paths. You're a pro and will be through all your sessions in no time." The receptionist stopped outside a door. "You're in Pod Four today. The suit is ready for you. Remember your pause word?"

"Baltimore." Amelia had never been there, and it was unlikely to come up in casual conversation, so it fit the safe word parameters.

The receptionist consulted her tablet and nodded. "Very good. Dr. Malachi has made a couple of suggestions based on your Performance Improvement Plan, but feel free to deviate if something else catches your eye. Every module Dr. Malachi suggests can be applied to your PIP. Any questions?"

Amelia shook her head. Dr. Malachi's suggestions were usually more interesting than the ones Jason in Human Resources and Development assigned to her plan.

The receptionist opened the door with a cheerful smile. "There will be water waiting when you exit."

Amelia stepped into the pod and closed the door behind her.

An omnidirectional treadmill took up most of the room. The prep area, tucked into the near corner, was cluttered with a bench and locker. The VR suit hung on a hook. Amelia stowed her purse and shoes in the locker and took down the suit and put her jacket in its place.

Amelia shucked off her skirt and blouse. Her shoulders dropped and her breathing steadied as she went through the familiar process of suiting up. She worked her feet into the slippers and pulled on the puffy control and haptic feedback suit. It zipped up the front like coveralls and the fabric formed micro-pleats as it shrank to a close fit. She worked the gloves onto her hands and pulled the mask over her face.

Amelia took two steps onto the omnidirectional treadmill. As she walked to the center, the rig verified her identity and started up. The goggles fogged over and instead of looking at the room, Dr.

Malachi's splash screen presented itself, followed by a series of menus.

Amelia navigated the menus with ease. There was no need to be anxious; she'd finish her twenty modules soon and be back to overseeing the firm's financial analysts.

Her options scrolled in front of her. *CBT: Reining In the Emotional Elephant*. Meh. *Reframing Obstacles as Opportunities*. Nah. *Through the Garden of Earthly Delights*. That was one of Dr. Malachi's suggestions. Amelia vaguely remembered that bizarre painting from her art appreciation class. Figuring that path would be more entertaining than the others on the list, she selected it.

As she dropped into the path's lobby, she noticed it was a multiplayer pair-up. For a moment, she thought about Baltimore-ing out and selecting something else, but that would be rude. She hoped the algorithm didn't match her with anyone who would impede her progress in closing out her PIP.

The path's lobby was a translucent dome about twenty feet in diameter. Outside, a fog swirled. Inside, a person in a sloth onesie stood in front of Amelia. She was young, near to Amelia's age, and of similar height and proportions. Amelia had modeled her avatar after her physical self and wondered if her new partner had done the same. The tag above her head read *Serena*.

"Hi, I'm Amelia."

"Rennie." Her pajamas changed into a basic black jumpsuit.

Amelia scrolled through her options while the environment loaded and equipped a similar outfit. She checked Rennie's stats. Her partner had a top-of-the-line Fahrsehn mask, a high-resolution full haptic feedback suit, and an omnidirectional treadmill registered to her public profile. "That's a nice rig you've got."

"Same to you."

"It's a rental," Amelia said.

The dome shifted to transparent and the fog cleared. Fields of green rolled up to distant cliffs topped by what might have been towers. A host of animals frolicked in the middle distance, and a huge body of water sparkled on the horizon. Beyond the dome, the vast pastoral landscape didn't appear to have roads or vehicles. "Looks like we're going to be doing some walking."

"I'm on the sofa," Rennie said.

Amelia stepped backwards. The omnidirectional treadmill responded naturally to her movements. "You're just headsetting it?" She'd encountered Setters in plenty of sims for tabletop games, but never in any adventures, or one of Dr. Malachi's therapeutic paths.

"Yeah. Don't really see the point of walking around. If this were some zero-G acrobatic adventure, maybe I'd suit up. This doesn't look worth the effort."

Was Rennie not concerned about reaching her movement quota? Amelia had sixty percent to go and her day was almost over. If it weren't for these paths, she would have missed her movement quotas for the last two weeks.

Amelia set her jaw and turned away to look outside the dome. "Seems like you're not getting the full experience." A door formed in the dome and they exited the lobby into the garden. Rennie's motions were smooth and natural even though the avatar was being directed by a hand controller rather than a bodysuit. It was disconcerting to think how they were perceiving the same simulation differently.

A dozen steps from the door, a circular reflecting pool sparkled in the sunlight. An old man stood in front of it. Dr. Malachi. He had been the guide for every path she'd walked. The real Dr. Malachi, if he even existed, wasn't logged in from another pod. This prerecorded avatar was a Non-Player Character, more archetype than person. He wore a salmon-colored toga cinched with a golden belt and spoke low, indeterminant words to an owl perched on his arm.

"Welcome to the garden," Dr. Malachai said, his words suddenly clear. Amelia had stepped into his trigger range. The owl flew from his arm and perched in the hollow of a tree.

"You have chosen to walk *Through the Garden of Earthly Delights*. Be not distracted from your path. Before the midnight hour, the key must turn in Two Boat Tavern and you both must exit."

Rennie interrupted, "If you don't, you'll be charged a failure fee and won't move on to the next level."

Her new partner didn't seem to be taking this seriously. Maybe she should have Baltimore-d out, but she could only imagine what her boss would say if the firm had to pay for a repeat session. It would come out of her bonus, and these paths did not come cheap.

The Dr. Malachi avatar ignored Rennie. His level of artificial intelligence didn't have enough agency to respond to anything but the most basic requests. He said to Amelia, "Take these two balls and follow the owl."

A red rubber ball, like a schoolyard kickball, hovered in the air in front of Amelia. Rennie had an identical one in front of her.

As Amelia's hands closed on the ball, it shrank to the size of a flat disk. She slid it into her pocket. When Rennie did the same with hers, Amelia's pocket felt a little heavier. An icon popped up in the corner of her vision. A shared inventory. When she put her hand in her pocket, Amelia had access to both discs.

"What are they for?" Amelia asked, but Dr. Malachi had disappeared while she had been distracted by their shared inventory. He had never been very helpful.

"Who knows?" Rennie answered.

The owl glided out of the tree's hollow and landed on the path. It cocked its head and then turned and hopped away from them.

"Follow the owl." Amelia started down the path. Rennie was two steps behind.

The tree-lined path made for easy walking through the unfolding hills. What had appeared normal while the world was forming around the dome—the plants, the animals, the structures

—became more bizarre. Chimera clustered on the hillside, sheep with beaks, birds with horns, and unicorns. Sharp spikes protruded from the towers and the air grew hot.

They soon came to a wide river. The opposite bank craggy and uninviting, the near shore a smooth beach, and a fast current divided the two. The owl made short flights down the beach until it landed on a large, ridged gray rock at the water's edge. It glittered, designating it as an interactable item. The rock was an overturned half shell from a monstrous muscle. Several feet long, it had the same proportions as a rowboat. It was the largest shell Amelia had ever seen.

The owl paced, back and forth, over the shell's crest then hopped off and walked to the river. Amelia had played enough games and walked enough paths to know they were supposed to use the shell as a boat and float the river. "They could have just programmed the owl to talk," Amelia commented as she dug her fingers under the shell's lip and tested its weight.

It weighed less than expected and Amelia managed to turn it over on her own. A bead of sweat trickled down her spine. Even without a full sensor suit, Rennie should have been able to help, but she just milled about, looking at the river.

The shell's mother-of-pearl interior glistened. Eager to get into the coolness of the water, Amelia grabbed two branches that sparkled with interactivity. She handed one to Rennie.

"What for?" Rennie asked.

"Oars." Amelia mimicked rowing. "To row."

Rennie's looked skeptical. "Pretty sure the current will take us where we need to be."

Amelia wasn't convinced. "We'll need these to get to the current."

Rennie shrugged and held the branch while Amelia put the boat into the cold water. "Get in," Amelia said. "I'll hold it." The shellboat bobbed, buoyant in the shallows as though impatient to reach the current. The owl perched on the bow. Rennie lumbered in with the makeshift oars and nearly upset the boat. The owl stayed put.

Amelia shoved the boat off and as the water took it, she rolled over the edge and into it. Her grip tightened on the makeshift oar. "If you don't help, we're only going to go in circles."

Except they didn't. The shellboat made straight for the middle of the river.

"Knew we'd make the current." Rennie leaned her head down against the side of the shell. The shore rolled by. "Walk enough of these and you figure out you don't need to do everything. The algorithm isn't going to let us get too far off track."

Amelia pulled her oar into the shellboat. Nearly everything in the world sparkled. Perhaps that was part of the distraction Dr. Malachi had mentioned.

A gigantic pink marble tower rose in the distance, its base half-straddling the river. Beyond it, a wide lake sparkled. Something gray and silver and as long as a parade approached the tower's base. It looked like a giant centipede. Amelia couldn't recall what it was in the original painting; just another strange creature from Bosch's imagination.

Hoping to avoid being noticed, Amelia kept her head down as the river carried them to the tower. Gigantic flower petals and pale leaves floated to the ground from tree branches hidden high in the sky or blown in from far distances. The low sound of snores came from Rennie's side of the shellboat. Amelia was about to nudge her, when voices distracted her. Amelia peeked over the shell's lip.

What she had thought was a giant centipede was a tight formation of people clad in silver bodysuits, some of them held large red balls in their hands. The centipeople splashed through the river delta. The strangeness pulled a small laugh from her lips, and she raised her hand to stifle it.

At the confluence, where the river joined the lake, a great golden fish twice the size of a human jumped in the water. To move past it, the centipeople occasionally threw a ball, which the goldfish played with until the ball sank into the water, no longer interesting.

The goldfish's attention fixated on one of the individuals in the centipeople; one who didn't have a ball to throw. Neither did his neighbors. The goldfish leapt out of the water and engulfed the man's head and shoulders before plunging into the depths. It returned a moment later amid a flurry of bubbles and faced the passing centipeople. Someone threw a red ball and the goldfish gave chase.

"So that's what the balls are for," Amelia said.

Rennie jerked awake. "Huh?"

Amelia tugged her up to look over the edge. "To distract the goldfish."

"Cool." Rennie settled back down and showed no interest in seeing what Amelia saw.

Amelia pulled the disk from her pocket. As their shellboat approached the base of the tower, she expanded it between her hands to the size and shape of the ball. The goldfish poked its head out of the water. Amelia threw the ball, and the goldfish leapt and bounced over a wave to intercept it. The current bore the shellboat into the main body of the lake. Amelia wiped her sweaty palms on her pants.

A tinkling of bells and a sudden weight in her pockets made her check the inventory. They'd received ten gold coins for passing the goldfish. Above, the owl flapped away from the pink tower and landed on one of the branching crescents of the central fountain.

The lake was crowded with people in similar makeshift boats of large leaves and flower petals. Mermaids surfed the waves, and men rode fish. The current maneuvered them along the shoreline.

"Guess we're going this way," Amelia said, miffed that Rennie had been right. They didn't have to row. It felt a little like cheating to not actually walk the path they were on. As a Setter, Rennie might be used to this, but Amelia had a sedentary day and still needed to reach her movement quota.

The near shore was a turmoil of humans and animals. Manic men and beasts raced circles while the lazy lolled about. Women clutched at birds as though they could take flight. A massive fountain rose from the middle of the lake. Giggles echoed from within. All around, swimmers sported in the water. Not all of them were human, and everything was a sparkling distraction.

Amelia couldn't remember all the bizarre things depicted in the painting. "Those animals aren't normal. And what are those people doing?"

"Do you have to keep talking? I could use this rest time."

"I'm here to do the work," Amelia said.

"Oh yeah? What did you do?" Rennie asked.

She'd laid into Derek for missing his deadline. She didn't recall exactly what she said, but the phrase "lazy bum" had been in there, and so had "worthless." It had been in the corridor as he had been slinking in at half past ten. The head of Human Resources and Development had overheard. So had everyone else. Hence the Performance Improvement Plan. If she didn't pass, she'd be up for termination at her quarterly review. But Amelia wasn't going to share that with Rennie, who seemed to delight in doing even less than Derek had. "Nothing. What are you here for?"

"Same as you. Nothing."

Amelia pursed her lips and turned her attention to the river. The owl took off from the central fountain and flew toward what looked like a blue tower in the distance. It landed, a small lump on one of its outstretched spikes. The blue tower pulled the shellboat as much as the current did, and soon it loomed above them. White specks crawled over it, an infestation of some kind of long-beaked bird.

Close by in the water, a trio of men rode large silver trout and chased the mermaids who flicked their tails and splashed. One of the men slipped his fish into the tower's shadow. The white birds squawked and squealed and swarmed over the tower, their long beaks scissoring open in agitation. Amelia put her hands over her ears and watched, transfixed.

A gigantic blue bird with a long beak stepped out of the shadow of the tower and dipped its head. Too fat to fly, it hopped along the shoreline. Its beak snipped the man with the fish in half and flicked the torso to the birds on the tower. The fish swam back toward the safety of the lake, the man's legs still straddling its back.

Amelia swallowed the bile in her throat. "Did you see that?" Amelia clumsily beat her branch-oar at the water, battling the current until the shellboat drifted in a slow spin. "We need a plan."

Rennie rose up on her elbows and peered over the side of the shellboat. "I don't want to try to get past in daylight," Rennie said. "We should take shelter and wait for nightfall." She yawned. "Take a nap to refresh ourselves. We can hide in the fountain."

Amelia shivered at the odd giggles emitting from the fountain. "It was occupied, and I don't think we want to interrupt them," Amelia said.

On a nearby boat, two shadowed figures watched them from under a gigantic leaf. More oversized leaves and petals floated nearby. Everything sparkled.

"We're going to hide under a leaf and float past." Amelia leaned out of the boat and grasped the nearest floating leaf. "Give me a hand with this."

Rennie didn't budge. Setters were never as invested as someone who was fully suited up. The algorithm should not have paired them up. She wasn't going to call Baltimore this far in. With jerky motions that betrayed her frustration, Amelia tugged the broad leaf onto the boat and over them like a little roof.

The current funneled them to the blue tower and Amelia adjusted the leaf. They were almost fully covered. Almost. She hoped the other floating leaves and petals were enough camouflage for the shellboat. The crackling birds increased in intensity.

Something rocked the shellboat. The shadow of the long-beaked bird appeared on the leaf. Its sharp, scissor-pointed beak poked at the leaf, working its way under, seeking them out in the shadows.

Amelia froze. At her side, Rennie was immobile. The beak jabbed down between them and scraped against the shell's interior.

"Use your ball," Amelia hissed. Rennie didn't move. Amelia couldn't tell if Rennie had gone back to sleep or was paralyzed by fear. The beak withdrew and the bird tilted its head and lowered its eye to the hole. Unblinking, it examined them.

Heart racing, palms sweating, Amelia wasn't going to fail this due to Rennie's inaction. She grabbed the disk out of their shared inventory. It expanded.

The beak came down. Amelia jammed the ball onto it like an olive on a cocktail pick. The bird jumped back, taking half the leaf with it, and hopped along the shore, unable to open its beak. Baby birds squawked and called, but their mother bird could do nothing.

Amelia and Rennie floated by, half covered by the remains of the leaf. Another tinkle of bells and more coins were deposited into their inventory.

Amelia sighed in relief. The current pulled them downriver and into a dusk that fell faster than Amelia expected. Shadows deepened, swallowing everything. Even the sky lacked stars. Rennie's snores cut through the night.

The clock showed a quarter to ten. It couldn't have taken them that long to cross the lake and float along the river. Passing the blue tower must have changed their clock. Maybe they were supposed to wait until nightfall.

One by one, fire-lit windows and doorways came into view, some nearby, others in the distance on darkened hills. The glow of a settlement lit the shore. The occasional surface break burbled the water from whatever creatures traveled the river.

The boat bumped against something with a hollow thunk. They

were dead in the water. Amelia caught a scream in her throat. It was only a dock.

The owl flew off, a black shadow soon lost to the night until it landed somewhere above them and turned toward them. The orbs of its eyes glowed orange amid the darkened waterfront.

The docks were deserted, but raucous music of discordant strings and arhythmic drums came from the distant buildings that weren't distant enough for Amelia's taste.

Another strange creature broke the water's surface with a slurp and then descended back into the depths.

The shellboat bobbed next to a ladder. "I guess we leave the boat," Amelia said and climbed.

"Probably safer than by boat." Rennie stretched and pulled herself onto the dock next to Amelia.

The owl remained at its roost as the shadows under his gaze took shape. Two large rowboats were secured to the dock. Each held a pillar that together supported a larger boat several meters above the water. It had been cut in half from port to starboard, exposing a cross-section of its cargo hold.

The whitewash inside was sea-worn and flaking. A grid of kegs covered one wall, a long table and benches ran the length of the hold. Instead of the cacophonous revelry of the village, the wheezing song of mournful bagpipes drooped from the musicians on the upper deck. The owl looked down from its rooftop perch.

"Two Boat Tavern," Rennie said. "Cool. I could use a drink."

A rickety ladder led to the boat's interior. "Would you like to go first?" Amelia asked.

"Nah," Rennie said. "I'm good."

"Maybe you should go first," Amelia prodded. She had done all the work up to this point. Her frustration was about to burst out of her. She had thrown the ball for the goldfish. She had impaled the other one on the bird's beak. It was time for Rennie to do something. Like trigger any waiting trap and be the one to take damage.

Rennie hesitated.

"I insist," Amelia pushed. Rennie had to take a step forward or fall on her face.

Rennie threw her a look. "Fine." She climbed the ladder and from the top shouted, "Nothing to worry about."

Amelia scurried up the ladder. She hauled herself onto the floor of the tavern and picked herself up, wiping her sticky hands on her pants.

Glassy-eyed people sat somberly on benches at the long table. They clutched pewter steins and stared at nothing. No one reacted to Amelia's and Rennie's entrance. The door at the far end of the table glittered in the dim light, and the keyhole in the ornate doorknob glowed. The game clock read 10:04 p.m. Just under two hours before they had to open the door.

Behind the bar, the tavernkeeper tapped a keg. Wearing a black dress, her horns poked out from under her white kerchief and a tail snaked out from under her white apron. A demon just like those on the darker side of Bosch's painting.

"This is the place." Rennie sat down and patted the bench next to her. "Buy you a drink?"

"We haven't found the key yet."

"I bet the key is somewhere in here and will show itself when it's time."

Rennie had been right about the river current. She had probably been right about the second tower. They should have waited for nightfall. Amelia sank onto the bench next to Rennie. It felt good to sit. She loved the idea of doing nothing, of letting the world go by. She was tired and deserved a break.

The tavernkeeper placed a stein in front of each of them. "How much?" Amelia asked, checking their inventory to see how much of coin they had collected.

"On the house," the tavernkeeper grumbled. She turned to leave, but Amelia reached out and caught her apron. The tavernkeeper's tail wrapped around Amelia's wrist in a warning squeeze.

"Please." Amelia's voice shook and the squeeze tightened. "We need the key to that door. Do you have it?"

The tavernkeeper yanked her apron back from Amelia's grasp. "No."

"Do you know where we can find it?" Amelia asked. "We can pay you." She hoped their twenty-five gold coins would be enough.

The tavernkeeper released Amelia's wrist and used her tail to point through the open side of the tavern. In a nearby boat, a fishing rod sat in the empty left socket of a giant horse skull. The line dangled in the water. Something took the bait, and the skull jerked back as though its absent skeleton had reared up on its hind legs. The hook came up empty, but its bait caught Amelia's eyes. A bronze key glittered red in the lights of the surrounding fires.

"The key," Amelia said. The skull continued to fish and each cast failed to catch.

"Yeah, I see," Rennie said, taking a swig from the stein.

"We should get it," Amelia said, but stayed sitting on the bench.

"Many travelers have tried," the tavernkeeper said. "Not all succeed."

Amelia toyed with the stein, spinning it in the condensation. "What happens?"

"The Equine Cranium gets them. Or the river does."

"But some make it," Rennie said and raised her stein in a toast.

The tavernkeeper's horns raised and dipped in a slight nod. "Some do."

Amelia watched the key as it bobbed in the water. The shadow creatures who called the river home made it too dangerous to try for the key from the water. But, every time the Equine Cranium reared, the key dangled just in front of its eye socket.

ANNIE TUPEK

Amelia stood, leaving her beer undrunk. "Are you coming?"

"Nah, I'll just stay here."

"Come on." Amelia really didn't want to climb up that big skull alone. "I'm sorry about pushing you up the ladder."

"This is where I belong," Rennie slurred and took a swig from the stein. "You've got this." Amelia climbed down the ladder by herself. At the bottom, on the dock, she looked back up. Rennie sat at the table, blending in with the patrons. She wasn't coming. The sting of betrayal was light, but it was there. She should have known better than to rely on Rennie's assistance. She should have Baltimore'd out when she'd first noticed the path was a partnership.

Amelia made her way to the horse skull in the rowboat. It rocked in the water, back and forth. The boat drifted further away with each lapping wave.

On its rocking upswing, Amelia jumped into the boat. She gripped the wet wooden planking and pulled herself up against the giant skull. There wasn't much room left.

The boat rocked, and Amelia pressed herself to the back of the skull, her shoulders level with the jaw joint. The bone's porous surface seemed to pull the moisture from her fingertips. She watched the fishing pole and the brass key that dangled just beneath the water's surface until the Equine Cranium reared and pulled it out of the water. Amelia slammed herself flat onto the skull and held on, watching the key come within reach of the fishing pole. She was too far back to reach the eye socket. She needed to get onto the horse's forehead. From there she should be able to get to the eye socket, and then, the fishing pole.

The key sank into the night river and Amelia rose to a crawl. The tavern's glow cast its light into the night. Rennie sat with the others, hand on stein, staring into space. The tavernkeeper watched Amelia, her gaze was unmistakable. And the owl remained at the tavern; its orange eyes adding light to the darkness.

158

Amelia crawled over the back of the Equine Cranium. It reared again. She slipped and caught herself on the eye socket and held on. She breathed slowly to control her panic as the key teased her, swinging just outside her reach. She wasn't steady enough to grasp it. She knelt on the bridge of the skull's nose and clung to the giant eye socket with one hand.

"Next time," she told herself.

The skull returned the key to the water and Amelia adjusted her grip. She reached out for the fishing pole, but it wouldn't move. She couldn't reel in the key, she couldn't change the fishing pole's angle. Long shapes circled in the water, waiting for her to fall.

For several breaths, there was nothing but the bobbing of the boat in the water. And then, when she thought she could wait no longer, the skull reared up and the brass key swung out of the darkness and nearly hit her in the face. Water spattered her nose and mouth. The key dangled within her reach.

Crouched low over the eye socket, she clung on with one hand and grabbed the key with the other. She wrapped her fingers tight and pulled it to her. The Equine Cranium whipped from side to side. Amelia flattened herself against the skull and clung on like she was riding a mechanical bull in a country bar.

She yanked the key from the line and the Equine Cranium calmed immediately. It dipped its mouth to the water, and had the key still been on the line, it would have returned there.

Amelia pressed herself flat against the bone and skidded her way backwards, over the forehead and down the back of the horse's skull until her feet hit the boat. She jumped back to the dock and returned to the tavern. The key's weight was heavy in her pocket, but her footsteps were light.

"That was fast," the tavernkeeper said as Amelia crested the top of the ladder and climbed into the cargo hold. "There's the door." She nodded her horned head at the door at the far end of the table that now had a golden light ringing it.

Amelia tapped Rennie on the shoulder. She turned and the slack look on her face tightened into an expression of surprise. "You're back," Rennie slurred.

Amelia showed her the brass key.

"Knew you could do it."

"Let's go," Amelia said and gave a gentle tug.

"Finish a drink first," Rennie said. "To celebrate." She pointed at the clock. It was 11:30. Time moved strangely here. "We've got plenty of time for a quick drink." She leaned back on the bench and called, "Barkeep! A fresh drink for my friend before she leaves."

"Before we leave."

"I'm not going anywhere. I'm staying here with my new friends." She gestured to the others at the long tables. "My compatriots." She tugged Amelia down onto the bench. "Have a drink."

Exhausted but wary, Amelia sat and waited while the tavernkeeper took her time tapping the keg. She hadn't expected that much physical exertion and felt like she'd been given a full body workout. From rowing the shellboat to riding the Equine Cranium and all the walking in between. They were both supposed to exit. Amelia wondered if she would get partial credit for coming out alone.

"Come on, let's get out of here," Amelia said half-heartedly. It seemed to take tremendous effort to stand.

The tavernkeeper gave her a smirk as she delivered a fresh stein of beer. Rennie threw her arm around Amelia and clinked her stein against it. "Drink up."

Rennie called for another round, jostling Amelia in the process. The weight of the key bumped against Amelia's leg, a sudden reminder. She looked up. There was less than a minute until midnight.

She stood. The motion knocked the bench back and earned her the disgruntled looks of the others. Even though Rennie hadn't contributed to getting them to the end, she didn't deserve to be left behind. And Amelia needed her to get full credit for the path. "Come on." Amelia yanked Rennie up by her collar and pulled her from the bench.

"Hey! Come on," Rennie responded, and sloshed beer all over the place.

"We're leaving. Both of us." She wasn't going to repeat this path just because she had an ineffectual and apathetic partner. It wasn't fair. Amelia dragged Rennie, stumbling, to the door at the back of the tavern. The horned tavernkeeper set down the stein she had been wiping clean and followed at a distance.

Amelia put the key in the lock. The door swung open into blinding light. Amelia stepped through.

The light dimmed to gray, the colors slowly resolving into Dr. Malachi's ending splash screen. They stood near a reflecting pool in a garden like the one they had started in, surrounded by tall trees, though this one was empty of animals. Dr. Malachai shimmered into existence next to the reflecting pool.

"Congratulations," he said. "You have passed level Sloth." A board appeared with the Seven Deadly Sins. A red line struck through Sloth. "A new sin will be chosen at random the next time you walk *Through the Garden of Earthly Delights*."

His wrinkles deepened as he grinned cheerfully. "You brought your companion with you. You didn't leave her behind or give up on her. It was no doubt difficult, but you've made progress accepting the slothful aspect of your nature."

Rennie's avatar winked out. An NPC companion wasn't what Amelia had expected for the pathworking sessions from Dr Malachi. Rennie's AI had been more sophisticated than Dr. Malachi's avatar and had been the path's true guide, telling her to relax and enjoy the ride. Amelia couldn't believe how stubborn she had been in forcing the path rather than letting it carry her along.

"Please see the receptionist on your way out. Take your time."

The slow, looped motions of the exit lobby began.

Amelia lifted her hands to her face and peeled off the mask and hood. She unsnapped the gloves and ran her hands through her hair. As was often the case after a path, she was a little light-headed and dizzy as she came back into herself. Her mind raced to process the journey as she exited the rig.

Amelia poured herself a glass of the cucumber-and-lemon-infused water that was waiting for her. She checked her movement quota. Ninety percent and her commute home would get in the final ten. Another day of squeaking by. And now she knew what to expect on the garden paths. There were six sins left on the list and six sims left in her PIP. She wondered which she'd face next. She hadn't yelled very loudly at Derek, but it would probably be wrath.

LION'S DEN

K. FUFKIN VOLLMAYER

"I didn't kill her. She just got what was coming to her." Tina could feel them behind her, all of them glaring, like when Moose was off-leash and his tail froze and he stood stock-still, ready to attack. Her cellmates were quiet and ready to pounce. She couldn't walk away or leave through the open door of the cell, because they all really did surround her. Besides, there was nowhere to go. But she couldn't meet their eyes either, so she glanced at Father Romero's card. One glance and the cursive was a dead giveaway. Sister Dorothy had written in her perfect penmanship and Father Romero had signed it.

Sister D. always had good answers about what the Devil was up to, how to spot sin in homeroom first thing in the morning. With her dark mustache drooping down on her upper lip, watching her mouth move as she talked was like watching a dark spider web twitch.

She always had the best stories. Like when she was with the Jesuit volunteers teaching farmworker kids down in Delano. As she told it, one afternoon she snatched a note the boys were passing around. On it was a drawing of her with the words *cara de perro*, or dog face, on account of her mustache and the rash on her face.

When an epidemic of giggling broke out, she growled and barked at the boys. Then she read Psalms to them. Even in Tina's confirmation class, when everyone would nod off after school, Sister D. would call out, "Let's get up and do some jumping jacks. Up you go and name your Saint!" All six feet of Sister D. would make you jump hard enough to wake you up. She never gave out Judgment under God or JUGS where you had to write out contrition stuff.

Tina tried a turtle move as her cellmates kept yammering away. Were they still talking to her? She lay down and retracted her arms and legs closer and clutched Sister D.'s card. Like she could grow smaller and escape their stares. She must've laughed somehow, remembering jumping jacks and Name-Your-Saint; laughed at how Sister D. would always read Psalms if you stared too long at her face.

Then, one of her cellmates coughed, her voice rising in an accusation. "What I say is: Nope. This ain't no laughing matter. Nope. You there, new girl, you jus' gonna lie down and go sleepy-weepy right now?"

Tina's turtle move of trying to disappear and huddle with her card and not argue was interrupted. Tina didn't answer her cellmates, because it was there on Sister D.'s card: *They will try to torment you.*

A grown-up voice came over the PA system. Maybe the office lady voice breathing too hard into the mic would distract them.

The girl coughed. Tina needed to look up, to pay attention, to face them. But she couldn't. One of them kicked Tina's bunk bed. "You. I am talking to you."

She rolled over as she stared at the card and read it to herself.

Dear Tina, When you go to Ventura, remember Daniel and the lions. You will be imprisoned, like Daniel in the fiery pit. They will tease you and, yes, maybe even torment you. You ask for strength and grace from God. Daniel held fast to God and to the Commandments. So you should, too.

Tina laughed, recalling grace. Was it a girl's name or a prayer? Her oldest sister was Grace, short for Graciela. Try to keep the Commandments.

Only Tina had broken the biggest one.

The intercom announcements at the juvenile facility sounded like those from homeroom last year. Same mic breaking up, same heavy breathing, same long rambling sentences. Last year, it was Mrs. Martin chirping away about home and away games, try-outs, and SATs.

But it wasn't last year. Tina was here, inside the muggy cement-walled room with metal framed bunk beds from the 1950s. The walls had a heat gradient like an August sidewalk. This voice on this intercom spoke about arithmetic, the AC down, and the GED. This year, last year, it was getting mixed up. Tina spoke to herself because Sister D. was right, it was as hot as a fiery pit.

Be like Daniel.

But her thoughts were cut off by another of her cellmates breaking in. "Hold up, hold up. She does not even answer. No way is she gonna do that here."

"C'mon Neecie, it was a pom-pom. You see any of that sport shit here?" one of the other girls said.

While they bickered, one of them kicked her bunk again, shoving the metal frame so it shuddered against the wall with that grinding sound like when she put the clutch in wrong on the Pinto. Tina squinted at her card and nodded as one of the girls, this one with a throaty laugh, poked Tina's back. This girl's voice matched her face, for she had a diaper rash of acne, angry and red. Tina sat up. It had to be a sign. Sister D. had face problems too, starting with that crazy mustache she had, her fringe on top of her lips. Her cellmate was saying something as the sound went out again, only this time Tina knew that when the soundtrack disappeared, it came from inside her own head. People were speaking. Tina could see their lips moving, but the sound was gone, *poof,* absent.

There was the girl with the bumpy face, there was another girl who was taller and wearing so much eyeliner her eyelids were black cracking lines. And a third girl who really was a girl. She had a kid's face, not a day past twelve years old.

"You answer, New Girl, because no way you are gonna pull that here. You deaf or what?" the coughing girl asked.

Tina looked down, she wasn't like Moose the Dog who froze and then could pounce and shred up the fur of another dog. Tina whispered, answering to this knot of girls. "I wanted to scare her. That's all. I didn't do anything."

But she had, which was why she was here.

The intercom lady announced dinner, the AC, and someone in the hall was mopping with bleach. Bleach. Tina smelled it. Bleach like Mission High.

Her coughing cellmate stabbed the air in front of Tina's face. "Look here, we is like R2-D2, only we is N2-D2, Neecie and Natasha."

"Tina," Tina answered.

Natasha shook her head. "Hell, the whole world knows your damn name."

"We is watching you," Neecie with the eyeliner warned.

Tina's mattress had no sheet and was covered with so many rust-colored stains, it was one of those Rorshach tests that the shrink had given out every week, asking: "What does this look like, Tina?" It was a mattress of patterns with blobs and petals colliding from a hundred girls who'd slept on it during their period. Neecie went back to braiding her hair.

Sister D. wrote a P.S. on the back of the card.

Daniel was surrounded by lions ready to devour him. They were hungry, starved. But Daniel survived, steadfast in his faith. You can, too.

All of it jangled Tina. The intercom voice, the bleach from the hallway that no way, no how, could cover up the toilet smell because here in Ventura, inside the beehive of dozens of windowless cells that was an echo chamber for every sniff, giggle, and fart, there was no AC.

"At least this isn't homeroom," Tina must've said aloud.

Neecie laughed. "Nope, it is way way worse than homeroom."

Tina was here in Ventura inside her cell, and from out in the hall, no working AC was becoming a bad toilet with the stink of hundreds of girls in their jumpsuits with nervous B.O. Like one big locker room. Whatever the bleach was supposed to do, it wasn't. The heat and no air was Mission High. The bleach from the hall was like her first week of her first year. The September heat, no breeze, just chlorine that was an exhale from the Olympic-size pool. At the back of Mission, the blue diamond pool glimmered in the sun.

A senior who had to be a Todd or a Dave or a Greg grinned and waved to her. Stunned, Tina waved back. He stood six feet something, as tanned and angular as a Macy's shirt ad. He laughed and shoved a friend of his, which seemed to cancel the wave. Unsure, she turned around. There it was. He was waving at her mom as she rattled out of the parking lot in the shame-event-on-wheels, the Pinto. This Dave or Greg or whatever called out to his huddle of varsity thugs, "Guys, it's as green as shampoo, a Prell-mobile, no, a Pinto-Prell mobile." One of them laughed so hard, he snorted.

Tina willed herself, *do not look back, do not look back, just keep walking.*

The school buildings wavered like a desert mirage. Sunlight bounced off the windows of the office and the cafeteria and the classrooms, blinding her as she wandered to the back to the pool. Forty-five minutes before first bell, when most people were just getting up, here was the girls' varsity, doing laps. She wanted to watch Kiki, wanted to see if she was as fast as everyone said. Only, as Tina stared at the pool, there was no telling who was who.

Besides, as she watched the churn on top of the pool, she didn't really watch swimmers doing laps. You heard them. The rhythm of their arms slicing the water down before they somersaulted against the pool wall in a flip turn. Then the steady stroke-stroke-stroke resumed, all of it bathed in chlorine and jasmine. The jasmine bushes beside the pool had leaves so waxy they looked plastic-fake until you stood near them and the tiny white flowers released a perfume counter of scent.

With his shaved, shiny head, and bulldog neck, Mr. Clean of the ammonia cleaner blew his whistle. He was the varsity swim coach. He yelled out, "C'mon, ladies. Tomorrow, all this week, you have to swim harder. No, you swim hard."

A giant clock counted seconds, which was odd to Tina, because swimming wasn't basketball, but sort of the same. Most of the team swam two laps in a minute twenty. The girls climbed out of the pool as he waved his clipboard around. Tina saw Kiki, as tanned and compact as a suitcase, like she was part of the luggage that included the guy versions of Todd or Dave or Greg. They matched. Same build, same tan.

The drill sergeant coach dismissed the team with a final complaint. "What is wrong with you wimps this morning? All of you's save for Kiki and Janet were off on the IM drills. We leave at six on Saturday. Until then, no homecoming parties, none of that. Practice, school, sleep."

Once he dismissed them, Tina smiled and waved over to Kiki.

Kiki squinted at her.

Whatever.

Here was another thing Kiki apparently did without effort, as if high school was still sixth grade Girl Scouts and she'd get a badge for organizing a pizza dinner fundraiser. God. It was so unfair. Sure, sure, Tina could dog paddle and float, but swim a lap in forty seconds? Nope. Never.

Tina suspected it all started back in kindergarten. While she was watching Sesame Street on Mrs. Murdock's sticky carpet while her mom worked her shift at Safeway, Kiki and all the rest of them on the girls' varsity were learning side breathing. They had flip turns down before they could read. To Tina's calculations, by first grade she was behind.

For first period, Tina pretended to fumble with her book bag in the hallway and then slipped into the back row as the bell rang. As luck would have it, all the seats were taken save for one behind Kiki. As Tina slipped in, Kiki turned and said, "Janet's sitting there."

"But it's the last seat," Tina whispered.

Which was true. Mr. Paoletti, who was too handsome to be a math teacher, but here he was, took roll and droned on about Algebra II. There in front of her was Kiki's hair, as wavy and silky as a kimono sleeve. Even her hair was perfect. Tina's own hair was frayed and, if she didn't gel it, it sprouted into a haystack. Three weeks ago, just before church on Sunday, Carlo came in, stood beside her, reached out, touched her hair, and laughed. "Ma. Come look. Tina has broken hair." Her mom poked her head out of the kitchen and said only, "Tina, you permed it again? Waste of money. Come on, I'll get you a scarf."

Kiki whispered to Dee-Dee sitting beside her, "See look, I have the copper green sheen, can you believe it? The chlorine just coats it up."

Kiki had hair that was like the word from the crossword, what was it? The fairy tale word. Tresses, like Rapunzel, she had golden tresses. Her hand must have been too close to Kiki's head for too long or maybe she actually touched it. Whatever happened, the sound around her stopped. A hole of silence poured in and she couldn't hear them. Thirty faces, like jackals all turned, and in the deafening silence they sneered and stared at her.

Kiki jumped up. "Stop touching me."

Tina could not hear any sound at all, but she saw them and then finally the sound snapped back on, with everyone grinning and Mr.

Paoletti holding out a piece of chalk, "Tina, perhaps you'd like to finish the equation?"

Tina scribbled out x and y and the slope derivative on the chalk board. Mr. Paoletti was usually on the defensive, even if he had good sideburns. But not today. He nodded, as stunned and silent as the rest of the class that Tina with the wrinkled hair wrote it quickly, then slipped into her seat.

Janet Meloni and Kiki gave her the stink eye the next day in the hallway, a look and then their two heads met together as they passed by.

Dee-Dee Miller stopped the two of them, looked at Tina, and announced to the hallway, "It's on the last stall upstairs."

And it was. In the girls' bathroom upstairs, there, above the too loud Kotex metal box, in black marker, was a drawing of a girl. She was wearing a scarf with tufts of weedy hair sticking out and a hand outstretched toward the back of a girl sitting before her in class. The caption below the drawing: Freak Show in Algebra II!

Tina could not remove the drawing with soap, with a sponge, or with her fingernails, because it really was permanent marker. So she locked the door to the stall. When she returned the next day, the door was unlocked and the stall was completely wallpapered with graffiti. Lines spun around the drawing: She's touchy feely and oh-so-creepy; No-touching-Tina; High school is like Kindergarten! We keep our hands to ourselves!; Be careful, the groper might get you; Don't Touch!; She's a Freak House!

At least the last one had a point. Who didn't like the Commodores?

She blinked and hit her ears, anything to knock out the sound vacuum. She couldn't hear anything, staring at the bathroom stall, now a shrine to No Touch Tina, all riffs and rhymes.

She skipped school for the week. When her mom found out she missed class, she didn't leave the house for two weeks except for school and confirmation classes. Which was fine, because it meant she could work on her routine for try-outs for the cheerleading squad.

Tina tried.

She had practiced all summer when she wasn't babysitting or cleaning houses with Jo. She tried to copy a summer Olympics routine, all those gymnasts from the Soviet Union that looked like they were still ten years old doing contortionist back bends. She lay on the floor, putting her legs on the wall to stretch them out and after falling asleep she would wake up like Gumby, all bendy flexible. She practiced doing handstands against the wall but her shoulders screamed and she had to tape her wrists. She tried a back flip off her dad's Barca-lounger that landed her on her head and seeing double the rest of the week. Jo slammed the bedroom door all week. "T, we have two party clean-ups and mom said OK on using the Pinto and now you can't even vacuum," Jo said.

Okay, okay, so her routine wasn't to Cyndi Lauper or Madonna, but she had it down to Phil Collins, who had a bigger sound.

Today was the day. The gymnastics coach, Miss Morrison, sat with Kiki and Dee-Dee Fisher, who were the two co-captains and had clipboards and stopwatches. The three of them watched Tina like cats on a fence waiting for a pretty bird to land. She began her routine and was running, spinning, doing the Olga Corbett, then with arms extended at the end of the routine like the gymnast Nadia Comaneci.

She'd double sealed her panties, but somehow her shorts ripped. Were they staring at her bloody crotch? Her outfit was kind of like her routine, kind of like the Pinto, kind of like her hair. She danced and bounced but had never done gymnastics, so even her final Gumby splits were strained.

If she could just do a routine like Kiki, she could upgrade her whole life. No more St. Francis Cancer Auxiliary bargain bag clothing for her. No Greg or Dave choking hard as they spotted her mom's Prell-mobile. No bathroom stall that was an encyclopedia of

Satanic writing in permanent marker to her touching of Kiki's hair. God, Kiki was that actress with the man's name in *Blade Runner*. Daryl Hannah who did Kamikaze back flips and then fought like a blonde demon with her scissor kicks.

Kiki smiled with hard eyes. "Phil Collins was an interesting choice. Thank you so much." Tina didn't need to see who would make the team on the athletics board. She could see it in their eyes. When Sister D. asked her what was wrong the next day, she reminded Tina that at six feet, she'd been a point guard in the CYO, not a cheerleader. She said gently, "Try softball, Tina. It's more forgiving."

What Tina settled into instead was joining the Candy Stripes. In the spring of freshman year, her unofficial project of trying to get close to Kiki was through their volunteer drives. The Candies were busy little bees, organizing clothing drives, a car wash, canned food, and a visit to the senior home in Walnut Creek. When she arrived at the meeting, it was a bunch of other honor roll nerds, two girls she recognized from Algebra. There was either no carpool available or no carpool offered for her. On Saturday, she pleaded with Jo to drive her out to Walnut Creek.

"I'll do your laundry chores. Don't look so mad. Okay, two weeks of laundry. Please?"

Jo put the petal to the metal and still the Pinto farted along. By the time they got out to the office of the senior place for the Candy Stripes canned food drive and reading to seniors, something was off. The place looked like a golf resort of endless lawns and oldsters in Easter-egg colors. Jo slammed on the brakes behind a long sultry line of BMWs.

"You sure we got the right place T., I mean look at all this?"

Even the gate attendants had matching turquoise polo shirts. One of them who could've been the older brother to one of the Greg-Dave-Todds. As they approached, the attendants waved and pointed down the road. "The service entrance is down the road."

Jo laughed and wound her hair around her finger as she rolled down the window to chat. With Madonna blaring, even if the Pinto looked lame, they weren't.

Jo rolled up the window and gazed out at the luscious emerald sheath that surrounded them. Two golf carts whizzed by in which were seated the golf version of Ken and Barbie. They were trim and tanned. "You sure you want to do this, T.? It's like Club Med for old people."

"Sister D. told us to sign up for a confirmation project. So, here I am."

Jo patted the dashboard and laughed. "Okay, but I'm not sure if this place needs volunteers. You're on your own getting back."

Tina lugged the box inside the door where all the Candy Stripes were. The box split open and out rolled the Del Monte cans that were so dented, so forlorn, immigrants from the Soviet Union or boat people would shake their heads, No.

Once she hauled it inside the office of the senior living, there they were, Kiki and Janet Meloni. Kiki stared at her and didn't smile or say hi, but turned to Janet Meloni and said, "The shoes." Then they both did this thing, it was another SAT word. They snickered. Kiki wore white ballon Keds that Tina had seen in a Go-Go's video, so they were cool.

Sort of.

The Candy Stripes put out used books. Tina put out the bargain bin canned food. Only the Del Monte cans were so miserable, they would not go to anyone living in this senior resort. Maybe the landscapers would take them? Everyone scattered for home. Janet Meloni left early, the Rogers twins and the Algebra girls all got picked up, leaving behind Kiki and Tina.

Tina smiled and asked, "How are you getting home? Could I get a ride with you?"

Kiki ignored her and went back inside the office. For fifteen minutes. So Tina started walking out to the road to get the bus as Kiki's mom glided by. She stopped the big station wagon.

Kiki rolled down her window and without looking at her said, "My mom wants to know if you want a ride back."

"Your first time with the Candies?" Kiki's mom asked.

"Yes."

"What did you think?" Her mom didn't even look like a mom, more like Kiki's older sister. Like she could do a lap in forty seconds, too, before hopping off to get highlights and a manicure. Tina wanted the whole package: Kiki's hair, hell, her mom's hair, the Volvo, all of it.

"They didn't look like they need books or canned food," Tina said.

"You might be right about that," her mom smiled.

"But," Tina offered, "I heard there's another Candies volunteer opportunity. At least that's what Sister D.—I mean, Sister Dorothy —said."

"What?" Kiki asked. "At the church?"

"You should go, Kiki," Tina's mom said.

"But I haven't heard of this, Mom."

"I guess St. Joseph's hasn't announced it yet. But it's definitely happening," Tina said. From the back seat, she could almost hear Kiki rolling her eyes. Staring at the mother-daughter team of perfect hair from the back seat, Tina had to stop her hand from touching her hair. A thousand pats would not subdue the broken wire look from the bad perm.

"Maybe ask Dee-Dee to go. It's a great opportunity, " Tina's mom trilled.

"Okay, okay, yeah, but weird that Dee-Dee doesn't know about it," Kiki mumbled.

"Honey, Dee-Dee doesn't know everything."

"I guess. But still," Kiki said.

Finally, Tina got a break. She was going to be with Kiki away from school, just the two of them, alone together, and she would finally see, proof positive, that Tina wasn't a freak and that all she wanted was to be her friend. Then Kiki would pass notes and invite her to parties and say, *hey come sit next to me on the ski bus up to Tahoe* and *hey, have you met Steve?* And maybe, just maybe, whatever it was that was Kiki would pollinate and grow on Tina. Everything was lining up.

Two weeks later, Jo let her borrow the Pinto even though they weren't cleaning houses. Tina packed them a snack from Molinari's like her mom and dad did when family visited: cured salami and crackers and a bottle of the bright red slimy peppers. She picked Kiki up and they sped off to Saint Joseph's.

"Where is everybody? No lights are on," Kiki asked as they waited in the church parking lot.

"They'll be here. I brought us a snack while we wait. Here have some salami and crackers."

"Are you kidding, Tina? It's like a million calories. And who stabs food with a butcher knife?"

Tina handed her a piece of salami on a cracker. "Try it. My dad got it special from the city."

Kiki sighed. "There's no other Candies. No other cars even."

"No, no they're coming. I got the time wrong. It's a special event Sister D. planned for tonight."

"Look, just take me home. I mean, I don't know what's going on, but this does not look like a Candies event. At all."

So, Tina drove Kiki back to her block. Kiki's house, a large Spanish Mission style with oak trees in front, was dark.

Kiki rummaged in her purse. "I, oh, I forgot my keys."

"You can just come back to my house and wait for your parents to get back," Tina offered.

"What? No. There was no Sister whatever, no Candy Stripes. You lied."

"No. I didn't."

Kiki slammed the Pinto door. "You did. You are like what everyone says."

No. That wasn't true. How could she be saying this when Tina was trying so hard? And then the sound went out again. Kiki was out of the car, a blue shadow moving toward her house with no lights on.

When she tried to piece together the sequence of events from that night, Tina could never be sure. Because of the sound gap. She'd fallen into a silent hole again.

She was standing over Kiki, who was thrashing around, scrambling to get to her feet. She stood and wobbled off, her hands at her chest, holding the dark syrup seeping onto her white shirt. Tina looked down at her dumb too-white too-big dorky shoes that were splotched. She laughed quietly, repeating the line from Miss Jamison's Shakespeare class, "Out, damn spot."

Everyone told her what happened, but Tina wasn't sure. She wanted to scare Kiki to get her to knock it off. Like in the summer when she was practicing her cheerleading routine. She jumped and fell and had the wind knocked right out of her. She was so stunned, she had to slow down for two days. She remembered cutting Molinari's salami, to Kiki crying, to the end of her old life. Then the beginning of her new one. Lots of time alone in the cell. The minute she was outside the cell, she was never alone, with everyone staring at her like she was, well, like she was No-Touching-Tina who is touchy-feely-and-oh-so-creepy.

Neecie and Natasha were shaking the bed and Tina woke up and finally someone turned the sound back on. She was not back on the block with oak trees and sprinklers turning on as Kiki staggered around crying like she was drunk.

She was in Ventura. She'd been dreaming about Daniel and the lions and Kiki from school, the two of them together. Natasha was yelling and Tina whispered only, "Daniel. I, I, just wanted to teach her a lesson."

ROSALYN

KATIE NELSON STONE

1904

Agust of wind rolled through the garden. At first, pleasant and warm, it breezed through the wisps that dangled from my chignon and landed against my champagne flushed cheeks. Then, it turned cold. The wind clung to my arms and traveled down the back of my neck, sending a shiver though my shoulders and reminding me of the earlier perfectly warm June weather.

I shook off the chill but should have taken it as an omen.

The event was nearly over. The annual Garden Party my estate hosted was, by most opinions, a huge success.

Drinks had been drunk. Food consumed. Strangers met. Friends reunited. Laughter shared. Arguments started. Dishes accumulated, and staff worked around the remaining partygoers to clean up spilled wine and abandoned appetizers.

The candles on the table, nearly burned to their nubs, flickered as another midnight breeze rolled through the garden.

A part of me felt relief it was over. I wouldn't have to host this event for another three hundred and sixty-five days. But, now that the party was nearly over, another part of me felt different. Not morose, nor regret. Something deeper and more akin to—panic.

The grandfather clock inside chimed twelve times, the gongs traveling through the open French doors and out into the garden's patio.

Midnight.

The long table in the garden at my father's house seated upwards of one hundred people. But now, just five guests remained.

Richard, Mr. and Mrs. Wainscott, Eliza, and an individual I knew not.

Guests attended the annual party to gorge themselves on the free food and drink. Or to beset their eyes on Conrad Mangum's famed estate and gather gossip that could be shared at dinner parties or luncheons for the next month.

Blood suckers, most of them, yet I couldn't see them go. Not yet.

The head of the table was my throne for the evening. I glanced to my left, where Richard Bosalin sat. He turned his shoulders toward me and leaned forward. Richard was a divorcé and nearly ten years my senior. The man was too dull to be slick, but too slimy to be endearing. Despite this, I'd entertained the idea of his courtship once—the man would wait on me hand and foot. He was handsome, with an even handsomer bank account. The prospect was appealing, and Mrs. Doherty, our house manager, begged me to consider. But could I commit myself to a lifetime of personhood living under the moniker Rosalyn Bosalin? Absolutely not. Atrocious. Despite my refusal to be his party date, or to be taken to dinner, Richard still tried, and I couldn't tell if I respected him more or less because of it.

Next to Richard sat Mr. and Mrs. Wainscott. Dale and Kitty, as they requested they be called, were transplants from St. Louis. I earned their acquaintance due to an unfortunate predicament I found myself in earlier in the week. My horse threw a shoe, leaving me stranded, and they happened upon my situation and gave me a ride home. When they saw all the pre-party activities in the garden, they practically invited themselves. Mrs. Doherty made sure they received an invitation.

Kitty giggled as Dale poured her another glass of champagne.

Across from Kitty sat Eliza Kennedy. Eliza was my best friend. We'd known each other since St. Bishops' boarding school. Back then, we'd been inseparable. Seats next to one another in every class. Dormitory beds pushed together. I often spent holiday parties at Eliza's parents' estate. But lately, things felt off between us— electric, charged, and cross. Eliza and I were close like sisters and fought like sisters. It was not uncommon for her to ignore me for weeks at a time. But we always came back together, eventually, and I shrugged these bouts off as the woes of early adulthood grating on our friendship. No bother, things would right themselves out, and why make an issue out of something when it need not to be?

Lastly, seated directly to my left—the priest. I had absolutely no clue how he came to be at the garden party.

Or why he was still at the party.

He sat relaxed, with one arm in his lap and the other draped over Eliza's chair beside him. He laughed easily and talked just the right amount.

From the moment I met him, I distrusted him.

"Lovely party, Miss Rosalyn," Kitty said.

"A total smash." Richard shrugged off his jacket and placed it around my shoulders. I made eye contact with Eliza, who stifled a laugh.

"Luckiest moment of our lives, bumping into you." Dale picked up his glass. "Such a lovely surprise."

Eliza sat back in her chair, the pink chiffon of her dress rustling slightly as she settled in. "I'm surprised as well."

Dale laughed. "That we received an invite?"

"No," Eliza said. "That Rosalyn saw fit to accept assistance."

The table laughed as one and I rolled my eyes in good fun.

Mrs. Doherty appeared beside me and cleared a few of the remaining plates on the table. A woman well into her fifties, she had been the manager of our estate for the last fifteen years, but she'd been with us for nearly thirty.

I avoided her gaze, because I knew one look would convey a litany of opinions; either displaying displeasure that the party crawled on, or worry if I was all right. Those were Mrs. Doherty's two extremes—annoyed with my behavior or concerned over my wellbeing.

"Everything well?" She looked at me.

"Everything is just splendid, Mrs. Doherty," Eliza said. "Please, keep the refreshments coming."

She gave a quick tight smile. "Happy to hear you had a nice time, Miss Eliza. You seemingly always do."

I snorted a laugh as Eliza lifted her chin.

"I heard someone say this party has been a tradition for nearly fifty years," Kitty said.

Mrs. Doherty cleared a few more of our dishes, my dessert plate included. I reached, taking it out of her hands.

She smiled at Kitty, warmer than she had with Eliza. Genuine. She'd been so appreciative when the Wainscots helped me home. "It is," she said. "Longer than I've been here, even."

"I was unaware that the Mangum lineage had established themselves in Boston for such a length of time," Richard said.

Mrs. Doherty smiled. "It's a Bethesda family tradition, actually."

"My mother's family," I said. "Her estate has upheld this tradition for generations—always upon the occasion of the Summer Solstice."

"Yes, it was Mrs. Mangum's family tradition, God rest her soul.

And Miss Rosalyn will not be the one to break that tradition," Mrs. Doherty said. "No matter how hard she stomps."

"I do not stomp," I countered. "Not anymore."

Kitty reached over Dale and placed a hand on my arm. "I lost my mother this year, too."

I moved my arm toward the dessert plate, dislodging Kitty's gesture. "My mother passed away years ago."

Kitty pulled her hand back onto her lap.

Mrs. Doherty squeezed my shoulder. "We're sorry to hear of your mother's passing, Mrs. Wainscott. It's hard and forever will be."

Kitty and Mrs. Wainscott shared a look, one that seemed too familiar. The champagne had my head feeling fizzy and I had to look away toward the garden.

My first memory was of my mother's annual garden party. Playing on the lawn with the other children. Mrs. Doherty tying a perfect bow on the back of my dress. My mother's arms as she picked me up. Fighting sleep while in my father's lap, his cigar smoke encircling the two of us.

The garden and our house had once been filled with laughter and family and love.

Now, I looked forward to midnight of the party. Because it meant the longest day was over, and the party would soon be, too.

Until next year.

I didn't say any of this to my guests. Not that they would have heard me.

"Nice to see you here, Father," Mrs. Doherty said. "It's not every year our Garden Party welcomes a clergyman."

I popped a piece of strawberry pie into my mouth then frowned. "Unfortunately."

Mrs. Doherty pinched the underside of my arm, harder than a tease, but softer than a punishment. "You are in God's company."

I scrunched my face together and looked up at her. "Funny," I said. "I didn't see him on the guest list."

The priest laughed and Kitty and Mrs. Doherty nearly swooned. "Thank you for hosting such a wonderful party. I feel honored to have been included."

"Yes, and who *did* include you?" I asked.

Mrs. Doherty's hand moved to the back of my chair. A warning. "I attend mass at St. Joseph's, so I'm afraid I've never witnessed your sermon."

"No bother," the priest said. "You've seen one, you've seen them all. All the Latin and such."

The group laughed and the candles flickered.

"Church is dreadfully boring," I said after the laughter quieted.

"Rosalyn don't be rude," Mrs. Doherty started.

"I didn't mean it maliciously, Father. It's only an opinion."

The priest placed a hand over his heart. "No offense taken. I appreciate your honest candor. I must wonder, however, if perhaps you just haven't found your church yet."

"I am well acquainted. I attended Catholic boarding school."

"A building isn't the only place for devotion," he said. "True worship can happen wherever you are."

I rolled my eyes.

The priest laughed again. "That sounded trite. What I mean is, faith can be found outside the walls of the church."

"Wonderfully said, Father." Mrs. Doherty leaned over me and picked the plate up off the table. I did not protest this time, as it was now empty. "We're so pleased to hear you all had a nice time this evening."

"Oh dear," Kitty said, grasping at the armrests of her chair. "We've overstayed our welcome."

"Nonsense," I said, waving Kitty down. "Mrs. Doherty is just being pleasant."

Mrs. Doherty squeezed my shoulder. "You all have a wonderful rest of your evening. I'll be in the kitchen if you need me."

She turned and walked toward the house. I watched her go. She'd worked for our estate since my mother was a child. She witnessed her marriage to my father. She knew my father, my family. She'd watched my father leave. Mrs. Doherty was the one person still on this world who knew me the best. And it was only because I paid her to.

"What a wonderful woman," Kitty said.

"Old Mrs. Doherty was practically born in this house," Eliza said. "She'll probably die in it, too—"

"Mrs. Doherty is a wonder," I interjected. "This party runs like clockwork because of her."

"It was very kind of her to invite us," Dale said. "Kind of you, too."

Kitty leaned forward, eyes big. "I did wonder if *he* might be here tonight."

I sighed and leaned back in my chair. Perhaps Mrs. Doherty could return and request they all leave in haste.

"I informed my dear wife that *he* is probably too busy writing his next book," Dale said.

"The *final* book," Richard said. I could almost see the dollar signs reflecting in his eyes.

"Sorry," the priest said. "Perhaps I've missed something."

"Conrad Mangum is Rosalyn's father, Father." Eliza hiccupped.

I forced a tight smile across my lips, hoping the crinkle in my eyes looked sincere.

"Sorry," the priest's head swiveled between me and Eliza. "*The* Conrad Mangum? Author of—"

"*The Sunset Cowboys.*" Kitty clapped her hands.

I took a sip of my wine. "That is my father."

Eliza sneered. "Rosalyn acts all coy, but her father's fame has allowed her quite a luxurious life. Fortunate, isn't it, that some can play at humility while standing upon a pile of gold?"

No one seemed to pay Eliza's tirade any mind. Perhaps because she was drunk. Perhaps because she was being rude. Or perhaps, because that's what Conrad and his books did to people.

Dale looked to the garden and sighed. "I remember the first time I read *Pal Comes Knocking*."

"The first, because he's read it multiple times," Kitty said.

"Of course," Dale continued. "When the gunman opened the trapdoor —"

"And found the undertaker with his wife—" Richard joined in.

"—I nearly awoke the whole block."

Kitty set down her glass of wine. "He certainly woke his wife!"

The table laughed again. I sipped my wine and looked to the kitchen door where Mrs. Doherty had been. A part of me wished she'd come check on me again. Tell all these people that the party was over.

But I don't want them to leave.

When I looked back at the table, the priest's eyes met mine. I quickly looked away.

"I was quite shocked myself when I found out who Rosalyn's father was," Richard said. "I'd known Rosalyn for months, but it wasn't until her father won The Literary Prestige Award that I knew of her relation."

"That award is inside," Eliza said. "Rosalyn, grab it for your guests."

I shook my head at the mention of my father's Prestige.

Eliza tutted, turning her lips into a pout. "Come now, guests. Let us change the subject. Rosalyn does not like talk of Conrad."

"Are you close with your father?"

"Kitty—" Dale admonished.

My eyes bounced back to the priest, who was still looking at me, before I settled on Kitty. "My father lives a separate life. I have not seen him in many years."

"I'm sorry," Kitty said, her cheeks turning red. "The champagne has loosened my tongue."

"He writes often." I didn't quite understand why I said that.

Eliza snorted. "And Rosalyn ignores him."

My collar itched. "I write."

"Only when necessary." Eliza turned to the priest. "He's invited her out to Oregon at least a dozen times. She ignores his request every time."

"Well," the priest said, "I understand travel might be hard."

"You mean for a woman of my upbringing?" I asked.

He shrugged sympathetically. "Or it might just be hard."

"My apologies for babbling on about him," Dale cut in, obviously feeling guilty. "I didn't realize you had a contentious relationship."

"No need to apologize. I could not care less," I said, not bothering to correct him or avoid the accusation. "If I were to travel to Oregon, I'd miss out on these types of dinners with wonderful folks like yourself." I lifted my wine glass in salute before taking a large drink and signaling the waitstaff for more.

Eliza leaned back in her chair and set her eyes on me. "Yes, poor, poor Rosalyn Mangum, left behind in a mansion, drowning in champagne, and gorging herself to death on caviar. We all feel utterly devastated for you."

"Come now," Dale said. "Let us not allow the champagne to create regrets for the morning."

"Rosalyn has no regrets," Eliza continued. "Nothing any of us ever said to her could hurt her or make her happy. She exists to indulge before moving on to the next thing she only partially decides to participate in."

The party grew silent as the air stretched between us.

Eliza and I made eye contact, and I held it, unblinking in silence.

She was looking for a rise out of me. Years of outbursts taught me indifference to be the most powerful weapon in this friendship. But —a small piece of me thought—she was right, and she was my only friend left because of it.

Richard cleared his throat. "Father, did you study at St. Joseph's?"

"Yes, do tell us a bit about yourself," Kitty said. "You're so young."

"This is only my second year after being ordained," the priest said. "I work as a chaplain for a prison."

Kitty gasped and covered her mouth. "Good heavens."

"How'd you get the unlucky draw then, Father?" Richard asked.

"On the contrary. I quite enjoy my assignment."

"Really?" Eliza gestured toward the rest of the table. "Then, you're a better man than most."

"I don't know about that," the priest said as I yawned. "I find working with the downtrodden invigorating. Rejuvenating. Inspiring. Among other adjectives."

The table laughed. Kitty beamed at the young priest. "Aren't you afraid?"

The priest shook his head. "Frustrated, yes. Sad, most of the time. But afraid? Never. Most of these convicts—these men—have been dealt an incredibly difficult hand in life. Each with their own sorrows, their own troubles, and their own techniques at dealing with those troubles. Most, if not all, are impoverished and have had to find alternative methods of survival. But they're the same as you and me. They dream. They worry. They fight. They laugh. They've just taken a different path than my own."

Kitty and Eliza tutted at the priest's monologue, while Richard and Dale grunted in admiration.

I yawned. Louder this time.

The priest looked at me, then down at his lap, smiling a little. "My apologies. Here I am, prattling on. I find that often I get carried away when talking of my work." He looked at each table attendant, his eyes finally landing on me. "What carries you away?"

Eliza set down her champagne glass. "A party question!"

"Haven't played one of these since boarding school," Richard said, leaning forward. "I'll go first. None of you would ever guess, but I'm rather passionate about trains."

The group oohed politely as Richard continued. "Ask me anything about timetables, engine, make, model, and I'm sure I'll be able to tell you."

"No, thank you," I mumbled.

But Kitty said, louder, "I wouldn't even know what to ask! What a fascinating hobby."

Richard turned to Dale. "Your turn."

Dale opened his mouth, but his wife intercepted him. "And you can't say work! Insurance shouldn't be anyone's passion."

"She's got me there," Dale said, placing a hand on his wife's. "If I can't talk about my career, well then I guess what most carries me is —the Spinone."

"The what?" Eliza asked.

"Lord have mercy," Kitty sighed as Richard chuckled.

"The Italian Spinone," he said. "A beautiful breed of a dog. Excellent hunters. Extraordinary retrievers. Smarter than any man you'll ever meet."

Kitty placed a hand on Dale's arm. "When Dale was a child, he traveled with his parents abroad. While on an excursion with his father's college, Dale got lost. It was a hunter's Spinone that found him. He's been obsessed ever since."

"I'd love to own one, but they haven't been made popular State side, unfortunately."

"One day." Kitty patted his arm.

"Indeed. Your turn, Kit."

"That's easy. Our son."

Dale planted a kiss on his wife's hand.

"And you, Miss Eliza?" the priest asked.

Eliza's hooded eyes scanned the table before landing on mine. "I love to write."

"How convenient," Dale said. "To have a best friend with a famous author for a father."

Like a switch, Eliza's charm was back. "I keep asking for an introduction but—alas."

"Dear Eliza," I said. "I've told you—the next time I see him, I'll be sure to make an introduction."

Eliza laughed. "At this rate, I'll be dead by the time you see your father again."

I opened my mouth to respond, but the priest cut in. "And what carries you, Miss Rosalyn?"

"Nothing."

"Nothing?" Kitty asked.

"Does planning dinner parties count?" I said.

"No," Eliza said. "You just attend."

"Agreed," Richard said. "It must be something that pulls you. That drives you forward. It can't be something passively participated in."

"Sorry to disappoint, but I'm carried nowhere." I leaned back in my chair and held my arms out wide. "I'm floating through life, nary a care in the world, as if I were a newborn babe."

Kitty patted the table in front of me. "You'll find something. Perhaps after you're married."

Richard lifted his eyebrows. "Yes, perhaps marriage helps."

I scoffed. *Said the divorcé.* "You are all being silly. I'm perfectly content."

"But not happy." Eliza's eyes hardened as they lingered on mine.

My brow twitched. "I think you've enjoyed too much of the free champagne, Eliza."

"Is it not free for you, too?"

"Rosalyn cares about money," Richard threw up his hands. "That's something."

"We *all* care about money." Kitty laughed.

"The greatest evil of the world," said the priest.

"I thought we said our professional careers couldn't count," Dale looked around, bemused. "If I can't list my work as an insurance agent then Miss Rosalyn certainly can't list her fortune."

The conversation had gone awry. I typically didn't mind being the center of attention. But there was a difference between attention and scrutiny. I shook my head. "I didn't mean—"

"Despite our spat, I quite agree with Rosalyn." Eliza took a long sip of champagne, then set her glass down. "We are being silly."

A wave of relief washed over. My friend was defending me. "Thank you."

"This debate surrounding Rosalyn's purpose is moot." Her eyes flickered toward me. "Because she has none. Ros will never marry. Ros will never have children. And Ros will certainly never work."

"Stop it."

"To do so, one must try putting forth a modicum of effort, and that is not how Rosalyn Mangum lives her life."

"Enough." I slapped my hand against the table. Kitty and Dale jumped.

"Oh dear," Eliza said. "Have I struck a nerve?"

"You'd just love that, wouldn't you?"

"At least it would mean you cared."

"But, dear Eliza, I don't care."

"You don't care about anything?" Kitty's eyes looked sad and full of pity.

"That's not what I meant."

"There's only one thing that gets under Rosalyn's skin," Eliza said. "And it's not money troubles or uninvited guests, and it certainly isn't annoying suitors."

Eliza pushed her chair away from the table and stood. The guests shifted, awkwardly, looking to one another.

"Perhaps it's time for my wife and I to call it a night," Dale said.

"Perhaps it's time for *all of us* to call it a night," the priest agreed.

If they leave, you'll be alone again.

I opened my mouth to protest, but Eliza turned to address the table.

"I'll be right back," she said. "I promise. Stay put!"

I took a long drag of my wine as Eliza's footsteps disappeared into the house. She'd had too much to drink again, and was probably asking Mrs. Doherty for something to nibble on.

"Look what I have here," Eliza emerged from the house, giggling. She stopped at the top of the stone patio staircase, jutting her leg out and lifting an object toward the side of her face.

I turned toward her. "Return that."

"Come now, Rosalyn." Eliza moved the crystal object from one hand to another. "You are responsible for your guest's entertainment."

"Eliza."

"And what do you have?" Kitty asked.

My stomach flipped as Eliza held the object over her head. "Conrad's Literary Prestige Award. Mrs. Doherty keeps it in Conrad's office. I've told Rosalyn—you should display that in the front room. But she never listens to—"

All it took from Eliza was a hiccup and an unsteady step, and the award toppled from her hands to the patio's stone steps, shattering into pieces.

Eliza's hands moved from her mouth to her heart.

The crystal pieces speckled the patio's floor, glimmering in the flickering candlelight. Mrs. Doherty would have to clean it up later.

I took a deep breath, lifted my chin, and turned to my guests. "No bother."

The table sat still, with their eyes on me. I looked from the priest then to Eliza, who stood with her mouth agape.

"No bother?" Shock creased Eliza's forehead.

I willed my heart to slow and my face not to flush. "Conrad has won other awards."

"But this was his first award," Eliza said. Her face shifted from worry to disgust. "Truly? 'No bother?'"

"Why are you picking this fight?" I asked, lightheaded due to my increasing anger and overconsumption of champagne. "Would you prefer I scream and curse?"

"I'm not picking at anything." Eliza shrugged nonchalantly. "Your behavior just shocks me, is all. You're—"

"I'm what?" I said, my annoyance uncontrollable.

"You're wasting it!" Eliza stepped down the patio stairs, kicking the shards of crystal. "You have the means to do what you please, but none of the drive to do what pleases you. Nothing bothers you enough to care."

"And you do?" I asked. "You could be writing. You could be meeting other people. You could be feeding the poor, or helping orphaned babies." I snorted. "But instead, you ruin my father's property."

"I apologized."

"You did not."

"You think you're the center of everyone's world, don't you?"

"No." I hated how my voice rose an octave as I said it. "I do not. I'm the center of nobody's world."

"Poor, poor, Rosalyn," Eliza said. "The daughter of a famous author, who has a maid and doesn't have to work." She snorted. "Nobody feels pity for you, I'm afraid."

"I don't care!"

"You're pathetic. You're a drain of resources. It's no wonder your father left."

"Ladies," Richard said. "Let's calm down."

Eliza turned on him. "Why are you even here, Richard?"

Confusion spread across his face. "I was invited."

Eliza laughed. "Not by Rosalyn. She can't stand you."

"No need to be rude, Miss Eliza." Kitty looked at Richard.

"What was it you said about him?" Eliza said to me. "Richard's too dull to be slick, but too slimy to be endearing." Eliza laughed. "But in the end, attention flatters Rosalyn, so she'll keep you around until she's bled you dry. Or finds another specimen for her to examine, a fan to fawn over her. But afterward, she'll never speak to you again. And you'll be left wondering if you made it all up."

Richard opened his mouth to respond, then closed it.

I could have defended him. Told the table it was a lie, or that Eliza had had too much to drink that evening.

But I didn't.

Dale, Kitty, and the priest looked at Richard and Richard looked at me.

He cleared his throat and thrummed his knuckles on the table. "My, the time's grown late. I better be going. It was a pleasure meeting all of you." Standing, he walked toward me and pulled the jacket from my shoulders. "Please give my thanks to Mrs. Doherty."

Eliza laughed as Richard draped his jacket over his arm and walked into the darkness.

"You're cruel," I said.

"You're the one who was speechless to his defense." Eliza plopped in her chair.

"That was uncouth," Kitty said. "Really. Poor Richard. You two should be ashamed of yourselves."

Both Eliza and I turned to her.

"You're about as useful as a hole in a bucket," Eliza shouted.

"You're not my mother," I said at the same time.

I took a deep breath and closed my eyes for a moment. When I opened them, the hurt was all over Kitty's face.

"Oh dear," she said. "And here I thought we were having a nice time together."

A wave of guilt passed over me. Kitty was sweet. She didn't deserve to be accosted by two friends in a disagreement.

"We were—"

"Come, Kitty." Dale stood so abruptly that his chair fell back behind him. "It's time we go."

"You don't have to. Please—"

Eliza interrupted me with a laugh. "Go ahead. Leave. Everyone leaves Rosalyn Mangum eventually. Isn't that what you've always said, Ros?"

I watched as Kitty and Dale disappeared, then turned to Eliza, narrowing my eyes. "You look down on my disposition when what you should feel is elation."

"Elation? At your indifference?"

"If I truly cared, I'd have you arrested for desecrating my father's property. But you mean too much to me as a friend, so I won't."

"A friend? We haven't been real friends in years." Eliza searched for her purse.

"Are you leaving?"

"Of course I'm leaving," Eliza said.

"Because of a stupid fight?"

Eliza gathered her shawl and gloves.

"Stay," I pleaded. Eliza turned toward me, her expression open and expectant. But why should I apologize when she'd been the one nagging me the entirety of the evening. "You'll never fetch a cabby at this hour."

"I should have dropped you years ago."

"But you haven't, because you need me." *And I need you,* I thought, but didn't dare say. Not right now. Not tonight.

"I do not," Eliza said. "Nobody does. And nobody ever will, the way you're behaving."

"Did you hear me?" I asked. "I don't care that you use me for my money. I can connect you to my father. Or perhaps his publisher. I—"

"Stop it," Eliza shouted. "Just stop it. You don't care about my passions or successes. You said so yourself. I've heard these promises time and time again, and they're completely empty. Just like you. You're as useless as a fifth wheel. Utterly good for nothing."

She turned on her heel and walked away from the table.

Eliza was leaving. My only friend. No matter that she was a bad one. At least with her, I wasn't completely alone in the world.

For years, I'd let her eat my food, drink my drink, spend my money. I'd listened to her complain about her family and her bad suitors. I'd sat through boring plays and bland symphonies. For her. And now, she was gone.

"Fine," I yelled at her retreating back. "Leave. See if I care. Good luck with your future. And your husband. And your babies. You're going to make a *wonderful* housewife."

But Eliza kept walking.

In all our fights, Eliza had never walked away.

The priest cleared his throat. "That was—something."

"She'll be back tomorrow." I was sure of it.

"Are you all right?"

I faced him. "Of course. This is a normal Friday evening for me and Eliza."

"Do you two always fight like that?"

"Not always. Sometimes we throw things. Other times we cry."

"Relationships can be complex."

"Really? Even for a priest?"

"Especially for a priest," he said. "My mother still cries every time she sees me, and my brother hasn't spoken to me in nearly three years."

"Heathens?"

He shook his head. "They just had a different view of how I should live my life."

"So—" I picked up a champagne glass. "We're both failures in following societal norms. Cheers to that."

The priest smiled. His champagne glass dinged as it hit mine, filling the dark night with its expensive song before he returned it to the table, the drink untouched.

I tilted the flute back and finished my glass. "It's bad luck not to drink after a toast."

Silence stretched between us and I watched the priest's face change in thought, then relax.

"What?"

"It's not my place."

"Oh, now you're shy. Out with it."

"You said you don't care that your friend used you for your money and connections. I take issue with that."

"It's not about you, I'm afraid."

The priest continued, as if I'd never said anything. "Perhaps you should care."

I sighed in a way that would let him know I was annoyed, or that the conversation was off limits. Either one, as long as he changed the topic. "What's the point?"

He considered me before turning his face to the sky. I followed his glance and was met by a blanket of stars. Despite being a night owl, it was rare that I stopped to look upwards when out on the town or pacing the halls of my house.

It was nice. To sit in silence and look at the stars, without expectations or judgement. With my head tilted back, staring at the vastness of the night's sky, I was reminded of the ocean. Swimming, specifically. My father hadn't necessarily taught me to swim, but rather to float. When we visited the shore together, he and I would spend hours in the water, belly up, watching the clouds move across the sky. Something I hadn't done since I was a little girl, but something I once loved—something I still loved, nonetheless. In the water, I always felt free.

Despite Eliza's assumptions about my position in life, this sense of freedom visited rarely in my adulthood. But as I gazed up at the star-laden sky, I was reminded, just for a moment, of the feeling.

At the table in the garden, in that moment, I felt peace.

A shooting star blazed across the blackened sky, illuminating its path for one fleeting moment.

"Look!" The priest pointed.

But I wasn't on the seashore, belly up.

I grunted in return, then turned my face away from the sky.

The priest continued to stargaze. Eventually, he said, "Apathy has always been my least favorite sin."

"Apathy? What's the commandment, Father? Thou shalt give a fig?"

The priest laughed, a genuine, big laugh that almost startled me. I laughed in return.

He wiped at the corner of his eye. "At least with the other sins, you have a bit of fun doing them."

"Gluttony and lust, certainly," I said. "But I'd argue there's no fun in envy." Eliza's departure flashed before my eyes, and for a brief moment a wave of hot shame came over me. I blinked, and shook the feeling from my heart. I did what I always did when I felt this way. I chose to forget about it.

The priest nodded. "Yes, but at least there's purpose in envy. You want something. You *need* it. You obsess, and you care enough to eat yourself away on the inside over how jealous you are. Apathy —or, sloth, as the Bible calls it—convinces its victim to live a life disconnected."

"Disconnected?"

"Detached. Aloof. Isolated."

"Those are just words to me, Father."

"Exactly." He pointed a finger at me and smiled. "Apathy leads to estrangement of one's mental and physical surroundings, for starters. And relationships are nearly impossible when one is overly apathetic."

"Is there a reason why you've brought this sin to my table?"

"I think it's obvious after what happened tonight," he said. "How you treated Richard, Kitty, and Dale. How you treated Eliza."

"I was mean."

The priest shook his head. "They were all mean, greedy, and opportunistic in their own right. But you—you were apathetic to it all."

"How come I'm the only one being scrutinized?" I asked. "Call the others back to the table. We'll tell Richard he suffers from lust. Kitty and Dale are prideful. Eliza is—greed, envy, wrath. She's most of them."

"You joke. The Devil's distraction from finding true light."

A slight sweat formed on my lower back. I was running out of ways to change the conversation. I leaned back in my chair and crossed my arms over my chest. "Why is it that you care?"

"It's my calling to care. How can you not?"

Heat rushed to my face and my head felt light. A wave of rage rushed through me. "You know nothing about me,"

He laughed. "I've just spent the entire evening with you."

"You attend one party, witness one fight with a friend, and feel justified assigning me sins?"

"I'm taught to read people quickly," he said. "One of my many priestly gifts."

"You think because you wear that collar that you're above the rest of them, but you're not. You're just another man who thinks he knows a woman because they shared a bottle of champagne."

"I think I know why you indulge in the sin you do." He placed his elbows on the table, steepling his hands, and tapped his lips with his forefinger. The crickets chirped, rhythmically. "Because to show that you actually cared—for others, for yourself—would open you up to feeling. And feelings are—"

"Frivolous," I finished, attempting to joke.

His eyes bore into mine. "Try again."

My smile faltered at the intensity of his stare, and I had no other option but to try honesty. "Feelings are dangerous."

He pointed his steepled fingers at me then lifted his hands into a shrug. "But—that's life, I'm afraid. People come and people go. Friends last and they fade. People are born and people die."

"And we're just supposed to sit back with this guilt, this shame, this unbearable grief, and take it?"

"What else can you do, Rosalyn?"

"You can furl into yourself." My voice was louder than I meant. "Avoid everyone that can know you or anything that can hurt you."

"Sounds a bit like cowardice."

"At least it's safe."

"Then I ask you, Miss Rosalyn, if you're not living a life exposed, then what is the point of living life at all?"

His gaze bore into me.

I turned away from him and gazed out to the garden.

In the moonlight, the garden was alive. Bugs swirling in the lamp light. Bats dipping between tree branches. A dark night sky set against a garden so thick and lush it felt impossible to decipher where the garden stopped and where the darkness began.

"What's your favorite sin, Father?"

He looked up at the stars. "I'd like to be greedier."

"I'm sure you could ask some of your fellow clergymen about that one."

He stood and pushed in his chair. "They need no reminding."

"Are you leaving? Stay."

"I must go. At this rate, the sun will be up soon."

"So, stay and see what God's created."

He smiled. "Nice try. I do hope to see you again soon, Miss Rosalyn."

"Perhaps later this week," I said. "We could get dinner?"

"You know where you can find me if you need me."

"I don't, actually."

But he'd already started his descent into the path through the rose bushes.

"You never said where you are stationed, Father."

The priest kept walking. Into the roses my mother once planted, past the irises I'd loved as a child.

"Father," I called, louder this time.

But he never returned my plea.

My lip quivered. Another person, leaving. Already gone.

The candle beside me flickered as it burned down to the stick, the wax spilling over and accumulating on the party's table.

I sniffed, then blinked before the tears could spill over my eyelashes.

To hell with them. All of them. The party guests. The priest. Eliza. My father. I didn't need any of them. I didn't need anyone.

I reached for the open bottle of champagne and placed it to my lips, tilting backwards.

"Rosalyn Bethesda Mangum!"

I didn't need to turn around to know it was Mrs. Doherty.

"Don't you think you've had enough? It's nearly one in the morning!"

"I'm not a child anymore."

Her footsteps slowed as she reached my chair. "What's happened? Where's Eliza?"

"She left."

Mrs. Doherty sighed. "Finally."

I turned toward her. "What do you mean?"

She sat down beside me. "She hasn't been a good friend to you in years, Rosalyn."

"Will you stay?"

"The night?" Mrs. Doherty said. "I suppose I have to, since the hour is late."

She was teasing, and I knew she was, but it undid me. The tears I'd held in poured out as my face crumpled into my hands.

"What's this then?" Mrs. Doherty said as she hugged my shoulders.

"Everyone always leaves me."

"I don't live here."

"You know what I mean. No one ever chooses *me*."

"About a hundred people chose you this evening, it seems."

"That wasn't me."

Mrs. Doherty stroked my head, like she used to when I was a girl. "It's your house."

"They came for my absent father's fame and my dead mother's legacy."

"Neither of which are here."

"Do twist the knife." I sniffed, then went to wipe my nose on my skirt. Mrs. Doherty stopped my hand and gave me a look before pulling a hanky out of her pocket and handing it to me.

"*You* are here." She sat back in her seat. "And you don't have to be."

I sighed. "Not this again."

"He wrote you again, you know."

"I know," I said.

"What did it say?"

"The usual."

"An invitation, then?"

"To go to Oregon," I said. "Meet him where he is. And what—watch him sit there and write?"

"Why not?"

"Oregon? Really?"

"What do you have here?"

"A house? A carriage? Champagne?"

"All of which will be here when you return," she said. "Go. Get some fresh air. Milk a cow. Flirt with a cowboy."

"Revolting," I said. "To all of that."

Mrs. Doherty stood. "You are expecting a different outcome from the same repetitive actions. It's time for something different. Now, get to bed. No more wine." She took the glass from my hand and walked toward the house.

The light grew dimmer as the lanterns were turned down and the candles burned out. But I knew that the darkness of my bedroom would be worse than the darkness of the garden.

Heels clacked against the stairs.

The waitress, a few years my junior, stacked plates and glasses on her tray, no doubt having been given instructions by Mrs. Doherty, regardless of whether or not I was there.

Mrs. Doherty knew I'd be here.

"Lovely evening," the waitress said.

It was after midnight at my dead mother's garden party at my absent father's estate.

And I wasn't ready for bed yet.

I turned to the young woman. "Care for a smoke?"

THE SISTERS GRIM

SALLY K LEHMAN

Once upon a time... that's how these stories begin, isn't it? Yet there are so many upon-a-times in the history of... well, history... that this once-upon-a-time stood out. And it all began with a single cell in a single body that grew and grew and grew until it split into other cells which grew and grew and grew. And when the growth of the cells continued unabated for many months, that body fell ill...

They met in a sterile white room with a gray patient table, two awkward metal chairs, and a short stool on wheels. When the doctor came in, he took the rolling stool making a gesture for Francine Rigby to stay seated in her chair. He didn't bother to look at the file folder in his hand—meaning he'd read the pertinent details before coming in.

"Ms. Rigby, the results are not good," the doctor said. "As you know, we caught your esophageal cancer at stage four, and the radiation treatments have not accomplished what we'd hoped for."

Francine sat a bit straighter. Her chin tipped a bit higher. Her brown eyes met the doctor's with defiance in spite of her feelings of fear and worry. "What treatment options are still available?" she asked.

He looked away, then down to the outside cover of her file as though he refused to meet her insubmissive gaze. "We will need to start with surgery to insert a gastric feeding tube below the blockage, which will allow us to access your stomach directly. Then we can begin a course of chemotherapy."

"No more radiation, then?" she asked.

The doctor frowned at his hands. "More radiation will make the damage to your esophagus much worse. It would likely make you unable to eat anything solid."

"I can't eat many solid foods now," she said. "Isn't that what the feeding tube is for?"

He met her gaze and cleared his throat with what sounded like a needless *a-hem*, then said, "Yes, the tube will allow us to feed you something called Enternal Nutrition each night. However, you can have some food and drink throughout the day as you feel up to it. But the formula will maintain your nutritional health to support the aggressive chemotherapies we'll be giving you."

Francine nodded and looked out the window to the elm tree whose leaves had just begun to turn yellow.

She did not know what we—the tellers of this tale—know. She would spend the coming months watching those leaves turn red then brown; would watch the limbs as they scratched naked against the window, and the buds as they grew to reveal new, green leaves in the spring. But Francine Rigby would never see those leaves change color again as summer once more bled into autumn.

As an astute reader may have guessed, this tale does not take place long, long ago in a far away land, but rather pretty-much-right-here and less than a score of years ago.

As with any tale worth any amount of muster, there were daughters... yes, sons could be there as well, however there were no sons—a fact greatly bemoaned by Francine's husband who handled his disappointment by causing a minor scene at a coffee house wherein he said he would be leaving forever, then scampering away to an elsewhere that is of little to no importance to the story at hand. (He was not missed.)

The three daughters were Maureen, Ophelia, and Beth, two of whom lived in lands which were very faraway from their mother...

The eldest, Maureen, lived in a large city where stories were told to make others believe in dinosaur parks, talking race cars, and mailboxes that delivered letters from one year to another. She loved to be part of creating these celluloid images.

The second daughter, Beth, lived on a farm with her husband in a land where the soil was rich in nutrients and able to grow nearly any kind of crop.

The youngest daughter, Ophelia, chose to be near her childhood home. This allowed her mother to mind her children when they were young and buy things that Ophelia could not afford on her own.

Calling her three daughters had been a difficult decision for Francine Rigby as she did not want to upset their lives with her worries. She was a private woman who had managed her life very well without a husband and without bothering her daughters for assistance. Yet, the doctors were determined that Francine speak to her family. Additionally, she knew that she wanted her daughters to be warned of what was happening, to know that the illness she had been living with was much worse than anyone had suspected, and yes, Francine wanted them by her side as she faced what was possibly the last sickness of her life, wanted their hands in hers, wanted to hug each of them and say goodbye. She also wanted to determine how best to divide the lifetime's worth of treasure she had amassed (because in these kinds of stories, there is always a lifetime's treasure).

When she called for Maureen, there was no answer on the line.

Francine left a message asking her daughter to call back, saying, "I need to speak with you about something important."

When she called her youngest daughter, Ophelia, again there was no answer. Francine left her message, "I need to speak with you about something important."

Lastly, she called Beth. This daughter had been the first to leave the Rigby home and start a life with her husband. Beth spent her days caring for her husband and their farm. Years before, Francine had expressed her doubts about the farming life and how well her city girl would adapt, and they had argued. There had been a distance between them since, leaving Francine hesitant to bother Beth.

"Hello, Mother," Beth said.

Surprised to not be leaving a message, Francine chuckled slightly and said, "Oh, Beth! I didn't think you'd be available. I know how busy you are."

Beth laughed. "Yes, the fields are thick with cauliflower and broccoli, but I'm never too busy if you need me."

Francine smiled. Happy to hear this from her daughter, but sad that she had only bad news. "I need to speak with you about something important," Francine said. "I'm not well. The doctor has found that my cancer is not responding well to the radiation. I'll need surgery soon—"

"That's terrible!" Beth exclaimed. "I'll come to help."

"It's not necessary, dear one," Francine said. "Ophelia is close by and can assist if needed. And I know how busy you are at home."

"Home is where you are, Mother," Beth said. "My husband will understand that I need to be with you. And, unlike my sisters, I have no children, so I'm freer to lend a hand."

"Won't this cause problems for your farm?" Francine asked.

"A farm grows new each year, but I only have one of you," Beth said.

And so plans were made to care for Francine through the

surgery and the first round of chemotherapy. So, on the morning before her mother's surgery, Beth would drive back to her childhood home (as, again, this once-upon-a-time happened fairly recently and a horse and cart, dear reader, would take far too long).

And the other daughters?

Ophelia called back after two days. When she heard her mother was sick, she burst into tears and said, "*But, Mom,* this can't be happening! Who will care for my children when I'm away? How will I pay for the new clothes I've been looking at? And my car is failing. Can you co-sign on a loan before you have the surgery?"

Francine negotiated over what Ophelia wanted and calmed her youngest daughter's concerns.

Maureen called back after four days. When she heard that her mother was sick, she said, "I am so sorry to hear this, but *Mother*, I cannot come to help. The stories my company makes are far too important for me to be away. We have deadlines and consequential people who'll be upset if we can't meet them. And I have a child, you know. And even though she lives apart from me, she depends on always knowing that I'm home if she needs me!"

Perhaps they were not so very horrible about it... but after all, this is a fairy tale, and when a woman gives birth to and raises three other women, she expects them to be more... sympathetic. She hopes they will nurture their mother as she once nurtured them. Thus, when only one of her children came to help her through this trial, Francine was disappointed, yet she straightened her spine and put her chin into the air and went on, hoping all would be well.

THE PURPOSE of a fairy tale is to tell you, dear reader, something which may lead you down a better road. And part and parcel of that task in this tale is to show you that Francine Rigby was not so blind a mother as this story might imply. She knew that her daughters lacked the little bit of the sparkle and refinement which she saw in her neighbor's children...

Next door to the Rigby house lived the Martin family with their matriarch, Tamsin, and patriarch, Caleb, and three daughters—Wendy, Iona, and Kate.

The Martin girls, all well into their third decade of life, had never moved from their family home. Francine watched through the window each morning as Wendy, in her smart business suits and low heels, went to work to help provide for her family, even though Tamsin and Caleb both worked and the Martins were quite well-to-do. Francine watched as, each afternoon, Iona came out to sweep the walk in front of the house, leaving the path safe for her parents to tread. And Francine watched as, every evening, Kate walked around the block with her parents, one on each arm as though the Martins were much older than their sixty-some years.

Francine wanted, at times, to ask the Martins how their children had grown to be so careful and thoughtful of their parents. However, to do so would reveal the concern Francine had that she hadn't been the best single mother, leaving her to explain to someone outside of her home how her daughters were, and she was truly unwilling to express that. Some things are simply too difficult to acknowledge.

AND SO, with plans made and a well-fueled car, Beth kissed her husband goodbye and drove back to the home her mother had made for her and her sisters long ago...

The day Beth arrived, Francine was overjoyed. She looked again at her daughter's golden hair and smiling gray eyes, and knew that, despite her worries, the surgery would go well. She knew that with the feeding tube in place, she could face the cancer with the hope that she could beat it.

Ophelia came to see her sister and to borrow a bit of money for a new armchair that had caught her eye. Ophelia was considered the beauty of the Rigby family with her deep blue eyes and auburn hair, and she had used that beauty to meet several suitors over the years, which had left her angry with men in general when they refused to take proper care of her... as well as being handsome... and rich... and hardworking.

The sisters exchanged a hug and kiss on the cheek, for they really did love one another even though they didn't spend much time together. Before Beth could sit down, Ophelia began to tell her about the latest paramour who had become a disappointment.

"His name is John," Ophelia said, "and even though he's not quite my type, I allow him to spend time with me." She leaned closer to her sister and almost-whispered, "He's not very good-looking, but I thought with some better clothes and a hair style that I had chosen, he could be handsome enough. He has moved me into a beautiful home where my children and I are very comfortable. But he has this odd habit of not coming when I call, which is rather unsettling. So I've decided I might need to leave him."

Never sure what to say about these things, Beth decided upon, "I'm so sorry for your loss."

"Not every girl can find a dependable man like yours," Ophelia said, and her bottom lip came out in that same adorable pout she used to get her own way as a child.

"Yes," Beth said, "I was very lucky to have met the right man so young."

"You know," Ophelia said, "it's really not fair."

"Life isn't always fair," Beth said, then turned to their mother, "About your surgery tomorrow, what do we need from the grocery store beforehand? I can take you there so you have all the things you like as you recover. Broth? Or juice?"

"No, no!" Francine exclaimed. "I've called your husband to

know which foods are your favorites these days. I've been to the grocery, and the larder is full for the both of us."

As Beth hugged her mother and thanked her for the thoughtful gesture, Ophelia cried out, "*But, Mom*! My cupboards are nearly bare. My children nearly starved. What about me?"

Francine gestured to the hallway where several brown bags sat on a table. "Yes, my dear, I have filled bags from the grocery for you as well. I would not want my grandchildren to go hungry. They are young still—only in their teens—and must be fed."

Ophelia jumped up from her chair, ran to her mother, and hugged her. "Thank you," she said. Then her voice became a bit quieter, "And the other thing we spoke about?"

Francine's cheeks flamed. "The shopkeeper has been paid. You may go pick up your chair today."

Ophelia thanked her mother with a kiss on the cheek, then lifted the grocery bags and scurried toward the door. "I'm sure the shopkeeper will want to carry the chair to my home for me," she said with a giggle. "He was quite taken with me, you know." And with those words, the youngest of Francine's daughters left without as much as a farewell or 'by your leave.'

Alone at last, Francine met Beth's gray eyes and smiled a smallish sort of smile. The difficult days ahead would be made easier, she knew, with the company of her middle child.

To take you, dear reader, through the trials and tribulations of surgery and chemotherapy would be asking far more of you than I would be so bold as to ask. Suffice it to say, the surgery went well and Francine was able to receive her nutrition through the gastrostomy tube just as her throat fully closed to food. She began her new treatments and held up well throughout. Eventually, Francine felt somewhat better and settled into a routine for her treatments. And Beth returned to her home as she was needed for the cauliflower harvest.

∽

UNFORTUNATELY, the medications the doctors infused into Francine's body did not kill the cancer. And so, she found herself once more calling her daughters...

First, she called Ophelia, who answered her telephone on the first ring.

As Francine said, "I need to speak with you about—"

Ophelia burst out with, "*Oh, Mom!* How did you know to call? I am so terribly distraught. John—the love of my life—has left me. After I made him dress better and wear his hair in a more becoming style, he found another woman. What will I do? Who will provide for me and for my children? Where will we live?"

"There, there, child," Francine said. "I'm sure you'll be fine just as I was fine without your father. You and your children can work and support yourselves. Perhaps this is a good thing."

"What do you mean by that?" Ophelia said as she continued to wail. "There are too many bills and too many things we need and the landlord asks for money *every month*. To remind me that I'm fatherless is just cruel. What will we do? We'll be left to live in the streets!"

Francine had had this conversation with her youngest child before, and the solution was always the same. She sighed. "Very well," she said, "you may all come live with me again. It will be a help to have you here. You see, the treatments aren't going as well as we'd hoped, and I'll need some assistance."

"Yes," Ophelia said, her tears gone on a butterfly's breath. "We will move in with you. My daughters can clean and cook. My son can drive you places if you're too weak to drive yourself. If Beth can do this, then so can we. We'll be so much help to you!"

Francine knew that they would not be of help, that her home would become a noisy hall of televisions and video games and adults who were children arguing over remote controls. But she couldn't live with the idea that her daughter might be homeless.

She then called her eldest child, Maureen.

Maureen answered her telephone on the second ring with excitement in her voice. "Oh, Mother, you must have called because of the honors my employer has received! Two of our stories have gleaned awards from an exclusive hamlet in southern France. Can you imagine how happy we all are?"

Francine smiled. "I am so happy for you," she said. "Such an honor!" Then she dampened her voice a bit. "However, I need to speak with you about something important."

"More important than awards? How about the fact that I'll be receiving a raise in my salary?" Maureen asked.

"Of course, awards and money are important and grand, however I'm still sick. In fact, I will not be getting better. The cancer hasn't responded to the chemotherapy. I'll be beginning hospice care at my home soon."

Maureen's voice hardened. "Well, *Mother,* surely you know that I have responsibilities here at home. My company needs me more than ever before. *And I have a child, you know.*"

Francine nodded slightly as she looked down to the table on which the telephone sat, and she said, "I understand. But perhaps you and your daughter can come to see me once more before I am gone."

And so tentative arrangements were made for Maureen and her daughter to come home for a long weekend at some to-be-determined future date.

Lastly, Francine called Beth, who didn't answer her phone as she was in the fields making plans for new crops. Francine left the message, "I need to speak with you about something important."

When Beth heard the message from her mother, she knew

things were not well. She packed her bag, kissed her husband, and called Francine as she drove back to her childhood home.

As PREPARATIONS WERE MADE to move Ophelia and her children back into the family home, Francine took a moment to visit her neighbors, stepping across the cracks in the sidewalk and over the neat path carefully tended each day by Iona Martin…

Upon ringing the doorbell, Francine heard voices.

"Get the door, please," called out Tamsin Martin.

"I'm in the middle of a game. You get it," called one of the daughters.

"I got it last time," called another.

"Fine!" Tamsin's voice nearly yelled. "I was only making food for you. I suppose *that* can wait." And the Martin matriarch opened the front door, red faced and wiping her hands on a towel. "Frannie!" she cried. "It's so good to see you."

"Yes," Francine said, wincing slightly at the unfortunate nickname Tamsin insisted on using for her. "Good to see you, too."

Tamsin turned and hollered, "See, it was just the next door neighbor."

Francine said, "I wanted to let you know that my youngest and her family will be moving back in. In case you're bothered by any extra noise."

"Oh, no," Tamsin said, "we can't hear anything over the noise of the girls' televisions and gaming systems. But thanks for letting us know." She turned to holler, "You three could learn something about being considerate about noise from Frannie here."

Francine nodded awkwardly and said goodbye, leaving the noise of the Martin family behind her.

As Ophelia and her children moved their many belongings back into the Rigby home, Francine wondered if she had misjudged

Tamsin and Caleb Martin's children. She shook her head, told herself that what went on in another home wasn't her business, and remembered that her daughters loved her in their own ways, and that Beth would be home soon.

~

DEAR READER, it is sad to say, but the planning of the end of a life is frightfully easy. One has only to make a list of all of their possessions and determine who shall have what, then write it all down for a notary to sign and seal. Beth and Francine managed the task in a few short weeks then went on to wait.

The waiting for the end of a life is slow business indeed...

"*But Mom*, why does Beth continue to live here with us?" Ophelia said on a fine June day as the two sat in the back garden and admired the orange rose bushes Francine had always prized. "She has a husband and home of her own. Why doesn't she go back to them?"

Francine sighed. She had heard these complaints from her youngest every third day since Beth had come back. First the questions were concerning how long the counting of things would be. Then about who would receive what; who would have the most and who the least. And when decisions had been made and signed as if in stone by the notary's hand, the questions turned to when Ophelia and her children would again be the only guests in the Rigby home.

Francine said, "Your sister is here to care for me. She takes me to doctor appointments. She prepares and attaches the liquid food to my body each night. She monitors my sleep in case..." Francine looked away from her daughter then back, "in case I die in the night."

Ophelia's lower lip came out in a pout.

Francine reached out and tapped the lip as she used to do in

Ophelia's childhood. "No pouting, dear," she said with an attempt of a smile. "Your lip might well stay stuck out."

She hoped for a laugh from her child.

She hoped for an adult's reaction from her child.

What she received from her child was what she had expected.

Ophelia's eyes squinted down into a glare and she walked away, mumbling as she went, "I am not a child."

～

AFTER THE PLANNING for dying was completed, Francine's eldest daughter, Maureen, came to visit...

Sadly, she was unable to bring her daughter as (much like her mother) work and life were heady things for Maureen's child. Maureen, however, was able to be away from her daughter and her work for three full days. She arrived on a Thursday evening and went to sleep early as she was tired from traveling. On Friday, Maureen had plans to see old friends for a luncheon which extended into dinner and ended in a lounge for late-night drinks. Saturday, Maureen went from store to store purchasing the delicacies she had missed from home. Francine was too weak to accompany her and had to wait until dinner for them to spend time together. Sunday, Maureen spent the morning packing up all of the things she had purchased, then left for an early-afternoon flight.

As the rest of the Rigby family waved goodbye to Maureen's Uber, Beth slipped an arm through her mother's. They walked back to the house in silence.

～

AS YOU HAVE BEEN TOLD, dear reader, (and as often happens to mothers in fairy tales) Francine Rigby died...

It was a dark night in July. More precisely, it was three short hours after the end of one day and into the beginning of the next. Beth had been sitting with her mother through the long night when it happened. One moment Francine was breathing, and the next she was still.

Beth sat for many minutes holding her mother's hand. When she had collected herself, Beth dried her tears and went to wake Ophelia and call Maureen.

"Ophelia," Beth whispered into her sister's bedchamber. "Come quickly and kiss your mother goodbye, for she has passed."

Ophelia sat up and whispered, "What do you mean *she has passed*? That makes no sense. She was fine through dinner. It just can't be."

"Of course, it can be," Beth said. "It's what we've been preparing for these last months."

Ophelia broke down in tears. "What will I do?" she cried out. "Who will take care of me?"

Beth's teeth clenched as she said, "Ophelia, dear, you should cry for the loss of your mother not for the loss of her care. She suffered so much these last months. We should be happy she's no longer suffering."

Ophelia's tears consumed her face and wet the collar of her pajamas. "*But what about me?*" she exclaimed.

Repulsed by her sister's words, Beth left the room and went to the telephone.

Maureen answered her telephone with a muffled, "Hello."

"Maureen, I'm sorry to wake you, but Mom died," Beth said.

"What can you possibly be thinking, calling me at this hour? I'm not some farm wench who's up with the cows and chickens every day!" Maureen said.

Beth clenched her teeth again. "I assumed you would want to know. Perhaps you would like to say a pray for her or arrange a trip to come see her before the funeral services."

Maureen yawned loudly. "Let me know when the funeral is. I

should be able to come then. But please, no more middle-of-the-night calls. I need my rest for work in the morning."

Lastly, Beth called her husband.

He answered promptly with not only a 'hello' but also an 'are you alright?'

"Sorry to wake you," Beth said.

"Nothing to be sorry about."

"My mother died."

"I guessed," he said.

"Can you come to be with me?"

"Yes."

So the Family Rigby collected themselves to lay Francine to rest...

The three sisters stood together and listened as the chaplain spoke lovely words about rest and solace and Heaven. They each laid a long-stemmed white rose on the mahogany casket before it was placed in the mausoleum.

Ophelia then went to her children to be comforted; went to be kissed by John (who had made amends upon learning that Ophelia's rich mother was dying). Maureen wrapped her arms about her daughter's waist and they spoke whispers to one another as they dried their tears. Beth's husband held her hand and gently wiped the tears from her cheeks with his white handkerchief.

The chaplain patted each of the Rigby sisters on the shoulder and said, "There, there."

The Martins shook each daughter's hand.

The Martin daughters shook each daughter's hand.

Each mourner came and went, while the sisters stood in their places and accepted the condolences offered. Then, Francine Rigby was left behind as her daughters moved on into a world without her.

As they walked from the mausoleum, Maureen asked Ophelia, "Was there a will?"

Ophelia waved away the concern. "Beth knows where the papers are. She can take care of that."

"But aren't you interested in knowing how much of Mother's treasure you'll get?" Maureen asked.

Ophelia smiled slyly and said, "I am the youngest. The baby. Surely Mom set things up so I'll be taken care of."

"But," Maureen said, "I'm the first born. Surely Mother would defer to me as the one to receive the most."

Finally, the sisters pulled Beth into a corner and asked her to weigh in. Asked her which sister would have what things.

Beth sighed. "I don't know," she said. "Mom and I made the list of what things there were, but only she and the notary know who receives what. I made sure of that. We'll meet with him tomorrow."

Ophelia crossed her arms and stuck out her lower lip. She stomped away with John and her children.

Maureen began to say something, but her telephone rang. She held up one finger and said, "I have to take this call. We'll discuss this later."

Beth sat on needles and pins worried about the talks she would have with her sisters, then neither came to her again that day. She and her husband, given a reprieve from uncomfortable conversations, went to a lovely and quiet dinner, then slept the sleep of two people who feel they have done the best in the circumstances presented.

AND SO, dear reader, we are at the last of this tale. The place where morals are revealed (if you look hard enough for them). The place where a lifetime's worth of treasure is divided up (some say equitably). And the place to which three sisters have led themselves over the courses of their lives...

The notary sat behind his small desk in the corner of a room to one side of the bank. In front of him sat the three Rigby daughters. Only the three were able to fit into the small room, and thus the others waited in the couches and chairs in the bank foyer.

The notary cleared his throat and began with, "I am sorry for your loss. Your mother was a fine woman. A good patron to our institution. She didn't owe a penny to anyone and her health insurance paid for all of her end-of-life care."

"Yes, yes," Maureen said, and she waved her hand as though to shoo away the notary's kind words. "What about the will?"

"Yes," the notary said, then cleared his throat again and slid on a pair of reading glasses. "It seems that the eldest daughter, Maureen, is to have the two paintings which hang above the sofa in the main living room as they are the most expensive of all the artwork in the home.

"The youngest daughter, Ophelia, is to have the bedroom furnishings in the room she was sleeping in at the end of Ms. Rigby's life. You mother adds the message that Ophelia has made her bed quite well and it is time for her to sleep in it."

The notary looked up with an awkward expression, his lips flapping a bit as if he were miming a fish. He folded his reading glasses and slid them into their case. He sighed.

The sisters waited for him to say more, but no more was said.

Finally, Ophelia asked, "But what else? What about the money?"

"Yes!" Maureen exclaimed. "Our mother saved throughout her life. Surely there's more for me than just two paintings."

He said, "Yes, well..." and his voice petered away to nothing.

"What happens to everything else?" the two sisters asked in unison.

"Your mother," the notary said, "left everything else to her middle child, Beth, with the understanding that she is not to give any of those funds to either of you. Otherwise, all of it is to be donated to this short list of charities." He fluttered a sheet of paper to show the sisters the list was a real thing.

It is said that, at times, a look can dissect a warty toad into millimeter-sized chunks. That look was lasering its way through Beth from either side.

Maureen yelled, "How could you do this to us?"

Ophelia screamed, "This is unfair!"

Beth stood and shook the notary's hand.

Ophelia yelled, "Who is going to take care of me?"

Maureen screamed, "*I have a child, you know!*"

Beth thanked the notary for his services.

Maureen stormed from the bank dragging her daughter behind her.

Ophelia ran to her suitor and flung herself into his arms.

Beth walked out of the bank with her husband by her side.

And as they walked to their automobile in the bank parking lot, Beth murmured to her husband, "It all went just as we planned."

THE GARDEN AT THE END OF THE WORLD

SHARON WOODARD

All the interesting people are missing from heaven.
— Friedrich Nietzsche

Not all creation stories are the same.

In one creation myth, the Lord took a handful of soil and, in His own image, created a man. And from the side of that man, He created a woman as helpmate, some would say servant. But before that, there was another woman. Created of the same soil as the first man, at the same time, in the same way. And the man, being the first man, and being in the image of his Creator, felt she should bow to him in all things. But being of the same soil, made at the same time and in all the same ways, she felt his equal. So when he pressed her, her only chance at freedom was to leave the place of their making. Her name was Lilith. This is the story of her return.

～

IN ANOTHER MYTH, the Inuits tell a tale of the beginning of days when the sky was made too low. So low, it pressed the people until they hunched. This problem brought the people together. First, they prayed to Ravens to ferry their request to the gods. Then, bearing long poles harvested from the forest, the people gathered and in communal prayer, in partnership to Ravens, with the gift of the forest, and in a fusion of head and heart and muscle, the people raised the sky.

Up, above their heads.

Up, above the trees.

Up, joining the sky to stars and planets.

Where a sky *should* be.

Their gods found it good and the sky has remained so since.

Meaning, prayers are physics.

That in Creation, mistakes are made.

And mistakes, even the height of the sky, are correctable.

In the Garden at the Beginning of the World, it's said, all was perfect. But it didn't last. The sky above it could not protect what emerged below, and the Garden at the Beginning of the World has become the Garden at the End of the World.

LAVENDER—AS she calls herself now—marches up to the broken iron gates of the Garden. Right up to its edge, a riotous wall of vegetation greets her. So thick and entangled she can barely see inside. With her back toward a dying world, her eyes draw to the vault of blue above, where the edge of trees unite the Garden with the sky.

In this last of all places, in the last moments, she arrives furious.

The timing is part of her fury.

AFTER THE MANHATTAN PROJECT, after mushroom clouds hung above Hiroshima and Nagasaki, horrified scientists dreamed up the Doomsday Clock to reflect the level of continuous danger humankind had crafted. Their midnight marked not just the end of a single day, but of all days. The inevitable conclusion of holes in the atmosphere, jet stream disruption, melted ice sheets, clogged oceans, devastated rain forests, fire storms, mass extinctions–all of it brought on by the men now scurrying into the end of days.

Tick. Tick. Tick.

LILITH GOES by Lavender now because, after the millennia of battle and persecution, why not wear a soothing name? Burdened by other names—Demon, Jezebel, Succubus, Witch, why not jeer at those who would name her and claim this? The light from a sweet purple shade. A calming magic that beguiles bees to conjure honey to medicate nerves. Surely reaching the Garden at the End of the World, nerve medicine would be welcome.

But Lavender's nerves are not beguiled and she is not prepared for what she finds.

Right up to the verge of the mangled iron gates, leaf and vine, briar and thorn, trunk and root weave a wall of vicious entanglement. She had dreamt of apricots and pomegranates, the enchanting call of peacocks in air alive with bird and water and insects and all the murmurings long forgotten except to the marrow of her cells. But the paradise of her memory is not what has become of the Garden at the End of the World.

She sneers.

Like everything else on Earth, the first Garden is defiled; no longer the paradise promised, but the one humanity has come to deserve.

But she has brought herself here and the first thing she will do is have the apples she's dreamt of. Apples in this place have a storied history. She will eat so many her belly will ache. Then she will destroy every inch of that tree, bring it to splinters and shatter its roots. As defiant as ever, she returns no angel, and though the Garden has fallen, her spark remains strong.

No one walks the Garden at the End of the World now. To be the first to flee paradise and first to return from the cataclysm left behind, the irony is not lost on her. Lavender squares her shoulders. No slinking in like a cowering serf, but as a warrior on strong legs, in a soldier's mantel, with a machete sheathed in leather slung across her back.

She pulls out her weapon and faces the Garden.

The Garden at the End of the World is not the same as the Garden at the Beginning of the World. How could it be? Oak trees birth acorns. Cached in an acorn's hard shell are dreams of the oak it could become. It is the way of gardens. Creation is the womb of the creator. The child stands on the mother's shoulders. New stories come to be. The villagers raise the faulty sky.

There is no welcome for Lavender here, there never has been, so she raises her blade to make one. Brambles snare her leather mantel. Her scarred hands wield the machete, slashing a path toward the Tree in the center of the Garden.

The wielding of her weapon brings memories of days past. When she made her way through the forest to save a child. When jungle vines blocked her path to fresh waters needed for a village to survive. Yes, she was well acquainted to the workings of a machete. She had taken down those obstacles, and she would take down these.

She aims her muscled body like an armed missile toward where the sky was never high enough for her. As she slashes at the entangled mass blocking her path, the vines and leaves seem to simply grow back. The opened patches close again before her eyes. New leaves unfurl, mocking her. Each step toward the gate a maddening one that results in a thudding heart, stinging sweat and rivulets of blood from a multitude of scratches.

"And so, the prodigal daughter returns."

Lavender wheels to face the voice. Posed on a span of vine, a scant foot tall, the burgundy demon spreads his leathery wings in the midday sun. She bows her head in disgust and defeat before raising it again and pointing her blade. "And, so it seems, have you."

"Where you go, I go," the demon singsongs on his perch. "For aren't I your guardian? Trailing you everywhere and evermore?"

She snarls at the thing he is, wizened with age and vileness. "Guardian? You plague and vex me. You are the fiction of those who take no claim of their own devilry, but instead thrust it upon me. You are no more to me than dust under my feet."

The demon howls in delight, grabbing his toes to laugh and rock and only his leathery wings keep him from losing his seat entirely. "Oh dear one, through all the ages of Man, you have not learned a thing. What a spiteful scourge you are."

Her strike is violent. The flat of her machete sends him down entangling in thorns and scattering a murder of crows filling the sky with raucous anger. Cautious, he crawls back to his seat.

Turning her back to him, Lavender slashes again into the heavy wisteria and ivy that have grown together in a blockade, hoping they are the key to this puzzle of entrance to the Garden. Already knotweed and morning glory amass around her ankles, seeking to twine their way up her legs. All of it impeding her progress. Drenched in sweat, she stops to rest, heaving a sigh, letting the machete's tip touch the ground.

The demon watches from his perch, out of reach.

"What are you looking at, you miserable cur?"

The demon surveys the lush mayhem of vegetation. "I expected something... different."

His melancholy surprises her.

He says, "All this time, all I ever wanted was to get you back here. To return you to Him."

"To Adam?" she asks, incredulous.

The demon's face twists in spite. "No."

She studies him, the twisted body, mangled and scarred, his skin stretched taught over the spare frame. Ugly, after so many lifetimes. "You wanted to come back? To Him? After what He did to you? To me?"

The demon shuffles his feet. "*He* did nothing to me. I chose to find you. I promised to return you to Him."

The shock of it makes her drop to her knees. All this time, she thought he was like the first envoy, the three angels sent to retrieve her. When Senoy, Sansenoy, and Semangelof found her in exile at the Red Sea, they'd spat on her. "Return with us to your Creator or suffer His wrath."

Long after she'd sent them away, when a new emissary arrived, she'd assumed him to be the same.

"You weren't sent? You volunteered?" Lavender asks, incredulous.

"I thought you belonged here. I thought I'd be returning soon. I never dreamed you would be so... stubborn."

"It wasn't stubbornness."

The demon's brow rose, exaggerating the frustration he had shown for eons. "I thought you could be reasonable. Find peace with Adam."

"Adam? Adam saw only a servant where I stood." It was an old argument that always ended in the same place. "Besides, I'd been forgotten. By then, Adam had Eve."

Lavender stands, picking up her machete, but all the passion has drained away.

The demon pokes along the tangled wall. "But now. Seeing what it's become. I'm not so sure."

"We both came from this." She pushes aside the leaves and grabs a handful of red soil. "Adam and I. Both of us, from the Earth Herself. The same. The same time, the same soil, the same intent."

"But in His image."

"Adam was in His image." She tosses the soil. "I am the other half of Creation. In Her image. With a womb. Different, but meant to be equal. Father and Mother. Son and Daughter. It was never supposed to be just Father and Son with no other."

The demon paces, listless and unmoored. "I thought this was home. Yours. Mine, but it doesn't feel that way anymore."

"It's why I wouldn't come back. That garden was a promise of a life that never came to be. A promise I didn't get to have." Resolute, Lavender steps past the gate to continue her fight with the thick vines.

"Because you fled."

The branch she throws sails past as he ducks. "Damn you! I'm tired of you and them. I'm tired of the blame for everything gone wrong. I only ever was what I was created to be. I can't help if they got that so wrong."

"But all those dead babies."

She throws her hands up in disgust. "Ah yes, the dead babies. That's rich, coming from you."

He doesn't return her contempt. He isn't himself at all. Real emotion floods his dark eyes.

"Beeza? What has gotten into you? What is this masquerade of concern?"

"I have always cared!" He slaps his palm to his forehead. "Now the whole world has reached its end."

"It was always doomed." Her exasperation falls away. "The end woven into the flawed fabric of the beginning. All of us actors in a broken tale."

He squints. "But it could have been different. When you didn't return with His envoy, He cursed every day you stayed away, a thousand babies would die. You caused those deaths. I've been angry at you this whole time."

"If—*If He* could tether the fate of thousands of babies to me, then *He* could also *not* do it. Of this infinite wisdom, you tell me, who is the Devil?" She spits her words at him, "*If* He even had that kind of power."

The demon shrinks his head into his shoulders. "You speak blasphemy!"

"Oh Beeza. *That* was God's pride. Those babies were to die anyway. Death is a companion to life. Flaw or feature, darkness comes for us all."

The pain on his face slides under her anger.

"Don't be like that. We helped, you and I. In the desert. Across all the lands, across eons." Her voice dips into spite. "And even so, every woman is alone in her birthing bed. Made worse by His decree of pain and suffering. *Death* and suffering. In the faults of His Creation, where was your God then?"

The demon turns from her. "I can't think like that. I was his angel, a creature of light. These were once wings of air. Not scars and gristle."

"I remember. But the road has been long, Beeza."

Turned away from her, his voice is muffled. "I hate that you call me that."

"Beelzebub?"

"I am not Satan. We are not in Hell," he mutters, hunching his elbows to his lean ribs.

"May as well be. Cast out. Shamed. Blamed. You've heard them call me the serpent that schemed and got them all kicked out. As if Eve didn't have a brain, and Adam his own conscience. Both using their God-given free will." Her voice seethed, "And what of me having lain with demons and populated the world with them?"

He winces, turning toward her, his eyes wide. "He proclaimed your defiance the cause of all pestilence and demonry. The Bringer of Storms."

Her lips curl into a snarl. "Isn't it convenient to blame the woman who stands for herself."

"But what of Truth? If light shines from the Almighty, any

darkness must come from a different source. You." He looks confused. It's not clear if he speaks in jest or in resignation.

She thinks to explain how shadow works, but the argument is tiresome and ancient. And what does it matter now? She swings her blade. "The joke is on all of them, because it seems I, of all of them, am the only one left to return."

The demon gathers himself as if to protest but drops down instead. "I suppose blasphemy is the least of our problems."

Lavender looks past the rusted gates, beyond the Garden at the End of the World, to the world itself. The sky is still blue, but the hem of a malevolent sky is not far. In the creeping apocalypse they couldn't outrun, fractions of time count them closer to the midnight of life.

"Now that we are here," the demon stands, rubbing off leaves, "and I have dreamed of this day, your return—why did you come back? Why now when all is lost anyway?"

"To destroy the Tree."

"The Tree?"

"The Tree of Knowledge and the warped teachings of good and evil it spawned. It wasn't based in wisdom, but something else." She glares at him. "I will take down that damned tree and everything it's come to stand for."

The demon inches back as he sits up. "What will that do?"

"That Tree allowed men to wield a corrupt sense of good and evil. To wield power and domination that birthed destruction." She gestures outside the gate. "It could have instead shone a light to exalt not subjugate. Everything could have been different." The fire in her eyes forces him further away. She is a goddess, after all. She escaped the Fall of Man and remains immortal. "That Tree deserves to feel my wrath."

The demon's face is troubled. "But even though our fates, the Tree's as well, are sealed? Even if it doesn't matter anymore?"

She glares down at him. "It matters to me."

The demon turns to the roiling sky. Is there less blue? He faces the wall of dense wood, briar, and gnarled root. His voice is resigned. "Even if it mattered, you could never get through in time."

Lavender laughs, deep and sinister, poking the tip of her blade toward him. "Ah, but yet I arrive! The Goddess of the Night. The Harbinger of Chaos. Queen of Vampires."

The demon cowers, his voice hushed. "I never called you any of those. I've never believed what was said of you."

She scowls at him. "Everywhere I travel, tales spin my eminence. All of evil spawns through my womb." She grabs her sex. "It is I alone that have birthed the lilum of the land."

The demon looks away embarrassed, ready to scurry. Pausing, he turns back, a light of rebellion in his eyes. "Yet, you didn't fight it. You let the people and their God goad you. Let your anger mold you."

She straightens to her full height. Scrambling, he flees behind a tree trunk as her voice bellows, "To be cast into shadow, anything not of Light is surely my mischief and my will!" She laughs seeing him cower and then quiets. "What choice did I have? Who would hear my voice? Who would believe me?"

Trembling, he doesn't answer.

The long-held anger drains from her. What does it matter? Lavender drops into a squat. "This is my hopeless legacy. Born into a story that never had room for me. A story that shaped me without my agency. The round peg where there are only square holes."

The demon's black eyes are shiny and wet. "I wish you wouldn't talk like that."

She grabs a rock to throw at him, but when she sees his face, the rock slips from her hand. "Are... are those tears?"

The demon squats, closer than he usually dares. "I know you. I've lived beside you this whole time. Your anger is righteous. But it's not all of the story." He points out to the sky where everything is ending. "You didn't do that. Greed bred that. They cleared mountains to mine treasure. They choked oceans with plastic, swelled landfills, poisoned waters. Greed engineered this end."

Lavender studies him, the swirl of emotions in her breast disquieting. "Yes."

His voice comes, cautious and low. "I don't think you should destroy the Tree. It wasn't ever about good and evil."

"What are you talking about?"

"It wasn't about knowing right from wrong. In the end, knowledge didn't slow it. Maybe it sped up the destruction." The demon creeps closer, shielding himself with his leathery wings. "The imbalance came out of a void." Tears splash his stark cheekbones, dripping into the foliage. His voice drops to a whisper. "I understand now. It's always been about missing you."

"Me?" Feeling the impending barb of his words, she grabs for a rock but finds her blade. "Can you stop mocking?" She stands, holding her machete. "Aren't we well past that?"

"Lilith," he says, his voice without its customary malice.

"Don't. After all this, after everything we've been through. I no longer bear that name." Their eyes lock. "Our God—your God—demanded my return, to serve Him, to serve Adam with no answer to my voice. Then He charged me with the safety of those babies at the Red Sea. Then all babies. Those miserable angels mocked this charge. As though the people meant nothing—the babes meant nothing. Like I meant nothing. You saw this. You know."

The demon swallows.

"And all the times after; every betrayed woman, every injustice, you saw. You know." She waved the machete above her head. "You know what this place has come to mean for me."

He winces, stepping back, eyeing the weapon.

She lowers it, meeting his eyes, "I have come back here, but even you can't burden me with that name. Call me anything. But not..." She touches the machete to his throat. "You owe me that, you little beast."

He stands to his full, though diminutive, height, not shrinking from the blade. "You abandoned this place."

"I had to."

"I know."

The machete drops to the ground, tension draining from her arms, her heart confused. "You agree with me?"

"Yes."

Lavender steps back. "For millennia, you've begged, battered, harassed, insulted, cheated, thrown every trick to make me swallow my pride and crawl back here. Torturing me with your meddlesome piety, and now. Now—"

"Now, I understand." He plops down, raising a puff of dust.

Outside the ruined gates, the flawed sky broils mustard yellow over a cracked and baked land.

Her shoulders slump, and she turns her back to her companion: an angel on a mission baked to a sun-crisped bitter demon, one who seems somehow more trustworthy.

"I was wrong." He searches her eyes. "I thought I was to bring you back to Him, but—" His hands gesture to the foliage. "I think my mission has always been to bring you back to this."

She follows his hands to the tangled riot of plants, the ruthless snarl of barb and briar that had once been a paradise, and scoffs. Just outside, the poison cloud creeps closer. She feels the clock taking away the seconds left.

Tick. Tick. Tick.

"It's too late. You failed. I failed, no matter what happens to that damned Tree."

"You were always going to fail."

"You're a spiteful, heartless, ass!"

He spins at that, outrage flushing his face. "I am all heart! How could I endure any of this, let alone all of it, at your side? I am the truest witness to your life. Your deeds. Your mistakes. Your growth."

He steps forward, well within striking distance. "I know the truth of your wild heart."

His passion shocks her. She has never considered what it might have been like for him; a loyal dog with his heart split between two masters. One, uncompromising, the other, God Himself. A sliver of admiration slips through her heart for this stalwart little being.

Standing tall, he says, "Though a true warrior, you've been hamstrung by this ridiculous story." His whole being seems to gleam with a new light. "Dominate this, dominate that. Bow to Creator but befoul and defame his partner in Creation–the Earth Herself. You've been tasked to hold up half the Sky with no reverence for the Earth you stand on to do it. All your work, all that you are, ever damned to shadow." He struts past her, hiding his impassioned red face, stopping abruptly at the verdant wall. "Destroy that Tree or don't." He turns to her, "It won't prevent what is coming. But now I understand what its destruction means for you."

Lavender sighs then, feeling the toxic sky outside the Garden, the far-off clouds creeping forward along the plain. "There is nothing left out there." She walks back, one step matching his three, bringing her alongside him. "It will take days, weeks to fight our way into this place. Even my machete may not be up for it."

He stands in front of the riot of razor palms and blackberry brambles, bull thistle and thorny roses. He stands still for so long, she bends to study his face.

"Beeza?" she asks, bewildered, having never experienced his calm studied quiet before.

He speaks, low and slow. "You were right to leave, even after all that followed." His feet shuffle. "But because of your dissension, this Garden and that—" he gestures out the gates, "fell short of what could have been."

He turns, a slyness on his face. "You left, in a fit of ego and rage." He holds out his hands in a hear-me-out gesture. "You've lived that outrage, but you've also lived lives inspiring love and service. Babies you've protected. Souls of women retrieved from pyres. Seeding hope, for sovereignty, freedom, and rebellion against tyranny. You must not continue in this place as you left it. In a cloud of rage, bent on violence."

Confused, she squats before him to be closer, to read his eyes and to discern trick from truth in this crafty creature.

"Your whole point was neither subservience nor dominance. Your return to the Garden at the End of the World must be as you truly are."

"A warrior," she says.

Frustration washes his face. "Yes, but no." He puts his bony hands on her shoulders, careful not to harm her with his claws. "The road honed your warrior self, but that's not all you are." He places his hand against a twist of vine. "You are Lilith, the first woman made of this place. You always belonged here. In your Mother's image." He spreads his hands encompassing the ground and feral plants erupting from it, his leathery wings cracking. "As a rightful part, full and equal. No master. But a part of Creation, destined to be Creator, too."

"How?" She dangles her machete, helpless, her shoulders slumped.

"Think, with your whole body. If you lived that life, here, welcomed as equal, your ties in the blood and soil of this place, your womb and soul welcomed and aligned with the womb and soul that this garden is, who would you be here?"

She stands, stunned, imagining all she has fought for, placed right there at her feet.

"Close your eyes. You don't have to set down your weapon. You don't have to trust me. Trust yourself," He steps back, his wings folding at his back. "There's no skill or lesson to chase. It's your birthright. Your place here. Close your eyes. Let it fill you."

Trembling slightly, touched by his words, she settles, laying the machete across her knees. Following the rhythm and earnestness of his voice, she does what the demon suggests.

If Adam had been persuaded, if his God had been persuaded, if the whole premise had been different and she had been able to stay, not beneath them, but on her own terms, what would have followed?

The space opening in her feels vast.

The sky above her feels higher.

The time left to her feels infinite.

She would know this place. She would know its creatures. She would not be slashing a path through it with an angry tool of war. The whole garden would be a part of her, and she an extension of it. She would understand it. She would love it, and it would love her back. Contained here and integral, a balance would have prevailed. The Tree would have borne a different kind of knowledge.

Her eyes open and she finds the demon, sitting before her, his clawed hands cupped gently in his lap.

From the wall of the forest, as if in answer, a doe appears. It dips its shy velvet head.

"How would you travel in this place if you belonged here?"

"Like a creature of it. Like I loved and knew this place."

The demon stands brushing the leaf litter from his leathery body. Lavender holsters her machete and bending slightly, enters the forest through the trail the deer has revealed.

As they wind their way along trail and stream bed, the ease of travel lends time to consider. The unhindered trek through the forest, clears space for Lavender to ruminate on the war within her.

The first to arrive in the Garden at the Beginning of the World was Adam. A handful of soil with the Holy Breath breathed into it. With Adam, pride emerged into the Garden. She grinds her teeth picturing the snarl of Adam's lip when he stood above, demanding she lay below him.

The fury leads her to slash at vines unfocused and vicious.

"When we get there," she spits, "I will splinter that Tree. I will take it to its roots then heave those up as well!"

The demon mutters but tucks his head and flies behind her.

The machete ricochets when it hits an iron-hard branch, striking Lavender and knocking her into a creek. She sits stunned, mud-crusted raven hair tussled in her eyes, and water soaked.

Before she can shift her anger to him, the demon wheels and ducks, finding cover in a small copse at the bank. "Are you injured?" he calls to her.

She doesn't move from her watery seat.

"Were you thinking about Adam?" Flinching, he spreads the fringe of leaves carefully to see her. "You lose focus when you think about him."

Lavender howls and flings a stone at him.

He ducks, barely in time. "I don't think the Garden will permit us to pass if you keep at it like this." He darts behind a boulder as another stone sails his way.

Lavender's guttural voice shatters the calm. "When I get to that Tree, I will rip every branch from it!" But when she stands, her feet slip and down she goes into the water.

The demon eases around the boulder. "I meant, She won't grant us passage if you don't go with respect."

Lavender whirls toward him. "Respect! What do you know of respect?"

"I'm learning!" he shouts, slipping back behind the boulder. "We won't get near that Tree if you don't figure out why you are here."

She slumps onto the bank rubbing her shoulder where a good-sized bruise blooms indigo. Rivulets of dirty water trickle from her clothing. She lies at the edge of the water, covered with mud and leaves.

He skirts the boulder slinking toward her. "You returned to the source for a reason."

"What reason?"

"How could I know?" he asks in a hushed tone, creeping closer. "I'm no goddess. I'm not even a god." His hands press his chest. "I am a bare scrap of heaven, sent to retrieve you."

She rolls her eyes.

"Maybe you don't know your purpose either." He creeps around her. "Is it revenge or to be true to your original nature?"

"What are you talking about?"

He squats, examining his bony hands. "You chose dominion over yourself. You always do. No matter the cost. Is revenge really why you are here? Revenge focuses on him and his Father."

"He's my Father, too."

"Be that as it may." Annoyed, the demon straightens, his wings half unfurled, his voice steadying, "I thought it wasn't about them, but about you. About Her. I didn't think you came to vanquish this world. I thought you came to save it."

Lavender snorts. "It's beyond saving. I'm here to avenge."

"Are you?" He is so earnest, it brings her up short. His face grows incredibly sad, his ugly wings drooping. "Then what was it all for?"

It takes a stalled heartbeat before she can regain her fury and turn away. "You are a pest sent to vex my entire existence. You are nothing."

"If you were the warrior you claim to be, you wouldn't be trashing this holy place like a Leviathan." He kicks at the machete. "You wouldn't need a weapon of war, here at your Mother's bosom."

"I don't answer to you, imp!"

His body shudders but holds steady. "No. You answer to who you once were. Who you were created to be. What would *she* do? How would *she* be?"

Tears burn Lavender's eyes. Rubbing her hands dry, she studies him.

And notices the change. "What is happening to you?"

The demon glances at his reflection in the pool, at the wings spread behind him. No longer burgundy-red but rosy-pale, the skin looser. His eyes no longer black onyx, but a warm brown. "It's this place. It's me coming home."

"Reverting to an angel?"

He shakes his head. "I don't think so." He marvels at his hands. The backs no longer stark veins and tendons, the claws shrinking. "I've been earthbound too long. I've seen too much. I am no longer just a sky creature. But this Garden..." Cautious, he steps forward. "I think it can change you, too."

"Into an angel?" she scoffs.

He shakes his head, solemn now. "To your essential nature."

"I have *never* been other than I am." But her haughty voice quivers as he shifts even more. Were his eyes even now revealing hints of blue beneath the brown?

"The Tree!" he shouts suddenly and takes flight.

As if responding to him, a rose bush gives way allowing easy passage through. The vines slide away from each other, their flowers no longer dense mobs of fragrant walls. The tree limbs bow and bend, leaving a path in front of the demon who is no longer a demon. Dazed, Lavender is forced to follow.

Until, there they are at the middle, back to the place where they both began.

She isn't prepared for the center of the Garden.

Rotten corpses of apples melt into a slick layer of slime on the ground, feeding a plague of black flies. Lichen-choked branches hunch above. Shattered graying limbs litter the ground. Gaping gashes of rot split the Tree's trunk.

Lavender covers her mouth. The flies swarm in a cloud. The fetid sweet of ferment permeates the clearing. Carnage has befallen what was once the heart of the Garden at the Beginning of the World. The very center of the Fall of Man. The Tree of the Knowledge of Good and Evil lies in ruin, fatally dwarfed.

As if the very sky had arrested it.

As if the sky hadn't been high enough after all.

The demon, who is no longer a demon, snaps to and flits about, worrying the area with his frantic flight. He springs back to tug her hand. "You have to move this! Clear it all. We must find it!"

In a stupor, she shrinks from his fervor as the stench of rot roils her stomach. She bats him away.

He stumbles, but rises, as if gravity has no hold. "This is the reason for your return. It called you here. Take your weapon." He grabs her arm, tugging it and the machete toward the center of the fetid mess.

Dumbfounded, she stares into the pile and back at him. "We're too late. It doesn't matter. Nothing matters." In all their travels, she has not felt the full weight of her grief. For her flight, for her life in exile, for the loss of everything that has ever been dear. The broken Tree has cracked her heart open.

"Pull yourself together, woman!" he yells, grabbing her collar and tugging.

His passion pierces her trance, and she looks to him, astonished.

He speaks with urgency. "The Tree of Knowledge became a pawn, it was never the jewel. It was covering what is true and ancient. What lies beneath it. What came from Her."

As she stands gaping, he flies to the pile and begins throwing off rotted limbs. The diseased shards cut and slice his tender skin. Crimson blood spurts forth.

She grabs his little body, wrestling him back. "Stop! You're hurting yourself!"

Shrugging her off, he escapes and hovers. "Don't you feel it? All of them reaching for you this whole time? The midwives, the witches, the suffragettes, the first wave, the second... you know what comes after the fourth wave?" When she doesn't answer, he lurches forward, making her lean back. "The fifth! The six! Another pulse. It's an ocean. It's how waves work. Generation after generation. All your daughters reaching for you all along."

Lavender stumbles backwards.

"Adam is long gone, but you persist." He speeds forward, sputtering, his hands gesturing to the ground. "They feel it and call to you even now."

Tears flow down her cheeks as she turns toward the Garden gates, worrying. Was the venomous cloud already licking its way in? "But, even if that were true, it's too late. It's over. We have lost everything."

"No!" The creature shoots upward as if his words were fuel. His arm points to the sky. "This reign, this age, is over. And His scion, too. And domination. Fear. Control. Taking to give back nothing... all their buffoonery." He flits toward her, fervent and impassioned. "They guarded a tree with a flaming sword! How did they think that was going to go?"

Humor grazes his eyes and even in her despair, she can't help but feel some stiffness easing, her scars softening. A buoyancy flows down her limbs.

His voice sharpens, strengthening through tears. "Your rage brought you back. But your passion, your sense of justice fueled that rage." Every fiber of him pleads with her. "What was severed from you, from all of us, you can save. Please, make haste!"

She wavers, between him and the debris. "But, the Tree is dead."

"Not that one! That only ever shadowed the deeper more ancient one. The Tree of Life!" He flutters, manic, between her and rotten foliage. "The communion of Earth and Sky; the source of everything." He flies behind, prodding her forward. "A Tree unable to flourish under a sky of fear and domination. Unable to feed on corrupted wisdom. A glorious being meant instead to dance with the sky."

He hovers before her. "It is meant to reach for light, for freedom, for nurturance and partnership, for what is raw and wild." He gasps, "For you Lilith. You are its scion."

Caked in dirt, mud in her hair, sweat-stained and bruised, every bit a wild child, she stares down past the spoiled broken Tree to the ground beneath. Was there something under the pile? Did a light falter, straining toward her? Using her machete, now not a tool of violence, but a scalpel of liberation, Lavender surgically removes necrotic tissues. Using muscles forged by pyres and passion born of injustice, and a heart broken by life, she labors, revealing, at its center, something alive.

Barely.

A seedling sprouts from the thick root of what had once been mighty. It springs into the light unfurling tiny verdant branchlets.

Lilith drops to a knee heaving, shedding tears, and sweat, as a knight at an altar, she lays down her machete. The creature flies to her side, alighting on her shoulder.

Here, in the darkest second, of the darkest hour, of the darkest of all days, they lean into the haze of light from the seedling.

He whispers, "You are here to heal this place."

Her choked sobs echo, "How could I possibly be enough?"

"Maybe you aren't." He tilts his head. "But maybe, you are."

The tree dances up into the sky. And with it, the clock of the world creeps forward into a new day.

CONTRIBUTORS

The Novelitics Writers Collective began as a haven for writers dedicated to the craft of storytelling and the pursuit of publication. Though the formal chapter of Novelitics has closed, the bonds formed within its creative, inspiring community remain strong. The writers featured in this final anthology continue to create together —offering one last, unforgettable journey into the heart of human experience.

Nicole Burron writes stories that explore the strange, the taboo, and the horrifying. She views the world through a lens that is both haunted and curious. Her soul resides in Portland, Oregon.

Kerry Cathers (editor) runs the website, A Curiosity of Crime, a research resources for writers of historical detective fiction. She published her first reference book, *A Writer's Guide to Nineteenth-Century Murder by Arsenic*, in 2022. Its follow-up is coming early 2026. She has given seminars on forensics, poisons, and weaponry for the History Novel Society North America's conference, various Sisters in Crime chapters, Mystery Writers of America, and Kiss of Death's COFFIN series. For more information on forensic science, crime, and policing in their social context visit her Substack "Bandits Roost" and follow her on Instagram @acuriosityofcrime.

Carrie Hayes writes historical fiction. Her first two novels, *Naked Truth or Equality, the Forbidden Fruit* and *Well Dressed Lies* were about the scandalous, trailblazing, spiritualist sisters Victoria

Woodhull and Tennessee Claflin. Her current work-in-progress is about a young American woman living in London during the Blitz. Carrie writes on Substack and Medium. Learn more at carriehayeswrites.com.

Sue Ann Higgens has been a pastry chef, a high school teacher and principal, a sweatshop sewist, a track coach, and a birth doula. Her writing looks at 20th century women, cultural friction, and entangled families. Her fiction has appeared in *Echoes: An Anthology of Short Fiction*, and *3rd and Oak: An Anthology;* she has nonfiction in *Our Hidden Conversations: What Americans Really Think About Race and Identity*. When not traveling, she lives and writes in Portland, Oregon, and works to make peace everywhere.

Sally K Lehman is the author of the novels *The Last Last Fight, In The Fat,* and *The Unit–Room 154*. Her serialized short novella, *Small Minutes,* was included in the Best Of edition of Bewildering Stories. She is the editor of the anthologies *Bear the Pall, War Stories 2016,* and *War Stories 2017*. Her work can be found in multiple literary magazines including The Coachella Review, Another Chicago Magazine, Lunch Ticket, and 34th Parallel. Sally has an M.F.A. in Creative Writing from Wilkes University where she worked as Managing Editor for River & South Review. She lives near Portland, Oregon. Learn more at www.sallyklehman.com.

Gail Lehrman is an expatriate New Yorker relocated to the Pacific Northwest. Though Gail traded the canyons of Manhattan for the mountains of Oregon, New York's voices continued to sing in her ear. Those voices are the force behind her debut novel, *Across Seward Park*. Gail holds a B.A. and M.A in English Literature and an MFA in Creative Writing. A frequent hiker in Oregon's lovely Columbia River Gorge, Gail is also an enthusiastic participant in the rich literary community of Portland, Oregon. Learn more at www.gaillehrmanauthor.com.

Trish MacEnulty is the author of a historical novel series, crime novels, memoirs, a story collection, scripts, and the award-winning, historical coming-of-age novel, *Cinnamon Girl*. She has a Ph.D. in English from the Florida State University and taught writing and film as a university-level professor for two decades. She currently writes book reviews and features for the *Historical Novel Review* and teaches magazine writing at Florida A&M University. She lives in Tallahassee with her husband and publishing partner, Joe Straub. Learn more at www.trishmacenultybooks.com.

Katie Nelson Stone lives and writes in Portland, Oregon. A Public Involvement Specialist by day and a historical fiction author by night (or early mornings, or lunch breaks, etc.), Katie's love for historical stories runs deep. She received her Master's in History from Portland State University and is a historical research consultant with her company River City Historical. Her clientele includes journalists, historical fiction authors, and documentary filmmakers. When she's not working or writing, Katie enjoys camping with her husband and dogs, bike rides, themed parties, good food, captivating books, and bad reality TV. Learn more at www.katienelsonstone.com.

Shirley Perez West was born and raised in the San Francisco Bay area among the remnants of cherry orchards, redwood forests, and Spanish ranchos. She holds bachelor's and master's degrees in journalism and is still trying to work out how not to let the facts get in the way of a good story. She currently lives on the north Oregon Coast where she enjoys paddling for a women's dragon boat team, and connecting with both local writers and far-flung members of the Novelitics community. She is author of *El Sueño*, a family saga of early California.

Micah Thorp is a physician and writer in Portland, Oregon. His first novel, *Uncle Joe's Muse,* won a 2022 Next Generation Indie Book Award and a Foreword Indies Book of the Year Award. His current novel, *Aegolius Creek,* will be published in September, 2025. His writing has been published in Cleaver Magazine, Fictional Cafe, and Blind Corner.

Originally from the Midwest, **Annie Tupek** went on a road trip to Alaska and never returned home. After spending over a decade in the frozen tundra, she moved south and now resides in Oregon. She is a licensed private pilot and when not making up stories, she can be found exploring the Pacific Northwest by land and air.

Journalism took **K. Fufkin Vollmayer** from Alaska to Washington, D.C. When one of her kids parroted the same frontier myth learned in school—of brave, white pioneers in covered wagons—she remembered the captivity and slave narratives she read with her professor, Michael P. Rogin. Combing through the Lewis and Clark journals, she focused on writing about York, the Métis, and the other enslaved member of the expedition, Sacagawea, in her novel *I've Known Rivers: York's Account of the Lewis and Clark Expedition.* In every Latin American country she's visited, she's learned about maroon communities and the Black African diaspora. Learn more at www.fufkin.co.

Sharon Woodard is fascinated by stories. The way they hold us, feed us, seed our dreams, and collectively knit us into existence. And what do those stories sit on? A peek behind the curtain reveals its stories all the way down. But what fascinates this writer are the edges and liminal spaces where stories are inconsistent or split apart to allow the birth of something new. The places where new understandings and ways of experiencing the world can emerge, and shift the whole Jenga tower of collective beliefs and thus subtly, change the world. Sharon is a licensed Naturopathic Physician practicing in the Pacific Northwest and mom of two fascinating and radically independent people. When she isn't lurking around gathering fiction fodder, you can find her paddling, hiking, or biking the verdant byways of her home in the Pacific Northwest.

Kim Taylor Blakemore writes historical novels featuring fierce, dangerous women—thieves, mediums, murderesses, and outlaws —each with tangled secrets and sharp edges. She's the award-winning author of *After Alice Fell*, *The Companion*, and *The Deception*, as well as *Bowery Girl* and *Cissy Funk*. Writing as K.T. Blakemore, she pens the Wild-Willed Women of the West series, including *The Good Time Girls*. She edited *Echoes: An Anthology of Short Fiction*, and *3rd & Oak: Stories* and led the Novelitics Writers Collective from 2020 to 2025. Kim is currently pursuing a Master of Divinity at Lutheran Theological Southern Seminary. Learn more at www.kimtaylorblakemore.com